Jan~~~~~~

Serial
Encounters

Table of Contents:

Introduction

Serial killers. Is there anything in the horror world that is more fascinating? Or more frightening? Unlike vampires, ghosts, zombies and werewolves, serial killers are very real. They walk among us, they work beside us, they ride the bus or the morning train with us. And some of us have met them, unaware of the nature of the hidden beast we are casually encountering.

These eighteen fictional stories examine the question of "what would happen if I met a serial killer in real life?" Most of the characters are made-up but the serial killers aren't. Jeffrey Dahmer, Aileen Wuornos, Ted Bundy, Jack the Ripper, and Ed Gein all make appearances in this anthology, as well as lesser-known but just as intriguing heartless killers.

Some of these stories are terrifying; some are heartbreaking; some engage in a little dark humor while delivering a solid punch to the gut.

Enjoy!

--Jane Nightshade, Editor

Everybody Loves a Clown
by Jane Nightshade

Ginny felt compelled to view the exhibit at the famous crime museum, even though she wasn't particularly keen on the idea. It was a deep-seated need—a bucket-list item—something she had to do.

"I was a witness a long, long time ago," she said softly to her husband, Lance, clutching his free hand while he bought tickets. "Not that what I saw would ever be admissible in court."

"I hope you get what you need out of that thing," said Lance, as they walked past the ticket-taker into an aisle of lurid exhibits from 19th Century London. "Because it's really weird to take this side trip to a remote mountain town in Tennessee."

"I appreciate you coming with me. I really do."

She dawdled in front of various gruesome exhibits, pretending to be interested in the crimes of O. J. Simpson and the complicated procedures of a forensic autopsy. After an hour, Lance took her hand gently. "It's time, Ginny. We've seen almost everything here. Now you need to see the thing you came to see. Unless you've changed your mind."

"I wish I could change my mind. But it doesn't seem to want to be changed."

They followed directions on a posted site map to the aisle they'd been avoiding. Ginny's eyes darted around, afraid to look straight ahead. But then she made herself look and there it was, a glass exhibit box, in which were hanging two old-fashioned clown suits, each with ruffled collars and pom-pom buttons.

Advancing slowly toward the glass box, Ginny took in her breath sharply. "One red-and-white, one olive-green-and-orange. Those ruffles were a bitch to clean." She noticed that the suits were covered with odd message buttons advertising ironic slogans, such as "Lead Me to Your Taker." He'd removed those buttons when the suits needed cleaning.

Ginny kept moving, until the tip of her nose touched the glass of the exhibit box. She read the signage posted inside, although she already knew pretty much everything it said:

"The clown suits of Killer Clown John Wayne Gacy of Norwood Park, Illinois, a Chicago suburb. The notorious serial killer murdered at least thirty-three young men and boys during a six-year crime spree lasting from January,1972 to December,1978. Some authorities believe he could have killed as many as forty-five people. Gacy buried most of his known victims in a crawlspace under his house at 8213 West Summerdale Drive. He threw the last few victims in the Des Plaines River after running out of burial space at home."

"Nice guy," said Lance, with a low, sarcastic whistle.

"He was good at lying. He lied to everyone, and they believed him. My mother loved him."

"Maybe we should go now? You've seen enough?"

Ginny didn't answer. She could almost smell the clown suits again—that decaying, mildewy odor that all of Gacy's clothes emitted when he brought them into her mother's shop for cleaning. She could almost see his chunky, falsely amiable face and hear his voice with its ever-present braggadocio.

What had she expected to get from seeing the suits again?

Closure. She expected to get closure. But there was nothing there. They were just grotesque lumps of cloth that once belonged to a very sick man.

She turned slightly to leave, disappointed. Out of the corner of her eye she saw a flash of movement and whirled back around. The left arm of the red-and-white suit slowly raised itself and reached out toward her, as if it recognized her.

Ginny fell into a whirlpool of darkness, fading to unconsciousness, while Lance shouted something irrelevant that sounded very far away.

* * *

Early June 1978

Briiing. Briing.

A middle-aged man jangled the bells on the door of the Fresh as a Daisy dry cleaning shop in Norwood Park and sauntered inside. He was whistling a jaunty tune and carrying a very large, zipped clothing bag.

Ginny cringed. It was creepy Mr. Gacy, her mother's newest favorite customer. Bulky and talkative, he bragged a lot about his successful construction business and his strong political influence in the Chicago suburbs.

Mr. Gacy was just another reason why Ginny resented having to work part-time in her mom's shop after school. Her father had died two years before, and times were tough. Mrs. Turner couldn't afford to pay anyone from outside even minimum wage, so she had to depend on her daughter. She did let Ginny keep tips from deliveries to the "special" customers.

She wished that Mr. Gacy would find another dry cleaners, but her mother gave him privileged service and he liked it—a lot. Mrs. Turner flattered his obviously inflated ego.

He unzipped the clothing bag and pulled out an old-fashioned clown suit. The voluminous fabric was olive-green, speckled with white, and printed all over with random orange patches. It had a large, triple ruffle around the collar and big orange pom-poms down the front. Mr. Gacy worked as a volunteer clown entertaining children at the local hospital and at birthday parties and other community events. This was the first time he'd brought in one of his celebrated costumes for cleaning.

"Why, Mr. Gacy!" Ginny's mother trilled, practically batting her eyelashes. "We haven't done a costume for you yet. It will be an honor to contribute in our humble way to all the great work you do for our children and communities."

"I'm wearing it at the annual Woman's Club Family Brunch on June 25th, Mrs. T. I've actually got two suits and two clown personalities. Pogo is the 'nice' clown who entertains young children and hospital patients. He wears my red-and-white suit. Patches is the 'mischievous' clown—he wears this suit. Patches isn't always… nice."

"My, that's fascinating! That'll be a dollar fifty, payable on pick-up," she replied, filling out a receipt. "It's a special job because of the fabric and the frills."

Gacy patted his clown suit with a fond gesture, and then Mrs. Turner scooped it up and placed it in the to-be-cleaned bin.

"That's fine, Mrs. T. Just get it ready before the brunch."

"No problem. We will have it for you long before then."

He gave her an ingratiating smile. "You're a champ, Mrs. T. One of my best girls."

" Go on, you charmer!" Mrs. Turner blushed. She rolled her eyes in mock offense, but was plainly pleased. "Ginny," she said, "make sure that Mr. Gacy's order goes to the front of the queue."

Ginny dutifully grabbed the to-be-cleaned bin and began wheeling it into the back of the shop, where the cleaning equipment was kept. "Yes, Mother," she said, stopping. She flashed Mr. Gacy her coldest look on his way out.

"Such a nice man," said Mrs. Turner, after Mr. Gacy left. "Does so much work for charity and never takes a penny in return."

"Really? He gives me the fucking creeps."

"Ginny! Your language! Mr. Gacy's a good customer! He's had his picture taken with the First Lady. Why don't you like him? Everybody loves a clown."

"His clothes always stink. That mildewy, rotten kind of smell—it's so gross. The neighbors complain that everything in his house smells like that."

"He's explained about that again and again. He has mold in his basement and can't get rid of it. He's probably got everything he owns sunk into that house and now can't afford to move. Lord knows it's hard enough to be a small business owner these days, with all of this awful inflation."

"Well, it isn't just his stinky clothes and house. The creepy way he looks at us high school kids sometimes—especially the boys."

Mrs. Turner sucked in air indignantly. "That's naked slander and we don't repeat gossip here, young lady! Now get back to work! We're behind on our orders because you spend so much time mooning over Tony Halbaum. Who you should forget, as the Halbaums are way too rich for our blood."

Ginny took the new orders into the back and began sorting them. She held her breath when she handled Mr. Gacy's order because it smelled bad—like his other clothes.

She remembered the day Tony Halbaum complained about Mr. Gacy staring at teenage boys: "I don't care what anybody says. He's a perv!"

"My mother thinks he's a saint," Ginny had replied. "She's so blind."

Tony continued: "He looked at me in this weird way when he came to discuss the Women's Club upcoming family brunch with my mother. I was practicing my dives in our pool, and he was staring at me through the sliding glass door."

"Oh Tony, that's so icky. Well, most likely you won't have to deal with him ever again, after the brunch is over. I, unfortunately, will have to see him regularly."

She took the clown suit off its hanger and examined it closely for stains. Stains were usually treated at the shop with a solvent before clothes were placed in the dry-cleaning machine.

On the left pant leg, she found a rusty mark. She held it up to her nose and sniffed. The coppery, salty smell was unmistakable. "Blood!" Ginny cried to herself, revolted.

Customers brought in clothes with bloodstains all the time. They cut themselves in the kitchen or got into fights. Still, Ginny shuddered. The blood just made the suit—and its owner—seem that much more sinister.

She dabbed the blood stain with the pretreatment solvent, and then hurried through the other recent orders. She dumped everything in the dry-cleaning machine, relieved to get the costume out of her sight, at least for a while.

After the dry-cleaning machine did its work, she finished the costume off with a commercial steam iron. It looked a lot better—almost new—and the blood stain was gone. Despite the cleaning, however, a faint, rotten odor of mildew still clung to the suit.

* * *

Ginny woke up the day before the Women's Club brunch. It was a bright, sunny Saturday in late June. She only had to work in the shop until noon, and was looking forward to having the whole rest of the day free. She had an appointment to get her hair cut so she'd look her best at the brunch—her first official date with Tony Halbaum. They would both be seniors in the fall.

She got up and walked sleepily to her closet, looking for the chenille bathrobe she always kept on a peg on the inside of the door. She grabbed the robe and was about to close the door when she noticed something odd poking out from among the packed pastel dresses and blouses on her clothing rod.

Cotton olive-green fabric printed with orange patches and a glimpse of big, floppy ruffles. It looked malicious, almost obscene.

"Wh-what!" Ginny cried. "It can't be." She forced a trembling hand to part the packed clothes around the olive-and-orange… thing.

Ginny froze, suppressing the urge to cry out.

It was Mr. Gacy's clown suit. No longer in the plastic bag she'd placed over it in the shop, but still clean and

13

pressed, as she had arranged it when she'd cleaned it days before. Mr. Gacy was picking it up at the shop later this morning.

Did I take this home from the shop without realizing it? she fretted. *Am I a secret klepto and don't know it? It seems unlikely, but what if it's true?*

Her mother would likely cancel her outing with Tony today and the brunch date, too, if she thought Ginny was taking things from the shop.

Unless… her mother was the one who'd put it in her closet in the first place. Maybe she'd arranged with Mr. Gacy to borrow the suit to play a trick on her. That was the only explanation Ginny could think of. They lived alone together and had no visitors that week. But why? To upbraid her for some perceived negligence of duty at the shop? Her mother knew that her daughter didn't like Mr. Gacy. Maybe she wanted to frighten Ginny into straightening up.

But it was totally out of keeping with her mother's personality, Ginny realized. She was a strict taskmaster, but she wasn't cruel enough to want to give someone a fright like this. It couldn't be.

Her mother knocked on her bedroom door. "Ginny, breakfast is getting cold. You need to come downstairs now or you won't have time to eat anything before we have to open the shop!"

Ginny slammed the closet door shut and hastily threw her robe over her pink Baby Doll pajamas. "Coming, mother!" she shouted. She visited the bathroom and then flew downstairs to breakfast. When she finished, she went back upstairs to get dressed. She opened her closet gingerly, expecting to see the olive-and-orange monstrosity, but it was no longer there. She pawed through all of her closet's contents and found nothing.

I imagined it, Ginny thought, giving up and choosing her favorite dress from the rod. Creepy Mr. Gacy would haunt anyone's dreams.

That was an explanation, but not a satisfying one. Ginny felt uneasy at the shop all morning. Mr. Gacy came to pick up his costume, and she couldn't look him in the eye. Her mood only lightened when Tony and his best friend Perry Waters arrived after lunch to drive her to the hair appointment.

* * *

Early November 1978

Ginny, busying herself in the back of her mother's shop, had been over the moon ever since her date with Tony at the Woman's Club brunch back in June. A couple of weeks after the brunch, he'd given her his letter jacket and announced to their gang at a summer pool party that the two of them were "an item."

Unfortunately, the announcement had been a little spoiled when Perry Waters showed up and told them breathlessly about some recent shocking news.

"Hey guys!" Perry exclaimed. "Did you know that a guy's body showed up in the Des Plaines River on June 30th? And it looks like it was murder, not an accident!"

Ginny was upset that her moment of glory was ruined, but quickly forgot it as she'd spent many happy dates with Tony over the summer. Everyone she knew reasoned that the dead guy was a drifter, or a runaway and those things happened to that kind of person.

Now it was early November, and Tony and Ginny were still going strong as a couple. This was their last year of high school and Ginny looked forward to spending time with Tony at all the social events the holidays would bring: football championships, Christmas dances, New Year's Eve.

Briing. Briing. The shop door's bells sounded, and Ginny ran to the front, thinking it might be Tony, who'd said he might drop by that afternoon. She caught up short when she saw it was not Tony, but Mr. Gacy. He was carrying a red-and-white mass of droopy fabric and ruffles on a hanger. Her mother was delighted.

"Why Mr. Gacy," Mrs. Turner trilled, "What have you been doing with yourself?"

"This and that," he replied, with an unctuous smile. "Mostly that. I need my other suit cleaned now—I'm doing a benefit for the new children's annex at the library."

"How lovely! You are such an angel in the community."

Ginny realized with disgust that her mother was flirting again with the fat, creepy clown dude.

"Ginny," she added, "be sure to give this order the usual extra special treatment we reserve for our best customers."

"Sure, Mom," said Ginny, eyeing the clown costume as if it were a snake. She carried it into the back at arm's length as she overheard her mother apologize to Mr. Gacy for her daughter's short manners.

"Kids these days!" her mother complained.

At home after dinner, Ginny called Tony from the princess phone in her bedroom.

"Sorry, I didn't drop by today," Tony said. His voice had a strange, distracted tone. "I was so worried, I forgot all about it."

"Worried—about what?"

"Perry's missing! He hasn't been seen since football practice yesterday. His parents are frantic. They haven't yet announced it at school because they thought he would come home. But it's been more than 24 hours and they're calling in the police. I expect there will be a special assembly tomorrow at school."

"Oh my god, Tony, that's awful. Maybe he hitchhiked to Chicago for fun and lost all his money and can't call."

"Maybe. But it's not like Perry to go off without telling someone. The last thing he said to me was something about a part-time job offer, but I don't know where or with whom. I'm driving all around the township tomorrow after school to look for him. Wanna come?"

"Of course! But I have to ask Mom if it's okay to skip work after school."

"Okay, bye Babe. Gotta keep the line clear in case Perry tries to call me."

Ginny hung up with a kissing noise and went to get a fresh pair of Baby Doll pajamas out of her dresser. She opened the second drawer and recoiled. Instead of her baby blue cotton set, there it was—

Mr. Gacy's other clown suit, red-and-white candy stripes and all. The one that was supposed to be hanging in her mother's shop, waiting for a special delivery to Mr. Gacy after she'd cleaned it.

Instead, it was folded neatly to fit into the drawer. She choked off a scream and then closed her eyes tight.

The suit was still there when she opened them again.

I'm not seeing this, she thought. *I'm not. It's an illusion. It will go away just like the other one I saw in my closet.*

She shut the drawer tight and flew quickly downstairs. She told her mother she wanted to sleep on the couch in the living room for the night because it was cold upstairs. Mrs. Turner said it was an odd request but didn't object.

At bedtime, Ginny made a makeshift sleeping spot for herself on the couch, using blankets and sheets retrieved from the spare closet in the hall. She was too agitated to sleep, and tried to read a mystery novel for an hour, but her mind kept drifting off into fearful territory.

The suit in the drawer and Perry Waters' disappearance. She felt that the two were somehow connected. But it was only a feeling. In the morning, she promised herself she would go upstairs and see if it was still in the dresser.

With the comforting thought that it might be gone by then, Ginny finally nodded off. Until she awoke at midnight, becoming vaguely aware of a particular sound that didn't resemble the usual night noises of the house settling or wind shaking the timbers.

A weird flapping noise, like straps of leather beating softly against something, in a slow, steady rhythm.

A slow steady rhythm that was coming toward her, *flap* by *flap* by *flap*.

Ginny's heart was in her mouth as she heard the noise get closer and closer. And then she saw it, illuminated by the headlights of a car flashing through the front window. A figure dressed in a red-and-white clown suit, complete with oversized leather shoes. Shoes that made strange flapping noises as their wearer trod across the floor.

Flap. Flap. Flap-Flap.

She bit the back of her hand, stifling the urge to scream. It was Mr. Gacy's clown suit, unmistakably. The red-and-white one. The person in it was staring but not apparently seeing as he made his way slowly toward her. He stopped and loomed over Ginny's terrified form on the couch.

Another passing car's headlights shone through the window, and she could see that her visitor's face was that of Perry Waters, who seemed possessed by some sort of trance.

"Perry!" She whispered loudly. "Where have you been? Everyone's been looking for you! And how did you get in here! This is not a great idea for a joke!"

There was no answer and no movement.

"Perry!"

He shook his head slowly from side to side. Then came a single sentence: "Dying—we are all dying in the dark place."

Then he turned away and walked up the stairs, still in an apparent trance, with the big, flapping shoes making their ominous noise.

Mother! Ginny cried to herself softly. What if this strange new version of Perry attacked or frightened her mother? She had to follow. Wrapped in a quilt, she forced herself to mount the stairs and then crept upwards in the dark on watery legs. She saw with relief that Perry was turning left at the landing toward her own room and not right toward her mother's room.

At the top of the landing, Ginny saw the shadowy shape of her bedroom door half-open in the gloom. She was sure she'd left it closed for the night. She moved silently through the opening, her hand reaching for the light switch on the right side.

Her fingers encountered something shockingly cold, which burned at the same time, like dry ice. Then a face suddenly pushed itself out of the dark, close to hers. Perry Waters's face—bruised and bloody, his eyes still staring sightlessly.

This time, Ginny screamed a real scream; loud, shrill and long. The face drew back into the night shadows and disappeared from her immediate sight.

Mrs. Turner flicked on the light. She was wearing plastic hair curlers, a flannel nightgown, and a frightened look on her face.

"Ginny what is it? Are you all right?" She put her arm around Ginny's waist. "You are shaking like a bowl of Jell-O."

Ginny trembled, speechless, for a good minute, but then calmed down. She looked around the now-illuminated bedroom.

There was no Perry Waters, no clown suit, no flapping oversized shoes. It was all perfectly normal and harmless.

"Bad dream, dear? You must be worried about your friend who's missing," her mother said kindly. "You poor thing. Would you like to sleep in my room for the rest of the night?"

Ginny nodded numbly. "Ye-es, Mother, I would. You go on—I'll be there in a minute."

Her mother gave her a quizzical look. "Are you sure you don't mind being alone in here?"

"I'm not staying long. I just want to check something."

When Mrs. Turner left the room, Ginny opened the second drawer of her dresser. There was nothing there except her spare Baby Doll pajamas and other clothes.

* * *

A day later, November 1978

"Are we really going to call on the pervy clown dude?" Tony asked.

"We have to! It's for Perry!" cried Ginny.

Tony gave her a skeptical frown, his hands on the wheel of his sleek, hard-topped convertible. They were parked on the sidewalk of West Summerdale Drive, a few houses down from Mr. Gacy's residence. They'd spent an hour canvassing residents of the street, asking if anyone had seen or heard of any information pertaining to Perry's whereabouts.

"You had a dream that Perry was wearing Gacy's clown suit and now you think Gacy kidnapped him? Admit it, it sounds ridiculous."

It wasn't a dream! Ginny wanted to protest. *Perry touched me! With a cold burning hand!*

But she remained silent; Tony was already too dismissive of her story.

"We're talking to everyone in the township, remember? Mr. Gacy may have seen or heard something useful from all the people he knows," she reminded Tony. "And besides, we brought along his clean clown suit from the shop." She'd thought a free special delivery might flatter him and put him off-guard.

Tony sighed. "I'm still thinking of that pervy way he looked at me when he was meeting with my mother about the June brunch."

"He can't be pervy if I'm with you."

"True." Tony drove to the curb in front of Mr. Gacy's house, a brick-faced rancher set well back from the street. There'd been snow that morning, but his walkways were neat and clear. The neighbors said he lived there alone, since his second wife divorced him a couple of years ago.

Ginny and Tony went up to the front entrance. Tony pulled open the screen door and rapped on the main door.

They heard a scuffling sound from inside, and then Mr. Gacy opened up, looking somewhat disheveled and uncomfortable. He was wearing a tan button-up shirt, a red cardigan sweater, and brown twill slacks.

Ginny was hit with a blast of foul-smelling air. It smelled like every single nasty thing possible: mold, mildew, rotten eggs, slaughterhouse offal—all rolled into one toxic brew. Tony suppressed a gag, looking ill.

"Yes?" Mr. Gacy said, through the screen door. "Oh, it's you," he acknowledged Tony, with a pained smile, straightening up and smoothing his hair. "And you," he nodded toward Ginny. "How is your mom?"

She held up his clown suit on its hanger, swathed in plastic. "I brought your suit back, nice and clean. My mother wanted me to deliver it personally, no charge."

Mr. Gacy pushed open the screen door and took the bundle from Ginny, draping it over one arm. "My, that's sweet of your mom, Ginny—she spoils me." Ginny thought his smile seemed "off" somehow.

Tony stepped forward. "Mr. Gacy, nice to see you again. My mother got tons of compliments on your appearance at the June brunch. We are also here looking for our missing friend, Perry Waters." He gave a quick description of Perry. "Do you know him? Have you seen or heard of anything suspicious?"

Mr. Gacy shook his head. "No, I don't know the young man. And I haven't heard anything about suspicious characters lurking around either." There was something furtive in his eyes and moisture above his upper lip that looked like sweat.

He's lying, thought Ginny. She saw it with sudden clarity. She threw Tony a sidelong glance, but his face didn't seem to register the same thoughts.

Mr. Gacy shivered. "Hey, you guys, it's cold out there. If that's all you want to know, I'm gonna hafta excuse myself."

Ginny felt a mild rising panic. She had to show Tony what she saw—that Gacy was lying.

"Wait! Do you have mold in your basement?" she blurted out, surprising herself. "My mother says that's why it smells sometimes."

Mr. Gacy was clearly taken aback. The furtive look in his eyes was replaced by momentary fear. Then he recovered smoothly. Tony took a half-step back and Ginny saw that he was starting to have some suspicious thoughts himself.

"Ye-s, yes I do. I apologize for the smell. I've called a specialist about it. Now I really need to go."

A thumping noise came from the inside of the house, and Ginny thought she heard something that sounded like a voice making a single, faint moan.

Mr. Gacy said quickly: "I was hanging a picture, and I think it just fell down. Gotta go fix it." He started to close the door.

"Sure. See ya around, Mr. Gacy." said Tony. Mr. Gacy shut his door tight with an unfriendly click.

"He's a liar!" exploded Ginny, when the duo was back in Tony's car. "He hurt Perry somehow, don't you see? I swear I heard another person in there, after the thumping noise. Oh, Tony, should we call the police?"

Tony snorted, throwing up his hands in a helpless gesture. "And tell them what? My girlfriend had a bad dream about a clown suit? The beloved neighborhood clown lives in a house that smells bad? A picture fell off the wall and made a noise? They'd laugh us out of the station. No, we need to keep looking for solid evidence."

A week later, another body of a young man was found in the Des Plaines River. Ginny and Tony held their collective breaths, but the body was not Perry's. Another drifter, the community consensus said. Not one of ours, they added. Ginny tossed and turned at night, thinking of Perry and then of the thumping sound in Mr. Gacy's house.

* * *

December 1978

The last month of the year rolled around and there were no new leads about Perry. Mr. Gacy was back in Mrs. Turner's dry-cleaning shop, carrying his olive-and-orange clown suit with the patches.

"I have a Christmas party at the firehouse coming up, so I hope I can pick this up in a couple of days," Mr. Gacy told Ginny's mother. "I'm gonna be Patches the Clown for those rowdy firemen." He gave her a broad wink and Ginny felt dizzy. All she could think about was the explanation he'd given before of his two clown personalities and how Patches wasn't always "nice."

Her mother put the suit in the to-be-cleaned bin. "Ginny, you know what to do with the suit. Always the head of the line for our wonderful Mr. Gacy!" She winked back at him, and Ginny suppressed a sigh of disgust.

"That'll be great, Mrs. T.!" said Mr. Gacy. He left the shop loudly whistling *Jingle Bells*.

Ginny rolled the bin into the back of the shop and started sorting the new orders as usual. She reached the clown suit and suddenly froze in her stance.

A fuzzy, light-headed feeling came over her and she almost fainted. She didn't want to touch the suit. She didn't want to clean it. She never wanted to see it again.

Finally, she grabbed her schoolbooks and her purse, opened the back door to the alley, and left, without telling her mother she was going. She hurried along the streets, head down to move faster, half-walking and half-jogging the twelve blocks to her house.

* * *

At home she threw her books and purse on the sofa and ran upstairs to her bedroom. She grabbed her princess phone and dialed Tony.

"He came back to the shop today with one of his suits," she told Tony. "I had a horrible reaction to it; I felt like I was going to pass out!"

"Ginny! I'm glad you left! Don't be so afraid. I'll protect you."

"I can't help it, Tony! I'm scared that I'll see one of the suits again in my house. Because I just realized, whenever he brings one in for cleaning, I see it in a place where it doesn't belong! And then another boy is found in the river or goes missing."

Tony made an odd, strangled sound over the phone wires.

"What's wrong, Tony?"

"Well, I don't suppose you... heard... yet." He paused as if debating with himself whether to continue.

Ginny pounced. "Heard what?"

"A boy is missing in Des Plaines." Des Plaines was the closest suburb to Norwood Park. "Younger than us, only fifteen! He worked part-time at that drugstore where some of us guys buy our baseball cards."

Ginny cried out in shock. "I've been there, too! I've seen that kid and talked to him! Oh Tony, I'm so scared— I don't want to see the clown suit again."

"I'm coming over. You shouldn't be alone in that house. And Ginny—don't look into any closets or drawers. I don't know about seeing things like you said, but I know it'll only upset you."

"Okay, I'll watch for you from the front window. Please come as fast as you can!"

Ginny hurried downstairs. She took the armchair close to the big front window in the living room. The minutes ticked down and it seemed like Tony was taking a very long time to arrive, and he only lived a half-mile away. After forty minutes she tried to call him from the wall phone in the kitchen. She got Tony's mother instead.

"Tony hasn't arrived yet?" Mrs. Halbaum asked. "He left for your house some time ago. Perhaps he had to run an errand first and it's taking longer than expected?"

"Maybe," said Ginny. "But he knows I'm not… feeling well. I hope he gets here soon—"

Mrs. Halbaum suddenly broke in. "Oh, wait. Someone called just before he left, and Tony said it was a person who had some information about Perry Waters. Tony was going to swing by their house before coming to see you."

Ginny felt instantly better. "Oh, really? That is great news about Perry—I hope it leads to Tony finding him! Did Tony say whom he was going to see?"

"No, he didn't say… he was in a hurry to leave."

Ginny hung up, feeling hopeful and relieved. Tony would get information from whomever it was he was meeting with, and he would find Perry safe and sound. Somehow. And all of the madness about the clown suits would go away. Surely it was just her imagination after all.

The wall phone rang almost immediately after she hung up with Mrs. Halbaum, and it turned out to be her mother.

"Ginny!" Mrs. Turner was angry. "What are you doing at home? We are behind on orders because of the holidays!"

"I'm sick, Mom," Ginny lied forcefully. "You were busy with a customer, so I just left. Tony is coming soon to bring me some medicine."

Ginny hung up before her upset mother could sputter an answer.

She returned to the chair by the window and started reading a chapter in her American history book for an upcoming test. She was lost in her studies for at least an hour, when finally, she heard Tony knocking on the front door. *Knock-knock-knock.*

That's weird, she thought. I didn't hear Tony's car running up. She pushed aside the drapes at the window and didn't see Tony's convertible parked in its usual place on the curb in front of her house. But it was indisputably Tony's distinctive knock on the door. Maybe he parked further down the street for some reason.

Knock. Knock-knock-knock. Knock-knock.

"Coming, Tony!" She called, rising eagerly from her chair. She would be so glad to see him!

She opened the door. It was Tony, all right.

Wearing Mr. Gacy's olive-green-and-orange clown suit. And staring at her with dull, unseeing eyes.

"We're all dying in the dark place," he said, in a toneless, mechanical voice.

* * *

Editor's note: A native of Chicago, John Wayne Gacy, aka The Killer Clown, was convicted of killing 33 young men and boys in the years between 1972 and 1978. Twenty-six of his victims were buried in a crawlspace under his house in Norwood Park, Illinois. Some authorities say there could have been more, as Gacy admitted that he had forgotten names and dates of some of his murders. He was sentenced to death by lethal injection, which was carried out on May 10, 1994 at Stateville Correctional Center in Illinois.

Close Encounters of the ER Kind
by N.J. Gallegos

I stepped into the hallway, nearly plowing over a radiology tech. "Sorry!" I called out.

"No big deal, Doc!"

From the examination room behind me echoed a cantankerous, "What'd ya say?"

Ugh. Conjuring a plastic smile, I turned. "Nothing, Mrs. Snell. I'll send the nurse in with your injection soon." She gazed up at me from the stretcher. Deep wrinkles puckered around her mouth—thanks to her standard sucking-lemon expression and chain-smoking habit.

She sneered. "I sure hope so. I'm in pain, can't you see?"

Weren't we all?

Nodding, I gently shut the door. "Bitch," I muttered. I *loathed* the woman; we all did. She feigned dementia— quite well—and under the guise of *illness* wreaked havoc on the entire town: running around ripping down Democrat campaign posters, shoplifting, and once, she stole an idling squad car and drove it to a Bingo game at the Knights of Columbus across town. When confronted about her shitty behavior, she feigned feebleness and turned on the waterworks. The police always sent her to the ER because *she's confused*. Not confused. A cunt, which—unfortunately—is *not* a medical diagnosis.

Rubbing my eyes, I walked up to the nurses' station. Berlin's *Take My Breath Away* drifted from the desktop radio's speakers. "Sally, did we run out of that elephant tranquilizer?"

"Fresh out," she remarked as she scribbled in a chart. "Mrs. Snell, I presume?" Sally's gum snapped, giving me a glimpse of artificial pink.

Rolling my eyes, I answered, "Weird, how'd you know?" I grabbed the next chart from the rack and skimmed the triage note:

Cammie Greene, assault.

"Oh, that one. She's in Room 9. Looks a bit rough but stable," Sally said. "Nasty lac on her head. Stitches for sure." Hands flashing like a Vegas dealer, she distributed a rainbow of pills into various med cups. "I already set up the tray and meds for you."

I took a drink of my coffee and grimaced. Sludge was a more apt term, but caffeine was caffeine, and I needed all the energy I could get. Especially as the clock ticked past 3 a.m. ever so slowly. "Thanks. I'll be in there making her beautiful again."

Sally chuckled. "I doubt that very much."

Entering Room 9, I saw what Sally meant. *Rode hard and put away wet*, my Meemaw would have commented over a cup of black coffee accompanied by a plate of off-brand cookies, as was her habit when gossiping.

"Hi, I'm Dr. Seline and I'll be taking care of you today."

Cammie Green gave me a distrustful look through her one available eye. A purple thundercloud overtook the left side of her face, swelling the eye clean shut. Stringy, dirty blonde hair hung limply around her shoulders—messy, thanks to all the dried blood. A quick glance revealed the source: a jagged laceration extended from Cammie's scalp to just above her battered orbit. Fresh abrasions spotted her chin and cheek. Cracked lips split and she grimaced, croaking out, "Cammie." Dried blood rimmed her mouth, reminding me of a kid who gorged themselves on fresh raspberries.

I pulled gloves on. "Nice to meet you… under the circumstances. I'm sure you'd rather be somewhere else."

"Sure would." Her gaze lingered on me. "Damn… you're real purdy for a doctor."

"Thanks," I replied, brushing her compliment aside. I was used to men commenting on my looks. *Why does a beauty like you need to be a doctor?* Puke. Leaning back against the counter, I asked, "What hurts on you?" Opening with *what happened?*—I'd learned through much trial and error—tended to make people defensive. *Cops* wanted details like that. For the most part, we doctors didn't give a shit. Sure, we're a curious bunch but I'd learned that minding my business was best.

Cammie paused, her one visible eye rolling back as if deep in thought. "Well… most everything smarts but… my head hurts real bad." She wore a man's white undershirt speckled with stains: dirt, food, and plenty of dried blood. A sizable rip in the armpit revealed anemic skin sorely in need of sunshine.

"Even a blind person could see that," I said.

Her lips pulled into a faint smile and her shoulders relaxed. "No shit! Purdy and smart. Ain't I lucky?"

I chuckled nervously. There was something lecherous about how she said that. "Is it okay if I take a look at you?" I asked.

"Hoping you'll do more than that," she remarked, nodding. *She's just joking*, I told myself. *Ignore it*. My fingers gently probed her jawline, and I took in the garden variety of bruises peppering her body. One the size of a fist on her side. Five on her upper arm in the unmistakable pattern of brutal fingers. More abrasions on her stomach and flank. I whistled and commented, "Damn."

"You like what you see?" she asked with a teasing tone.

Ignoring *that*, I asked, "Did… he… rape you?" I knew a man's handiwork when I saw it—women didn't do this type of shit to each other… usually.

Her muddy eye found mine and glittered. "No." Five o'clock from her pupil, a crimson stain bloomed—a subconjunctival hemorrhage that did nothing to improve her looks. "He tried like hell though." Her mouth pinched tightly.

I pulled my Mayo stand to the side of the stretcher, sat, and rolled a silver stool to Cammie's bedside. Exchanged my gloves for sterile ones. "Go ahead and lean back. Don't worry, I won't do anything without telling you first." Clutching the syringe filled with Lidocaine, I commented, "I hope he fared worse than you."

Teeth appeared—yellow-stained and oddly pointy—and her lips twitched upwards for the barest second, but Cammie remained mum.

"Have you had stitches before?" I asked.

She nodded. "It ain't my first rodeo. But I ain't never had such a babe doing 'em."

Should I call Sally in here to chaperone? Cammie was really laying it on thick with the come-ons.

Nah, I reasoned. She's just drunk and scared. Harmless. I gestured with my gloved hand. "Okay, this syringe is filled with numbing medicine. It pinches and burns like a bitch, sorry."

"I know. It's okay. You're just doin' your job. Go ahead."

"Okay. You're gonna feel a pinch," I said, leaning in cautiously, ready to withdraw quickly at any moment. Needles tended to spook most people and I'd had too many patients try to grab my hands, usually while I clutched sharp implements. Cammie remained still, enduring the injection of all ten cc's without a peep. Sally had washed the scalp laceration earlier, rinsing out gravel, bits of tissue, and plenty of blood—fresh and dried. Time and the injected epinephrine slowed the bleeding immensely, which was good. Head wounds bled like stink, and I couldn't see shit if she was gushing like a stuck pig. I poked her—hopefully—anesthetized skin with the suture tip.

"Sharp or pressure?"

"Pressure."

Satisfied, I sunk the suture needle into her skin. I had my work cut out for me: her wound extended to the galea—the fibrous tissue that covered the cranium. Fucking up the repair could mean a serious cosmetic defect… not that Cammie was a beauty queen on her finest day. Still, I took pride in my work.

I'd placed the last subcutaneous suture—knitting the galea together—when I felt something wet on my forearm. Looking down, I saw Cammie's lips only millimeters away from me. "Sorry 'bout that. Was just licking my lips and your arm got in the way," she remarked, as if it were the most normal thing in the world for her tongue to meet my bare skin.

"Don't do that again," I admonished. What in the fuck was wrong with her?

"You got it boss." She waited a beat before adding, "Thanks for takin' care of me."

No apology for licking her doctor I noted. Plucking the 5-0 suture from its package, I clicked my hemostats closed. "You're welcome. Taking care of people is the job."

Keeping blessedly still—most patients wiggled like fresh nightcrawlers plucked from the dirt, especially the drunks and crackheads—she snorted. "You'd be surprised, not everyone thinks like you."

"What do you mean?" I asked, snipping my suture. Perfect tail length too; all the time spent in the Operating Room being berated by surgeons with God complexes had paid off.

She shrugged. "People are turrible. And not just men more apt to use their fists instead of talkin'. Military men. Cops." She paused and I mentally added: *creepy women like you.* "Doctors. No offense."

"None taken," I replied. She wasn't wrong… I knew a few docs running around with undiagnosed personality disorders that counted in that number. "In fact, I agree with you. People with power often abuse it because… well… they can. I see it all the time." And I did. The prominent Senator with a blood alcohol of four hundred roaring down the highway who got off with a stern warning instead of a DUI and jail time; children of influential folks avoiding punishment while money changed hands; men beating hookers just because they could. "Listen, do you need a break? You've been holding still for a while."

She shook her head, fatigue stamped in each crease and wrinkle. Even though I was three years her senior, Cammie looked like she had twenty years on me—at least. Smoking and drinking contributed, but her premature aging was born of something different: pain. "Go ahead. Might as well get it done."

Hemostats and forceps flashing, I worked in silence until Cammie spoke, "I bet you're wondering what happened, huh? I know I'd be curious. Hell, sometimes I can be right nosy!" She chuckled.

She wasn't wrong, I was curious. "I mean… sure I'm curious but I'm not gonna pry—"

Cammie cut me off, "Hell, it ain't pryin' if I wanna tell you, right?" Her eyebrows pinched together, lending her a Frankenstein's monster appearance.

My hands paused before tying the suture. "I guess so."

"You keep goin', just tell me to shut it if my yappin' gets in the way." She flapped her hand dismissively, giving me a glimpse of her fingernails: jagged—making me wonder if she was a nail-biter—and rimmed with red. Blood—what else could it be? Nodding, I continued with the repair.

She cleared her throat—a phlegmy, wet sound—and started, "You can tell lookin' at me that I ain't got no money. No prospects. Got knocked up at fourteen and they took him after I pushed him out, before I even passed the placenta."

"Shit." No wonder she was fucked up.

"Yup. I ain't got no family. Don't got a home. And I ain't gonna lie, I gotta do whatever I can to get by. Hookin'. Turnin' tricks for dinner." She snorted. "I ain't got a car so I ride my thumb a lot. That's what got me in this mess tonight."

I glanced up. "You were hitch-hiking?" I wouldn't dare. I saw *The Hitcher* in theaters when it came out a few years ago and it scared the living shit out of me. Now I made sure my doors were locked and I sure as hell wouldn't stop for hitchhikers.

Cammie nodded.

"Dangerous," I remarked. And stupid.

She grimaced. "Hell, yeah, it's dangerous! This fella too… he acted real nice at first. *Miss* this, *Ma'am* that. Respectful-like." She rolled her eye and winced. "Then, once we got out in the boonies, he started gettin' handsy. I pushed him away, said stop but he didn't give a tin shit. Next thing I know, he's turnin' the pickup down a dark road and lookin' at me from the corners' of his eyes. You seen the road rash, right?"

Oh yeah. All over her face and body. "Yeah."

"I tried to jump out the pickup when it was still movin'. Scraped myself to shit and slick as snot, he was out of the car and on top of me anyway. Punched me a couple times." Based on her wounds—most of his punches found her face. "Almost passed out too." She considered. "Probably woulda if he kept punchin' but he was too busy undoing his belt and shovin' my pants down."

I abandoned my stitching. "Wow. What a piece of shit."

Nothing pissed me off more than rape; after taking care of innumerable sexual assault victims with shattered souls, I sincerely hoped that rapists resided in a very special Hell. Even Satanists thought rape was bad and—following that line of reasoning—their boss, Lucifer didn't condone it either. Even if Cammie was disturbing, she didn't deserve that.

When I saw the movie *Hellraiser* with my girlfriend, I leaned forward, spilling popcorn everywhere, and said: *This is it.*

What? She asked.

Hell for monsters, I replied. And it was. Awful humans paying for their sins, being torn apart by demons with gory, splatter-filled... *pleasure*. God, I hoped Cammie beat the ever-loving piss out of that prick.

She hacked into her fist—a rattly smoker's cough. If she didn't get murdered on the side of the road somewhere, she'd probably die from lung cancer. When she got control of herself again, she croaked, "Can I get some water, please?" A faint wheeze burst from her lungs, audible even without my stethoscope.

Looking around, I spied the collection cup we used for urine sitting on the counter and grabbed it. Held it up to the light. Eyeballed it. Clean. I undid the lid and filled it with tap water. "Here," I said, handing her the cup.

Cammie's weathered hands shook, dribbling half the water down her front. "Tha... thanks." Eye shut and her limbs stilled, delivering the cup to her mouth. Her left bottom lip was a swollen blackberry, stark against her pale skin tone. She swallowed deeply and the wheezing stopped; Cammie regained her composure.

"Sorry, 'bout that." Hands gestured to her throat. It wasn't exactly *bruised*, more so a purplish red, the color of a severe sunburn... suspiciously in the shape of, say— two hands throttling her throat just short of crushing her windpipe. The fucking bastard. She didn't have to say it; we both knew what he'd done.

Then she let out a low chuckle. "Stupid fucker didn't know I had a gun."

My blood chilled.

She thrust her hands up. "Don't worry. I don't got it on me."

"Well, that's good," I said, striving for a sarcastic tone, frantically hoping to God she didn't have a fucking gun. "How about we stop talking about the gun though?"

One look at Cammie told me that her story was true—her exam verified that this crime occurred, thankfully stopping at brutal sexual assault. But I *didn't* need to know; didn't want to know. Once patients started sharing details pertinent to a crime… shit started getting real and I didn't feel like spending one of my days off testifying in court.

"No more," I lowered my voice, "*gun talk.*"

Her hands went up again—*I surrender.* "Sorry, Doc. I won't say anything 'bout…" she paused. "*That.*" I eyed her jeans for suspect bulges roughly the size of a firearm while trying not to be totally obvious about it. Nothing I could see, not that it assuaged my anxieties. She lowered her voice and leaned forward. Hot musty breath gusted out—reeking of decay and booze—and she said, "I grabbed… *somethin'* from my pocket. *Somethin'*, I take when I gotta hitch, you know?" My eyes widened and she let out a hoarse laugh. "How long did it take?" she asked.

"Did… what take?" I asked. The abrupt change in topic confused me, made me off-balance.

She waved. "Your schoolin'; how long did you spend in school studying' like hell?"

I mentally counted. "Counting grade school… like… twenty-four years, give or take?"

"Ha!" Cammie thrust a finger into her chest. "I been hookin' longer than that. And I've seen a lotta shit in that time, lemme tell ya." Her eye got a little misty. "Done a lotta shit too. This prick done fucked up crossin' me tonight. I grabbed the gu—"

"Don't say it," I warned.

She paused. "I grabbed the thing and before he fixed to rape me, I gave him a *Pop, Pop, Pop*!" Cammie's right hand mimed a gun shape and after each *Pop*, her hand recoiled. "Boy… you shoulda heard him scream. Blubberin,' beggin' me to stop. Bastard didn't give a shit when it was me beggin,' I'll tell ya that." She peered down at her jeans and pointed. "See that?"

I did; a huge bloodstain covered the thighs of her jeans. "I see it," I replied.

"That's his, not mine. Blood spurtin' everywhere, him bawlin' somethin' pitiful up. An awful waste of good blood."

What the fuck did that mean? I wondered.

"I plugged 'im again—extra insurance—and I watched the light leave them nasty eyes." Even with the swollen and bruised lip, she grinned—revealing a front tooth that poked further out than its neighbors.

Unable to help myself, I asked in a low voice, "He died?"

Another laugh. "Shit, hon! I didn't check 'im for a pulse so…"

I waved my hands. "Never mind, it's better if I don't know." I peered at her laceration, only a few more sutures and I'd be done. Picking up my tools, I said, "You ready for me to finish up?"

"Go at it," she replied, leaning back. I resumed suturing. "You ever kill a man?" she asked casually.

Goosebumps prickled my forearms. "Um… not on purpose." Every doctor lost patients—sometimes through no fault of our own. Death comes for us all, but we can hasten his arrival with one bad decision.

"There's somethin'… about it. It's like cummin'. You outta try it sometime."

"Uh—" I started and without warning, her hand shot up, clutching my face in a death grip. Her skin against me was pure ice. Unbidden images rose in my mind—vivid and terrible. Dark alleys, ringing gunshots, flashing eyes filled with fear. Slurping sounds. A man's fat neck and my mouth latched to the side, imbibing hot, salty blood. Strength filled my weary bones. A pickup with its driver door ajar, headlights illuminating the swamp beyond.

Cammie bent over a body, eyes closed in utter ecstasy as she licked her fingers clean.

I let out a moan and willed myself to run.

My body remained rigid.

Like skittering spiders, her fingers crawled up the delicate skin of my neck. "Death tastes *so good*." My pulse thrummed, racing faster and faster. Sweat bloomed in my armpits. Then, her mouth was on me—quicker than a striking viper. Enamel rested over my carotid. Not enough pressure to break through… yet. "God, your smell. Imagine your taste." Her bumpy tongue rasped against me. *No, no, no*, I thought but, as if I'd been injected with a paralytic, I was rooted to the spot and rendered immobile.

"I don't kill women, though," she commented. "Only men. They ain't worth nothin'." The scent of stale sweat filled my nose and tears bloomed in my eyes. She brightened. "But… I can make you like me. You'd like that, wouldn't you?" *No, No, No*, chorused through my mind and my bowels clenched. Her teeth broke through, sharp spikes burying themselves in me. Something inside me gave way—my soul fracturing into a billion pieces— and blackness bloomed in the corners of my vision. More images cycled through me: tombs reeking of rot, wooden coffins, swarms of bats swooping and wheeling in front of a full moon, crucifixes, and bonfires. Before I succumbed to blessed unconsciousness, I heard:

"Don't worry, you'll thank me later."

Rough shaking woke me.

"Doc! Holy shit, are you okay?"

Huh? "What?" I said, lurching upright. Electricity crackled between my ears and the side of my neck throbbed. "What happened?" I asked, letting out a groan.

Sally leaned over me, eyes radiating concern. "I dunno. I heard a crash and came running. Found you on the floor." She gestured. "Like this. Out cold."

A glacial chill raced down my spine. "Where's Cammie?"

Sally shook her head. "Gone. I didn't even see her leave." She fixed me with a hard look. "What the fuck happened?"

I considered. What the fuck happened indeed? I cast my mind back, but a dense fog surrounded the memories. Amnesia? Or something else? "I don't know," I admitted.

"Should I call the police?" Sally asked.

I swallowed, tasting copper. "I guess." Must have bitten my tongue when I passed out.

"I'll call them." Sally raced from the room.

Damn, my neck hurt like hell. I gently probed. "What the hell—" Two perfect holes; already scabbed over. The bitch bit me! She fucking bit me, like she thought she had a starring role in *The Lost Boys*! Nuttier than a squirrel turd.

Once the police arrived, I recounted the events of the night—careful to leave out the murder details—but nothing came of it. It was like Cammie didn't exist, like she'd burst into a cloud of bats and disappeared. Went completely off the radar.

I didn't know it then but that wasn't the last time I saw Cammie.

Not by a long shot.

As time passed, I thought about her less and less. Life got busy, as it did. I bought a house and got an orange cat: Oliver. We fell into a routine. I'd come home from work, heat up a TV dinner, and flop on the couch with Oliver for some boob tube and snuggles. A nice, simple life.

But… some nights, I felt a pull: a *hunger*. Off came the scrubs in favor of revealing clothing. I'd troll the bars, picking up desperate men who thought they were about to get lucky—I played the part of an easy lay.

Not so. I was the one getting lucky.

It was so easy to coax them into handcuffs. I'd drive them into a frenzy until their blood roared through their veins—hot and fresh. I dined on the sounds of their screams when I buried my incisors in them—over their femoral artery or carotid. Sanguine wine flooded my mouth, strengthening me. Once I sucked 'em dry, disposing of their bodies was easy enough. The hospital's incinerator made short work of the evidence, and no one batted an eye.

My shift the day I rediscovered Cammie? Horrendous. Everyone tried their damnedest to die—all at the same time, naturally. I shuffled through my front door, jonesing for TV, junk food, a steaming shower, and a bottle (or two) of wine. I'd gone out the night before and drank my fill so my cravings for other vices were minimal.

Shower came first, washing fatigue and germs away. With my wet hair twisted into a towel and glass of red wine in hand, I sat on the couch.

"Mrrrrow?" Oliver said, standing on his hind legs, peering at me with emerald eyes. His front paws rested on the couch cushion, his intent plain: *you gonna invite me up, Mom?*

I patted the cushion next to me. "Get on up here and snuggle your Mommy, Oliver." He hopped up, kneaded some biscuits, then curled up against my leg. His body heat and purrs always calmed me. "What should we watch?" I asked, having fallen into the habit of talking to myself—of course, if Oliver was nearby, I wasn't alone… right? Flipping through the channels, I settled on an episode of *Attack of the Killer Tomatoes*. Nothing more fun than campy ridiculousness.

At the commercial break, I refilled my wineglass and flipped through the channels—always keeping my viewing options open. Sports? Nope. Soap operas? Hell no. The News Channel? Eh… finger poised to change the channel, I stopped, and my mouth gaped open.

What.

The.

Fuck.

A mugshot splashed across the screen. "Holy fucking shit," I said, gripping my wineglass tightly. "It can't be." Oliver shifted and cracked open an eye. Shut it. Resumed his purring.

The mugshot shrunk and a man in a blue blazer appeared on screen, his neatly manicured hands resting on a desk. A white coffee cup sat off to the side and not for the first time, I wondered what it was filled with: water, coffee, beer, or wine.

"Breaking news tonight, especially for those of us residing here in Florida. Experts are calling her "The First Female Serial Killer" while others say she's misunderstood. Regardless, she will stand trial for multiple murders, and it's said that the prosecution will be pushing for the death penalty. She claims it was all in self-defense but…" The reporter's voice droned on, but I heard none of it.

Still clutching my glass, I crept up to the TV screen and studied the mugshot. Same hair and if I squinted, I made out a faint scar on her forehead. I couldn't help but congratulate myself on the repair; it healed up great. She looked different from when I took care of her—both eyes were open and her face wasn't marred by bruises and bumps, but it *was* Cammie Greene.

Otherwise known as—

Aileen Wuornos.

Not one mention of her other proclivities. That was our little secret.

* * *

Editor's note: Aileen Wuornos was sentenced to death in Florida for six murders of male clients while working as a prostitute. She was executed on October 9, 2002, by lethal injection. Allegedly.

David and His Dog
by Bret McCormick

I thought Fort Worth, Texas was a shithole before Dad got reassigned to Minot, North Dakota. I spent the whole two years we were at Carswell Air Force Base, bitching about how there was absolutely nothing to do, whining about the hot summers and mosquitoes. I was clueless.

In retrospect I say cluelessness is just part of being a teenager. Fort Worth was heaven compared to Minot. At least there was Mexican food. In Minot, those poor dumb fucks had never even heard of chips and salsa. They may have discovered such delicacies in the intervening years, though. We're talking about the Seventies here.

Minot was cold as fuck in the winter.

I quit drinking sodas or coffee or water because I had to dress in so many layers of clothes it was like a Houdini escape trick to just get out of them and go to the bathroom. Maybe I was depressed. I didn't eat much either. Bottom line is I lost some weight and for the first time in my short life, boys paid me a little attention. I had been the fat girl back at Carswell and if I had not been

45

best friends with Lana Chalmers I would never have gotten within ten feet of a guy.

Everyone liked Lana—wanted her—so they tolerated me.

Minot was the asshole of America and pickings were slim. That helped, too. I about fell out of my chair when Darby Tanner invited me to a party. Would I go? Hell, yes!

The party was at a Teen Center set up for dependents of the Air Force personnel. It was okay. At least it was warm. There were pinball machines, lots of board games, a TV. No videos because that wasn't even a thing yet, but they did have movie nights sometimes. They'd set up a projector and show something like a spaghetti Western or a monster movie. It was something to do. Thankfully. there were no commercials.

So that party was a major turning point for me. Darby and a couple of other guys asked me to dance. They were sharing whiskey someone had smuggled into the center, pouring little doses of it into the punch cups of whoever wanted it. Everyone else did it so I did, too. I liked that feeling of being drunk, rattling around inside your own skin, laughing at everything. The next morning was a different story, but I'll skip that.

There was this guy named John Carr. He was sort of the leader of the pack. Everyone looked to him to set the pace. It was probably John who brought the booze. And right away, Darby and the others let me know there were other things available for those who wished to partake: pills, grass, maybe even acid.

That word acid made me really nervous. I was about as inexperienced as a sixteen-year-old girl could be and I'd seen the films they made us watch in school. *This is your brain being fried like an egg.* My life sucked bad enough as it was and I didn't want to even consider what it would be like with brain damage. I wasn't going to take acid but I was pretty much up for everything else. Within reason.

Pretty soon I was invited to other parties outside the teen center. Sometimes at an old building that had been some sort of a mechanic shop before. Sometimes at people's houses.

Drinking became a regular thing and I smoked a little weed. They accepted me. Dad was busy, Mom was dead, and I had a lot of freedom. I felt good about that. I stopped feeling like Daddy's little girl and more like my own person, more like a woman.

John Carr was from back East, Brooklyn or the Bronx or something. He was a big city kid.

He came and went from Minot on a regular basis. Sometimes he'd bring his brother Michael with him. They were like the dynamic duo, always stirring up shit. Sometimes they'd bring other people with them to visit. There was some important connection between the people in New York and the people there in North Dakota. I couldn't really figure it out for a while. Once I saw John and Michael getting out of a big black car, like a limousine. Inside there was a heavyset guy who looked really rich. Of course, he *was* rich. He was in a limo, right? But why was he hanging out with a couple of troublemakers like John and Michael? My first thought was, oh, yeah, he's the drug connection.

I first met David during a party that was held at a ranch house just outside the base. He was cute in his own way. Still, he was a little pudgy. Maybe more than a little. He made me think of a cross between John Belushi from the movie *Animal House* and Andy Kaufman from the Eighties TV series called *Taxi*, if you can picture that. Kind of a cherub face with big red lips. Always smiling.

HellBound Books

We noticed each other and I guess we sort of connected right away.

The other girls probably weren't so interested in David because of his weight. But I knew what it was like to be the fat one, so it didn't bother me at all. I thought he was okay and he was really close to John and Michael, so that gave him some status. I'd lost my virginity to Darby about a month before, but he'd already moved on to Rebecca Hightower. So, I was available. And David was definitely interested in me.

It was right about the time that David showed up that it became obvious these guys weren't just reckless partiers, they were part of a cult. I started hearing things about 'the Children' and 'the Process.' I didn't pay a lot of attention; I was too busy getting drunk and stoned.

The music at the parties had always had a sort of cultish quality, like Black Sabbath, Blood Rock, maybe Zeppelin. That was just a trend in the music back then. The flower children had enjoyed their fifteen minutes of fame and now we were off into the world of witchcraft and Satanism. It wasn't exactly my cup of tea, but it beat the hell out of disco music. I said it then and I still say it, disco sucks.

Long story short, I started hanging with David. We went to a ritual outside the old mechanic shop. It was really kind of cool, like a scene from a movie. There was a big bonfire and some of the people there, ones I'd never seen before, were walking around bare-ass naked. Guys and chicks. That was new. I was still a little self-conscious about my body so I wasn't about to peel, but I admired their bravado.

The music they played that night was nothing I'd ever heard before, stuff recorded by some band back East. Most of it was instrumental, no words, and it made you feel high even if you hadn't had a drink or a toke.

Spring was coming on, so it was still a little chilly out. David wrapped his arms around me to keep me warm. I wondered how the naked folks were feeling. They showed no signs of discomfort. The chicks' nips were hard and the guys' peckers were shrunken but other than that, they seemed fine. I was having a great time until they brought out the dogs.

These dogs were big and beautiful. My dad always called them Alsatians, but most people just call them German Shepherds. I wondered what was up. I'd seen John and Michael walking around with dogs like these before, but never at a party. The crazy thought popped into my head that those naked women were going to let those dogs have sex with them. I had no reason to think that and frankly I grossed myself out by dredging up that thought from my subconscious.

Where had that come from?

That wasn't it, though.

They killed the dogs. Quick, savage, without warning. Just cut their throats, then hung them over a wash tub to collect the blood.

I think I screamed. I'm pretty sure I did. Then David was shushing me, calming me, kissing me, and looking at me with those angelic eyes. I kind of went into a different space. Like I was outside my body having a dream. The fear left and I watched with fascination as the naked ones smeared the blood on their bodies. They made it seem almost orgasmic.

Then a lot of the others stepped up and drank dog's blood from the tub. Just scooped it up in a coffee mug and swallowed it right down. I didn't, but David did. I still remember that goofy childlike look on his face like a kid caught in the cookie jar, he's just grinning and nodding at me, blood running down his chin.

I didn't drink the blood but even if I'd wanted to, I would not have been allowed. That was just for the Children and I wasn't a member. It was like their Communion, you know?

David had his own dog there that night. A big black dog. Maybe a Labrador? I don't know I'm not much of a dog person. But that dog kept coming up and rubbing against us. It kept sliding between my legs, looking up at me and panting. David called him Sam.

"I didn't know you had a dog," I said after the shock of everything had worn off a little.

"I don't have him. He has me," David said. He knelt down and let Sam lick the blood off his chin. "Like that Sam?"

He was talking to his dog the way pet owners always do. You know that sappy kind of talk, baby talk, like women do with their toddlers.

What made this different was that Sam said, very clearly, "Yes, David. You know I do."

That dog sounded like a fucking college professor. Perfect diction.

"What did you dose me with, David?" I said, scared and angry. I'm thinking he must have put LSD in my drink.

"Nothing, nothing baby, I swear."

I pulled away from him. "I just heard your dog talk for fuck's sake! That's not normal, David!"

"Chill! Chill!" He shushed me and wrapped his arms around me even though I was resisting. "It's not normal because Sam's not a normal dog."

Sam sat down on his haunches and looked up at us, mouth open, tongue hanging out.

"Tell her how old you are, Sam," David said, giggling.

"In dog years?" Sam asked. They both laughed really hard. I felt sick. I bent over and vomited on the pavement.

"That's right," David said to me, "let it out."

"Time means little to me," Sam said. "I live both inside and outside of the restriction you call time. But since it's such an important thing to you humans, the best approximation is six thousand years."

David laughed and squeezed me. "Isn't that a fucking trip? Sam's over six thousand years old!"

"I made my first appearance on this world in Babylon. You've probably never heard of Babylon," Sam said, clearing his throat.

Now, that pissed me off. I wasn't great in school, I admit that. But I'd be damned if I was going to let a dog talk down to me. "Of course, I've heard of fucking Babylon," I said. "It's in the Bible."

"Good," Sam said. To David he added, "I like her; she's got spunk. You should bring her into the Children."

"Yeah." David beamed, looking back and forth from Sam to me. "That's what I thought. She'd fit right in."

I have other memories from that night. I mean, I think they're memories, they feel like memories. But if you think a talking six-thousand-year-old-dog is insane, the rest of the night would seem so far over the top that … well, I just don't want to go there. Okay?

When I woke up the next morning I hurt everywhere. All my muscles ached. My head was throbbing. I hurt inside, you know? Like in very private places. I'd bitten my tongue sometime during the night. It hurt like hell. I could barely drink water or talk. Most of all there was a pain in my brain. It was an idea of pain, a very serious idea that would not let up. Every time I even thought about how to make it go away I'd see mental images of Sam, the dog, shaking his head and warning me not to try. My head was splitting.

Dad and I finally had a major showdown. When he saw the condition I was in he flipped. He screamed at me full blast for over an hour. He said I wasn't hanging out with that "criminal trash" ever again. I didn't really disagree with him, but I was angry.

You know, I thought I was all grown up and beyond Daddy telling me what to do. I would've argued back more than I did, but my tongue was killing me. And my head was in agony. Every time I felt a surge of pain, I'd see that black dog Sam in my mind's eye, panting, wagging his tail, soaking up the misery just like licking the blood from David's chin.

I never saw David again. Not in person. Later, Rebecca told me he'd gone back to Queens or Bronx or Brooklyn or whatever.

Within two weeks, Dad had me on a plane to California. His sister, my aunt Heidi, had agreed to let me stay with her a while in Berkeley. She worked at the university as a secretary or something. Heidi was good to me. She helped me get my head on straight. Taught me how to have a little self-respect. She explained I could still be a girl, still have a life without making myself a doormat for others.

Berkeley was cool. It seemed every bit as trippy as Minot, but it was not Satanic. Sort of like the flip side of the coin, the flower child version, minus the blood drinking and Satan-worshiping. There was a real smart vibe there. Everyone leaned toward the intellectual, less toward the sensual.

Sometimes, when I least expected it, Sam would burst into my consciousness like a bat out of hell. He was trying to convince me he still owned me. Like I was his human and I couldn't do a damn thing about it. Once I saw two dogs engaged in sex on somebody's lawn. We were just driving by, I looked out the window and saw these dogs fucking. Then it was like I got hit by a freight train, slammed into a wall and Sam was humping me and snickering as he whispered things into my ear. It hurt. It hurt bad. It seemed completely real. And the scariest part was that part of me actually liked it. My aunt Heidi was driving the car. She said I looked like I'd gone into a coma. I was drooling and unresponsive. Then I snapped out of it. I couldn't bring myself to tell her what I'd really experienced. Or dreamed. Or… oh, God, whatever!

Another time I was shopping at the local grocery store. I happened to be passing down the aisle where the dog food was on display. I heard someone whisper my name. When I looked over, I saw the grinning face of a big, black dog—a dog like Sam—leering at me from the label on a twenty-pound bag of kibble. I froze. He barked at me and for a split second I was on rocky ground and Sam was tearing into my abdomen, stringing my guts out all around me, prancing and whining, laughing and growling the word, "Yummy!" I dropped a jar of pickles on the floor of the supermarket. What a mess. Glass, brine and pickles everywhere. A woman with gray hair, wearing a string of pearls muttered, "Stupid girl! Drugs!" Then she licked her lips in an exaggerated way and I would have sworn it was Sam looking at me through her old, blue eyes.

It took some time, but finally I quit seeing Sam in my head. I convinced myself it was all just a bad trip, an acid thing, a fictional experience brought on by the drugs. I was living a normal life and preparing to go to college. It wasn't easy because I'd never really focused on schoolwork. It was a chore but I surprised myself and my dad. Aunt Heidi said she always knew I had it in me.

I was so wrapped up in schoolwork and my new circle of friends I paid no attention to current events. Then one evening as Heidi and I sat down to dinner, I heard the name David Berkowitz coming from the news broadcast on the TV. I looked up and saw David smiling like a naughty boy as the NYPD led him away in handcuffs. Same pudgy cheeks, same red lips. They said he'd shot a bunch of people.

I started crying and I could feel Sam digging away with those big paws of his, trying to burrow back into my mind. Heidi shut the TV off and forbade me to watch the news after that.

She was shocked at the way I'd just freaked. I didn't tell her about my connection with David. I believed then, and I still believe, that all that stuff, that dark magic, rides into this world on our thoughts. The less we talk about it or even think about it, the harder it is for six-thousand-year-old dogs to dig tunnels into our reality.

I've done okay for myself. I've had a good life. Worked as a registered nurse most of my adult life. I did my best. I think I can honestly say I've done some good in the world. And that's important. Not just to me. To all of us. Who knows what would've happened to me if I'd stayed in Minot. Maybe I would've ended up in Brooklyn or whatever, squeezing the trigger and killing strangers.

I'll probably have bad dreams tonight. I hope not, but I probably will. Just because I talked about it… *them*… David and Sam. But I thought you needed to know.

* * *

Editor's note: David Berkowitz, known as the "Son of Sam" killer, pled guilty to six killings and eight shootings in New York that he committed from 1976-1977. He is currently serving six life sentences in the Shawangunk Correctional Facility, New York State.

Happy Face
by Jayna Locke

Keith Jesperson — Riverside California, August 1992

The road rolled beneath his wheels, thrumming with a force so powerful that it still thrilled him. It reminded him of the rushing Columbia River in Oregon where he had tossed a woman's body two years ago into the otherwise scenic gorge the river wound through. He passed the spot sometimes on his route and thought of her. A simple girl. Playful as a kitten. Too trusting.

Something about her, perhaps her irritating innocence, had reminded him of the stupid little cats he had tortured and annihilated as a child when rage overcame him—when his father berated him, and the school kids and even his brothers called him Igor. He'd been a big kid. Oversized.

Yet somehow powerless against them all.

Paul Young was on the radio, singing about a guilty face. Feeling so out of place. How did songs mirror real life sometimes, as if drawing something from your very consciousness? The song knew how he felt. Horny. Pent up. Angry. Alone.

That simple girl, Sonya, had been his first. There would be more. He knew that. It was just a matter of time. A matter of when. And how.

He gripped the wheel of his rig, as the sun lowered toward the horizon, and he thought about where he'd spend the night. Long-haul trucking wasn't for everyone. The lonely nights, the endless road, the truck stop coffee and the girls that just wanted to take your money for half-assed sex. But it wasn't a bad life for a man who liked to take different women to bed. Even slap them around sometimes if they annoyed him. He took pride in leaving it at that. Hurting them and then letting them go. It took a lot of willpower to send them stumbling off into the night, bruised and crying, but alive. In fact, it required more and more willpower each time. It was an almost exquisite sensation that he nursed along for now, until he wouldn't be able to control himself any longer.

Maybe that was the best thing about his wife taking the kids and moving away. Maybe it was the silver lining to the fact that his dream of being in the Royal Canadian Mounted Police had crashed to the ground when he sustained a shoulder injury. He'd recovered, and yet they still rejected him. Oh, he was so very angry. But it wasn't all bad. Now he could roll. He had the freedom to think, to plan, to do what he wanted, with whomever he wanted. Even sick things, sometimes. And there was no one to stop him.

He slowed down, passing through the outskirts of Riverside. He checked his watch and took the exit. He was still on schedule. Maybe the time was ripe for a little roadside attraction.

News Report, August 30, 1992, Blythe, California

Discovery of Murdered Woman in Blythe, California Sparks Investigation

BLYTHE, CA - The body of an unidentified woman has been found on the outskirts of Blythe, California. The victim had been sexually assaulted and strangled, according to local law enforcement.

The woman's body was discovered by a passerby early this morning, who alerted authorities. The Riverside County Sheriff's Office responded to the scene, and detectives have launched an investigation into the circumstances surrounding the incident.

The victim, whose identity is unknown, is described as a Caucasian female, approximately in her late twenties, with curly blonde hair. She was wearing blue denim shorts and a white crop top.

The button to her shorts had been roughly cut off with scissors or a knife. She had no personal identification.

In a Blythe truck stop, a scrawled note was subsequently discovered on a stall in a men's public restroom, which authorities believe may be related. The note reads: "*I did it. So you can't take credit, Laverne. Have a nice day.*" This was followed by a drawn smiley face.

Authorities are appealing to the public for assistance with any tips that may support the investigation, including information relating to missing persons. Investigators hope that with the public's help, they can swiftly bring the killer to justice.

Martha Singleton — Spokane, Washington, October 1992

The cool breeze wafted in through the windows like a restless spirit, signaling a change in the weather.

Fall in the Pacific Northwest was lovely, but it brought on a peculiar sense of melancholy too. Since her divorce from Keith two years ago, she had been on something of a roller coaster, wondering how things could have turned out this way. How she became a single mom, raising three young children under the age of ten on her own. It only took a cool autumn morning, and a look at her kids playing in the yard without their father here to mind them, throw a ball with them, or kiss them goodnight, and her emotions went spinning. Yet, she had left of her own volition. She'd done the right thing. The man was an ass.

She turned the pages of the newspaper while drinking her coffee. Keith would be coming for a visit today. She'd have to brace herself. His visits were infrequent, but had a powerful effect on all of them. The children would become over-excited and petulant, all wanting gifts from his travels, which he brought just often enough to fuel their anticipation.

At least he cared. That was something. But then why had he thrown all this away by sleeping with other women? She would never forget the phone calls to the house from various girls claiming to be his girlfriend after he landed the trucking job. "Well, I'm his wife," she'd say to them.

Not anymore. *You can have him, bitches*, she thought. Her coffee was growing cold, as if the life was slowly draining out of it.

She shivered. Considered pouring a fresh cup. Then an article caught her eye. Another woman's body had been found in California—beaten and strangled—and investigators were beginning to consider the possibility that a serial killer was responsible. Some creep had been taking responsibility for the killings from here to Southern Cal, adding a smiley face to notes he sent to the police and scribbled on bathroom walls, then signing them with, "Have a nice day. Happy Face." Three women had been raped and strangled since September.

Bizarrely enough, Happy Face was also claiming responsibility for the rape and murder of Sonya Barrett, that poor mentally challenged girl in the Northwest a few years back. A terrible, heartbreaking case. Martha shook her head, remembering how they had found Sonya's body, beaten and strangled, in a ravine by the Columbia River Gorge. The girl's sister was watching a news report on the murder and recognized her clothes. Horrible.

But it made no sense that it was the same guy, because a woman named Laverne Pavlinak and her boyfriend John Sosnovske had already confessed and been convicted for Barrett's murder.

Why would this Happy Face killer want to claim a murder he didn't commit? Well… there was just no accounting for sick minds.

His note had read:

"I killed Sonya Barrett January 21, 1990, in Portland, Oregon. I beat her to death, raped her and loved it. I'm sick but I enjoy myself too. Two people took the blame and I'm free."

She wiped her face with her hand, thinking of Sonya's sister. Imagining the sickening discovery that something like that had happened to someone you love.

Her thoughts were disrupted by a sound like thunder that she quickly recognized as the powerful engine of her ex-husband's semi. It wasn't something you heard much in the suburbs off the main highway, and it always caused a palpable anxiety deep in her gut, with its low, menacing rumble like a caged beast. Time to steel herself to see him again. He was her children's father, after all.

The children raced in through the back door into the kitchen, shouting, "It's Daddy! It's Daddy! He's coming!" They ran in circles and leapt like jackrabbits.

"Calm down, kids," she said. "You know Daddy doesn't like too much squealing. It puts him off. Come on, now. Let's see your best behavior."

A moment later, the front door opened, and her giant of an ex-husband was there standing in her doorway, all six feet, six inches of him. He seemed bigger than ever, blocking the light coming through the door. No wonder they had called him Igor as a child.

The children ran and were scooped up into his arms. "Hi Martha. Hey, kids," he said.

His voice was joyless, distant and nervous. He glanced around the house, as if he thought someone unexpected might jump out of a closet or something.

He held up a slightly battered sack. "I've got presents," he said. "But you kids have to be calm to get them."

Martha smiled at the kids. She could see they were doing their best, switching from frenzied jumping to bouncing up and down on their heels.

"Look," he said, pulling three enormous multi-colored lollipops from the sack. "You'll never guess where I got these."

Renee, the oldest, found a sticker on her lollipop. "Oh!" she said. "They're from Disneyland! Will you take us there sometime, Dad?"

"Yes! Yes!" the other two squealed.

He quickly stood up from where he was crouching with the kids, a taut smile frozen to his face.

He ran his hand through his hair and looked around again in that disturbing way, unnerved by his own shadow.

"All of us in Southern Cal? No, I don't know about that."

The door still stood open, and outside a car passed by on the street, kicking up fall leaves.

Martha squinted, watching him. This edgy, odd behavior seemed like a piece to some puzzle. But there were too many pieces missing for her to put it together.

"Someday," he said finally. "We'll see."

The children peeled the wrappers from their lollipops and began licking them. What was she going to do with these things? She imagined weeks of trying to keep them from getting stuck to couches, and helping the kids to keep straight whose was whose. And ultimately, they would break. They would get dropped or stepped on. And these gaudy symbols of their father's affections would only lead to tears.

"Daddy," Renee asked, "where are you taking us today?"

Keith ignored his daughter and turned to Martha. "Hey, uh, do you have any coffee made by any chance?"

"Sure. Yes, I just made a fresh pot."

He nodded and went out the door and down the path to his truck. A moment later, he came back with a stained thermos, and walked past her and the kids to the kitchen. Soon, she heard the sound of him emptying the entire pot into his thermos.

"Well," he said, when he returned to the front hallway. "I'd better hit the road. Good to see ya, kids."

The children protested. Wasn't he going to play with them? Couldn't he take them to the park, like last time? The girls began tugging at his hands and his clothes. Robby sat down on the floor and began to cry. "I wanted to show you my new kite, Daddy. Can't you help me fly it?"

"Come on, Dad, pleeeeeeze," Lucy said.

Martha held her breath. Something came over him at times like these. A black shadow that changed his countenance, as if rage was boiling within him. And a disturbing thought came to mind. A memory of a time he had killed some little kittens out behind the house. And other times, other small animals. Squirrels. Bunnies. He'd said it was important to keep rodents from proliferating. Then one day, he actually killed the family dog for misbehaving. It had traumatized all of them. And the way he seemed to light up when he was in control, tormenting beings that were small and weak, made her feel ill.

He appeared to be vacillating now, considering whether to stay and take them to the park, which was part of the deal. He had always taken them out somewhere, to a play area or McDonalds, and then she enjoyed the short break from the demands of single motherhood. But now something terrible gripped her. She couldn't shake the feeling that had come over her at the start of the day when the cool wind blew in like a ghost delivering a message. Something was wrong.

"That's okay," she said. "It's good to see you, Keith. I can see you have to get going. Say goodbye to your father, children."

Keith bent down and hugged the kids once more, promising to stay longer next time. Then he was out the door, with the kids staring after him, holding their sticky lollipops. A few moments later, he started up the truck and rumbled away, taking with him the sense she had felt, of something sinister and menacing that bordered on terror.

News Report, June 4, 1993, Santa Nella, California

Woman's Body Found Near Santa Nella

Santa Nella, CA - Police are looking for a suspect in the murder of an unidentified woman found along a dirt turnout on Highway 152 in Santa Nella, California yesterday.

The woman had been sexually assaulted and strangled. Jane Doe, as she is being referred to at this time, is described as a Caucasian female of medium height and build, with auburn hair.

Local authorities are asking for leads. The victim had no identification. Forensics specialists are seeking to determine her identity based on dental or medical records, but so far, no additional information has been supplied to the public.

Authorities stated that over 200,000 women go missing each year in the U.S. alone, and over 500 bodies are found without identification, creating a highly complicated task for homicide units.

Many of these cases go cold and are never solved. However, modern forensics and genetics are continually advancing and there is hope that new tools will increasingly support more effective crime-solving in these cases.

Keith Jesperson — Florida, September 1994

He sat at the counter of the truck stop cafe with his breakfast and newspaper, watching the waitress as she dumped out the coffee grounds from the big industrial coffee maker, refilled it and started up the machine. Each time she reached to open, lift, pour, her uniform raised up so that he could *almost* see her panties. He smiled when she looked his way. The kind, comforting smile that always won them over.

He thought of the last four years and everything he'd done. Terrible things. How each time it started with an urge, like curiosity, anger and desire all swirling together in his gut. Sometimes he would sweat. Or his hands would shake. Until it was done, he got his release, and a dead woman lay beneath his hands. Then there were bodies to contend with. Mess. He would cut off the buttons of their pants, which always seemed the most likely place for his fingerprints to be recoverable. He would dispose of those separately. Then he'd dump the bodies.

He should stop. Then he could live a normal life and cleanse his mind of the images of death. The closed throats, bloodied lips and twisted expressions. But each time the next one beckoned. And the need was like thirst in the driest desert. He had to quench that thirst.

The prostitutes had mostly gone down easy. Perhaps they were just so beaten down by life that you could knock them over with a feather. Catherine, the one he'd picked up in Riverside and dumped in Blythe, whom the police were still calling Jane Doe, had been the easiest of all. Like she felt it was coming to her. When he got fed up with her simpering and her affectations—for what? To impress him? Make more money?—he held her mouth shut, raped her, and then closed his hands around her neck. Tighter and tighter. She had looked at him, plaintive and scared with her eyes full of tears, yet resigned to her fate as her life left her.

The waitress topped up his coffee. He smiled and pushed his empty plate toward her. She returned his smile as she slipped a tip into her pocket.

He began to count on his fingers. Sonya in Oregon. One. Not a prostitute. Just a simpleton. Catherine from

Riverside. Two. Then there was Nina in Turlock, the bitch who made the life-altering mistake of climbing into his truck while he was sleeping and propositioning him. Three. Lisa, the prostitute in Salem, Oregon who tried to jack up her rates. Four. Then the woman in Santa Nella. Betsy, or maybe Brenda. Five. He didn't always ask their names. But he'd gotten better at the whole business. Now he kept duct tape and zip ties handy, for the ones that became unruly.

With the truck stop waitress brushing past, collecting his plate, bending down to set it in a bus tub so that he could see her cleavage... well, that made things simple. She wore a name tag.

Mandy.

"They're keeping you busy here, Miss Mandy," he said, turning a page of his newspaper. He kept his tone light, almost indifferent. A man who wanted to get somewhere shouldn't come off as one of those predator types. Women had their radar up for that.

"Weekends are always like this," she said. Then she leaned on the counter right next to him for a moment, and in that enticing proximity she emitted an aroma of food and coffee and a faint whiff of perfume. "Been on the road long?"

"You might say that," he said, adding a wistful air to his voice. "Years, actually. Sometimes it feels like centuries. Lotta miles pass beneath those wheels." It sounded romantic, even to him. There was a certain allure to truckers for some people.

"Is this what you grew up wanting to be? Did you just always know you'd be a trucker?" She straightened again, reached for the coffee pot and filled the cup of a grizzled man reading the paper just a few stools to his left.

Fortunately, she missed his involuntary flinch, which happened whenever he thought of his slaughtered dream of being a Mountie.

"Yeah, I think so," he said. "It was a choice between this and joining the Royal Canadian Mounted Police. They wanted me, of course. I have the right build for it and all. But I guess you could say this job won." He sighed. "I like the freedom of the open road. There's always another town, another adventure."

"It does sound nice."

"It suits me," he said, with another one of his winning smiles. They were getting along just fine.

He began imagining what would come next. A date, perhaps. A little ride when she got off her shift. Florida was nice this time of year. It was always the question of how to take that next step. Or better yet, to get the girl to suggest it. Because invariably it all went more smoothly if it was her idea.

He reached for his wallet, signaling that it was time for him to pay, to get going. And now that they had a connection, she wasn't going to just let him go. He was counting on that. He felt the telltale sweat in his palms. The thirst and desire.

But then something happened. In the very next moment, it was as if a cosmic shift interrupted his plans. And certainly, it changed the fate of Miss Mandy. The door jangled, and a young woman with a backpack came in and plunked herself down at the counter two stools away.

"Whew!" she said. "It's good to sit. I have walked and *walked* this morning, without getting a ride."

Mandy held up the coffee pot and the girl nodded. "Oh yes, please. In fact, it's a medical emergency." She smiled at Keith then turned back to Mandy. "Not to mention eggs over easy with bacon and toast, please. Thanks honey."

Mandy wrote down the girl's request on her order pad, tore it off, and pinned it to a clip on a rotating order holder, which she then turned so it revolved its way into the kitchen. On the other side of a steel window with heat lamps, a cook in a white chef's outfit snatched the ticket and went to work.

"Oh my God," the girl said. "It's like 'open sesame.' Or 'Your wish is my command.' I love how that works!"

Keith couldn't help but smile. This girl was not his type. Not one bit. She was way too spunky. Too lively. Like those fish that take hours to reel in. And yet…

"I'm Alanna," she said. "How about you, Mr. Long, Tall Drink of Water?"

He laughed. How many times had he been called that—a long, tall drink of water? It sure beat *Igor*.

"Johnny," he said at the last moment. Because if this was the last place anyone remembered seeing this girl, he didn't want them saying she left with a man named Keith. What had she said her name was? Elaine, he thought. Something like that.

Elaine sipped her coffee and looked along the counter at the others seated there, in various phases of drinking coffee, eating breakfast, chatting with their neighbors or paying up. Then her eyes came to rest on him. It was as if she wanted to compare her prospects and finally decided she was in the right place at the right time. "So, where are you headed, Johnny?"

He took a stab and said north, though he added that he might consider a detour, if needed.

Elaine tilted her head, evaluating him. She was older than she seemed at first. In her thirties, he suspected. Fine wrinkles collected around her eyes when she smiled.

"What about you?" he asked. "Where are you going?"

Mandy set Elaine's breakfast plate down in front of her. The charms on one of Elaine's bracelets jingled as she picked up a piece of bacon. She laughed. "I've been asking myself that very question. Just depends on which way the wind is blowing."

"No particular destination, then? What do you do, just see who's going your way?"

"Pretty much," Elaine said. "It's gotten me to some pretty cool places, all across the country. The Grand Canyon. The Smoky Mountains. The Florida Keys. It's an incredible country we live in."

She began to eat her breakfast in earnest, as if worried she would miss a ride if he was getting ready to head out.

She needn't worry. He was curious about this one. He could have some fun with her until he could get back home to his girlfriend Suzy in Washington. He gave her a smile as he paid up.

And the next thing he knew, she was paying too, and he was giving Mandy one last look as he and Elaine separately headed for the door, as if they each were on unrelated missions. As if they had nothing to do with one another.

In the cab, Elaine asked if he'd take her to Cairo, Georgia.

"Why not?" he said. "It's not too far out of my way." He was enjoying having someone to talk to, even as he imagined what might happen between them later.

But things did not go well. Not like he anticipated. Cairo was small and boring. They ate lunch in a diner, though the charm had worn off. When they returned to the truck, Elaine asked him to take her to the coast. She wanted to see Savannah.

He shook his head. These detours would cost him. He had a route and deliveries to think of.

"I still have business in Florida," he said. "Why don't you come along for the ride?"

She had become quiet and edgy, like she sensed something about him. Like maybe he couldn't be trusted. "Actually, I think I'll just get off in the next town," she said. "I feel like I need to get out. See some things."

So… she changed her tune. He'd thought she wanted to travel, and that she'd go anywhere he needed to go. What was wrong with that plan? He began thinking of ways to detain her.

"Oh, come on," he said. "We're just getting started. I'll take you along the Gulf Coast. It's very scenic."

"No thanks. I want to go to the Georgia coast. I've already seen the Gulf."

This was not good. Not good at all. "No," he said. "Now just settle down. You wanted to come along on the road, and that's what you're going to do."

He watched her as she turned away from him to look out the window, as if contemplating the possibility of opening the door and jumping out. When she looked back at him, there was fear in her eyes. She was trapped. Out of choices. And she knew it.

"Look," he said, with a mollifying tone, "It's going to be alright. You want to see the sights, and I need someone to talk to. Let's just see how it goes. If you're still wanting to go your own way by the end of the day, we'll part company. I promise. I'm sure you'll be able to hitch a ride back that way."

She stared at him for a long moment, as if weighing the likelihood that he was a man of his word. Then she nodded and seemed to relax a bit. She looked very tired.

"Why don't you go back to the bed and rest? Have a nap. I'll wake you up when we get to my favorite spot on the Gulf. You can see the most beautiful sight there is to see in the continental U.S. Then you can decide what you want to do from there."

She looked out the window again, at the trees and signs passing by at 70 miles an hour. "Okay," she said. "I'll take a nap."

What she didn't know was that he was well equipped with various restraints. His zip ties would do the trick nicely. Once she was asleep, he would pull off the road and shackle her to the bed. It was all so simple.

Or it could have been, if she hadn't screamed. She woke up, just as he secured her wrist and emitted an ear-piercing shriek.

"Stop that," he said, putting his hand over her mouth. "You can't make all that noise. I don't want to hurt you, so you have to stay quiet."

They were in a truck stop and he could see a security vehicle parked nearby. He wasn't supposed to have people in his rig, and he couldn't risk losing his license. What had he been thinking, parking here?

But she didn't stop. She screamed right through his fingers, then tried to bite him. He clamped tighter. "Shut up!" he hissed. The screaming continued, though muffled. She was strong. And he was sure her voice could carry.

He had no choice, really. What else could he do? He punched her with his powerful fist, right in the throat. She buckled. Then he took one of the zip ties and quickly wrapped it around her neck, tightening it against her throbbing voice box.

"Say hi to Happy Face," he said.

Her eyes grew wide, panicked. And he found himself smiling at her—pulling the zip tie tighter and tighter, high on adrenaline and triumph—until there was no life left and her dull blue eyes stared lifelessly at him. Accusing him of murder.

Yet the screaming seemed to go on and on in a torrent of grief and misery. In fact, it would echo in his ears for a very long time to come.

News Report, September 15, 1994 Holt, Florida

Unidentified Woman Found Murdered

HOLT, FL - The community of Holt, Florida is reeling today after the discovery of a woman's body near Interstate 10. The woman had been strangled and beaten. She had no identification and is currently being referred to as Jane Doe.

Local authorities are asking for anyone with knowledge of the incident to come forward, and will be reviewing reports of missing persons in the local area.

The victim is described as a Caucasian female, in her early thirties, with wavy, ash blonde hair. She was wearing a light blue jacket, blue jeans, and jewelry, including several charm bracelets. The button of her jeans appeared to have been cut off with a knife. There is no known motive, and the killer remains at large.

Keith Jesperson, March 1995, State of Washington

No one was paying any attention. He was known as The Happy Face Killer. Great. But he wasn't getting credit for the women they were calling Jane Doe, or for the other victims he'd claimed. The stupid police weren't putting all the pieces together, even with the notes he sent explaining what he'd done, with his happy face signature. What's the fun of getting away with murder without anyone knowing about it?

Meanwhile, Laverne Pavlinak and John Sosnovske were serving life sentences for the murder of Sonya in 1990. His murder. It just wasn't right.

He didn't want to be caught and blamed. He just wanted the Happy Face Killer to get credit where credit was due. There were seven, damnit.

His brain sizzled. Depression and anxiety were consuming him. And he kept hearing the screaming. Why wouldn't the screaming stop? It was possible—perhaps even inevitable—that he would have to come clean. But first, there was one more thing to do.

News Report, March 11, 1995, Spokane Washington

The Body of Local Woman Found Murdered

Spokane, WA - Suzy Worthington, a woman from the local area, has been found dead. She had been strangled and left by the side of the road. Police are questioning those in her circle in connection with her death, including her boyfriend, Keith Jesperson, who has denied any knowledge of the incident and has told authorities he is in deep grief.

Worthington had a long-time career as a long-haul trucker and is said by her sister to have had a free spirit and a loving disposition. The family asks anyone with knowledge around Worthington's murder to come forward.

News Report, March 30, 1995, Spokane Washington

Local Man Arrested in Connection with the Murder of Suzy Worthington

Spokane, WA - Keith Hunter Jesperson, surviving boyfriend of recently deceased Suzy Worthington of Spokane, and a long-haul trucker by profession, has been arrested on suspicion of her murder. Jesperson is said to have confessed to killing Worthington, and has also taken responsibility for the murders of several other women over the past five years. At times he claims to have killed over 160 women between California and Florida, while traversing the country on his trucking routes. At other times, he reverts to a list of eight women, beginning with Sonya Barrett whose body was found dumped in a ravine in the Columbia River Gorge in 1990.

Jesperson claims he is the infamous Happy Face Killer. The investigation is ongoing.

Martha Singleton — Spokane, Washington March 30, 1995

Holy Mother of God. Her hands shook as she stared at the newspaper item in front of her, which included a mug shot of her ex-husband. Pieces of a long unsolved puzzle fell into place one by one.

She called the children into the kitchen—the symbol of warmth and home, of safety and family.

And then she told them. There was no keeping this to herself. They needed to know. She needed to hold them close and cry.

"Daddy?" they asked. "Is that… our dad?"

"Yes. This is the man who was your Daddy. But please don't call him that anymore."

The children stared at her, and at the newspaper article showing their father in a jail uniform, glaring at the camera with cold yet triumphant eyes.

They all had the same question. Why?

The journey to understanding had only just begun.

Keith Hunter Jesperson, The Happy Face Killer, September 1995

So he confessed. His attorney said not to talk. But then he asked about the letter Keith had sent to his brother, where he described what he'd done since 1990. And he blurted out his entire confession. Sonya in Portland. Catherine in Riverside. Nina in Turlock. Lisa in Salem. Betsy or Brenda in Santa Nella. Elaine in Holt. Angie in Laramie—the one he dragged beneath his truck to obliterate her identity. No one even knew about her yet. But when he told them where to find the body, they would. And all he had to do was tell them about her Tweety Bird tattoo, and they'd know he was telling the truth.

And finally, Suzy, his girlfriend. An error in judgment. Damn it. Of course, they traced her back to him.

But you see, he had to take her life. She just wanted his money. They all wanted something he didn't want to give.

He'd get life, probably. And he deserved it. Maybe worse. He just didn't want to fry.

News Report, January 7, 1996, Salem, Oregon

Today, more than five years after they were convicted of the murder of Sonya Barrett, Laverne Pavlinac and John Sosnovske were released from prison based on a full confession by serial killer Keith Hunter Jesperson, aka The Happy Face Killer. With the assistance of his attorney, Jesperson provided convincing evidence linking him unequivocally to the crime. The victim's purse was not found at the crime scene at the time of Barrett's death in 1990. Jesperson was able to provide its precise location to police officers, leading to its recovery.

News Report, April 20, 2022, Santa Ana, California

Identity of 'Jane Doe' Victim of The Happy Face Killer Revealed

The Happy Face Killer, whose real name is Keith Hunter Jesperson, confessed after his arrest in 1995 and was convicted of a felony first degree homicide in the 1993 sexual assault and murder of a woman whose body he dumped along a dirt turnout on Highway 152 in Santa Nella, California. Investigators found her body on the side of the road on June 3, 1993, but they could not identify her until now.

On April 13, 2022, 29 years after her murder, the DNA Doe Project (DDP) and cold case detectives at the Santa Clara County Sheriff's Department identified the once-unknown woman as Jennifer Pringle. She is believed to be Jesperson's fifth victim of eight murders he initially listed in a confession in 1995. Two victims, one found in Blythe, California and another in Crestview, Florida, are still unidentified.

News Report, October 4, 2023, Okaloosa County, FL

The Happy Face Killer's Sixth Victim Identified After Nearly 30 Years

The sixth Happy Face serial killer victim, who was dumped on the side of a Florida highway in 1994, has been identified as Alanna Keller, aged 34 at the time. Keller was a hitchhiker who was murdered while making her way across the country.

In a press conference on Tuesday, October 3, Eric Aden, the sheriff of Okaloosa County, described how his team had worked with a private lab and used genetic genealogy to identify Keller.

In order to locate a match, they used the DNA of the victim's remains to develop a genetic profile of her and compared it to the millions of profiles on public databases like Ancestory.com and 23andMe. With the use of DNA technology, investigators were able to create a family tree for the subject and they identified relatives of Keller's living in Wisconsin.

"A family member gave a DNA sample, and it became a 100 percent DNA hit for Alanna Keller," Aden said.

Keller's family members were grateful for the tireless work of the team who persevered until she was identified and could be put to rest at last. They have asked for privacy. "Alanna deserves a voice," said Sheriff Aden, adding, "We're that voice for her today."

Keith Hunter Jesperson, October 2023

That voice. He woke to the sound of that woman screaming again. Even now, all these years later, she haunted his dreams, disrupted his sleep, and hammered his brain with her screaming, like the horrid drip of water torture. He had killed her in Florida almost thirty years ago, but she had never left him.

They had identified her at last. It wasn't Elaine, as he thought all along, but Alanna. He'd hoped that now that she had been put to rest, she would leave him alone. But she didn't. Maybe it wasn't her lost identity or her last terrible moments that caused her to remain restless and unforgiving. Maybe the screaming was not just for her, but for all of his victims. Perhaps she screamed for all the silenced women whose lives are cut short at the hands of men.

He lay back on the bunk in his cold cell and closed his eyes, wishing for the endless quiet you'd expect from the dead. Instead, it came ever louder. That voice, as endless as eternity, never leaving him in peace. She screamed, and screamed, and screamed.

* * *

Author note: This is a fictional story based on the murders of real life serial killer Keith Hunter Jesperson, known as The Happy Face Killer. The names of the victims have been changed, but the dates of death, and most of the details surrounding their murders are true. The news reports and many of the details are fictionalized versions of what truly happened. Jesperson's victims continue to be identified with modern genetics and genealogy, but at this writing the identity of Jane Doe from Turlock remains unidentified. This story was written a month after the identification of his sixth victim, in Florida. It is not known if Jesperson is truly haunted by his crimes, but one can hope.

Return of the Ripper
by Tom Howard

After a long day working for the London
Metropolitan Police, I'd returned home to sit at
my desk, as I did every evening at my London
flat.

Since the East End murders had returned, I hadn't
had much time to appreciate the crackling fire in my study
and the glass of whiskey from the American state of
Kentucky after dinner. My housekeeper had left a cold
chicken plate on the sideboard. It, and my nightly
whiskey, remained untouched.

An unexpected and uninvited guest held a Tranter
revolver pointed at my chest. The woman sat on the divan
facing me. Although the Tranter had two triggers that had
to be pressed to shoot, I knew I couldn't reach her before
she fired.

I cleared my throat, keeping my hands firmly on the
desktop.

"I don't understand." I didn't. Why was she holding
a gun on me in my study, dressed provocatively in a red
dress and wearing a ridiculous straw hat?

"Is Jack the Ripper back?" she asked.

I took a deep breath and lied, trying to allay her fears.
"These new murders have nothing to do with Jack.
They're the work of a sick mind, belonging to someone
who reads too many newspapers."

*Why was she here? Had Jack sent her? She looked
more like one of his victims than an accomplice.*

She stood, her full shirt springing around her. With
one hand, she removed the hat festooned with too many
silk roses after pulling out all of her pins. The gun barrel
didn't waver. "You told *The Gazette* the new murders

were the work of an amateur." She tossed the hat on the divan. "They are not amateurish. Are you trying to make Jack angry?"

How had she known what I told the Gazette? The police had discovered the second victim sliced open with her intestines removed and arranged around her head, recalling the grisly murders attributed to Jack in 1888, a decade earlier. I had been one of the policemen who had prowled the urine-soaked alleys in search of a clue, any clue, during those dark days of hysteria and frustration. Jack disappeared without being identified. A few similar murders occurred afterward, but I and the Criminal Investigation Department didn't consider them part of the original killings.

After seeing the latest victims' mutilated bodies, I had no doubt that Jack was back.

"I told the reporters the surgery was laughable," I said, "more the work of a pig butcher than the infamous Jack the Ripper. I hoped he would come looking for me."

Constable Cullen was stationed across the street as a bodyguard for me, but he hadn't stopped this woman from entering my house. Perhaps he thought ladies of the evening visited me regularly.

"When you appeared at the police surgeon's office," she said, "I feared as much."

I had seen her before, although she'd worn less rouge at the time. "I recognize you now! You're Nurse Moore from the pathologist's office."

I hoped she'd keep talking until she lowered her guard or Constable Cullen got suspicious.

"When I saw the bodies," I continued, "I knew that Jack had returned. If anything, the incisions were more precise than they were with the previous murders. We surmised he has been imprisoned or institutionalized for the past decade."

* * *

Earlier in the day, I'd visited the morgue to see if Dr. Patterson, the police pathologist, had discovered anything about the recent bodies.

The old doctor bent over the body of the first victim. "If it's not the same man, it's someone as knowledgeable." Dr. Patterson had examined the victims a decade earlier. "He removed the spleen without puncturing the intestines. That's difficult to do."

"Did he take anything?" I asked. Jack the Ripper had removed internal organs and displayed them around the five bodies he'd eviscerated. He'd occasionally taken organs or body parts for reasons unknown.

"From the first woman, this new killer took the spleen," Dr. Patterson said. "However, he didn't carry it away. He dissected it there and left the slices on the woman's forehead. With the second victim, he removed the heart and took it with him." Their names were Kira Nelson and Abigail Stevens. Ladies of the evening who worked on Whitechapel's Brothel Row.

"Will that be all, Doctor?" a nurse asked, suddenly appearing at his elbow.

"No, Nurse Moore. I'll let you know when I'm ready for the bodies to be washed. You're excused."

The nurse didn't move. The thin-faced brunette stared at the body cut open on the doctor's examining table. The organs appeared bloodless.

When the nurse didn't move, Dr. Patterson looked at her and frowned. "I said that will be all, Nurse Moore."

When she turned and left the room with a slight limp, Dr. Patterson sighed. "She's not been the same since she returned from that nurses' college in America. I don't know what they teach there. How much does one have to know to change a bedpan?"

***

Now, as the evening wore on, I'd become reacquainted with Nurse Moore, under somewhat unbelievable circumstances. I couldn't take my eyes off her pistol. "I remember you from the pathologist's office. I was there to find out what I could about the victim. It's my job."

"Your job? That's what men always say. Just as it's my job is to change bandages and bathe fat sweaty bodies while doctors slice open patients with no knowledge of what they are doing."

"Do you know what you are doing?" I asked, more to give me time to concoct a plan than to learn about her feelings of inferiority. Was she an accomplice? Had Jack sent her to find out what I knew?

She sat, adjusting her skirt around her. The pistol didn't waver. "Have you heard of the London School of Medicine for Women?"

"No." My duty pistol lay in a drawer of my desk, unreachable. Was she stalling? Would her murderous associate appear to repay me for insulting his surgical expertise? "Is it a nursing college?"

"You're like the rest." She scowled. "It's a doctors' college for women."

"I don't understand. You wish to become a doctor?"

"They turned me down. That's why I went to America to study. Even there, I had to attend schools for surgical nurses instead of a doctors' academy."

The windows behind her glowed from the street gaslights as workers were lighting them. I thought that if I tossed a book or a lamp through one of my windows, the noise might attract Constable Cullen. I'd likely be dead by the time he arrived, but at least the Ripper's possible accomplice wouldn't get away.

"If you shoot me," I said, "how would you explain it?" I could play the delaying game, too.

"You arrest criminals every day. Scores of miscreants would love to put a hole in your occipitomastoid suture. But you're asking why I'm going to kill you."

"It's because I almost caught Jack once," I said. "He's afraid I'll accomplish it this time. I scared him so badly he hid for ten years."

She rested the heavy pistol against her knee, still pointed at my chest. "Tell me about that night," she said. "The night you almost caught Jack the Ripper."

* * *

I'd been a bobby then. The detectives assigned to the case thought spending time and energy on prostitute deaths was pointless, but as the newspapers reported and fabricated stories, every woman in London feared a killer with a scalpel would climb through one of their windows in the middle of the night. The explicit illustrations accompanying those stories had made Chief Inspector Rawlings take an extended vacation in Switzerland rather than deal with an angry visit from the Lord Mayor.

It had been late, almost sunrise, on my patrol. I walked the alleys between brothels so often the working girls offered me a discount. When that happened, I just grinned and continued my patrol. I'd learned that groaning noises coming from a doorway didn't always indicate that someone's throat had been cut.

A strange, bubbling noise arose in front of me, but it didn't sound like running water. I spied a shape in the darkness, huddled over a figure lying on the cobblestones. As I approached, the man did not see me; he was quite busy, doing something to the prone figure, the nature of which I at first could not ascertain.

I blew my whistle and ran forward. "Stop!"

The hooded man turned and threw a knife at me. I turned at the last minute, and his slender blade stuck in my upper arm.

At the pain, I stopped and pulled it out. The cloaked attacker disappeared into the darkness. I rushed forward to help the victim, but I was too late. Her throat had been slashed like the others, but she had not been sliced open.

***

"It wasn't a knife in your arm, was it?" Nurse Moore asked.

I shook my head. "No. It was a scalpel."

"And did you note anything unusual about the killer?"

I thought back. "He was small. I included the possibility of him being a young man in my report, but it didn't help us find Jack."

She snorted in disgust. "Do I have to spell it out for you, Detective Inspector?"

I looked at the exasperated expression on her face. The clues fell into place. Jack's ease at approaching the prostitutes. The small size of the attacker. Nurse Moore's anger at not being allowed to perform surgeries.

"Jack the Ripper isn't a Jack," I said. "She's a *Jacqueline.*"

She smiled. "I can see how I avoided capture for this long, with such inept detectives."

"But why kill those women?"

She pulled up her skirt to reveal cheap stockings and a lattice of scars on her right leg.

"When I was a child, a carriage ran me down. My parents had little money, so they took me to a street surgeon. He operated on my shattered leg. I watched as he sliced me open and put the pieces of my tibia back together. In spite of the pain, I was mesmerized by the exposed tendons and bone."

She lowered her skirt. "He did a good job. I only limp after a long day."

"The rouge, the red dress," I said. "We thought the prostitutes didn't fear Jack because he was a client, but they didn't fear Jacqueline because she looked like one of them."

"Very good, Detective. Now, if I'm to practice my skills this evening, I would appreciate having my old scalpel back."

"It's in the drawer." I'd kept it more as a souvenir than evidence. I stood slowly.

"Step back." She raised her pistol. "I'll get it."

I backed away. "But why kill those women?"

"Because I wasn't allowed to learn anatomy with the men, and I wanted to see the organs working." She moved to the drawer and pulled it open. "The harlots were approachable. Afterward, it helped convince people I was a man."

She removed my pistol and the scalpel from the drawer. She tucked the gun in the sash of her dress. A cloth enfolded the scalpel, and she struggled to unwrap it with one hand while holding her gun in the other.

I pounced; afraid I'd not have another opportunity. If her pistol went off, it might bring Cullen to my rescue. At the very least, he might hear my dying declaration.

We hit the floor with me on top. Not as spry as I once was, I wrestled for the gun in her hand. With her pistol

85

hand waving above her head, she stabbed me in the stomach with the other hand, holding the scalpel.

I grunted and rolled off her, surprised at how much a gut wound hurt. I couldn't breathe for a moment and feared I'd lose consciousness. Would she cut me open while I was still alive?

She sat up. "Put pressure on it."

I gasped as my pressing added to the pain. My life's blood spilled through my fingers and onto the carpet.

She stood and looked down at me. "You'll die knowing you could have stopped Jacqueline the Ripper earlier if you hadn't been an idiot."

I kept pressure on my abdomen. "Everyone gave a different description of the man last seen with the murdered women. Tall, short, dark, light. Shabbily dressed, richly attired." I paused to breathe. "We thought we had a gang killing women, but the medical skill confused us. It didn't change from killing to killing."

"Why didn't you look for a woman?" She straightened her clothes.

I groaned. "It was inconceivable a female would butcher another woman in such a way."

"Idiots. If I hadn't shown up here tonight, you'd still be looking for a man."

"They will find you," I said between gasps. "You can't stay angry at your station in life forever. You'll make more mistakes, and they'll catch you. It'll be the gallows for you if you're lucky. Bedlam if you're not."

"With a gaggle of witless detectives running around thinking only men can commit murder, I'll be safe for a good while. It's not your concern. You'll be dead from blood loss before help arrives."

I tried to sit up, but pain washed over me. "You went to America to learn additional skills with a scalpel?"

"What? Yes. I've years more experience now." She put the medical instrument in her pocket. "You're trying to distract me. Why? You don't care what I learned in New York."

"I do." I bent my right leg. "I've been to several police presentations in the Americas. I learned a great deal from them." I'd also developed a taste for Kentucky whiskey while I was there.

She studied my face. "Are you in shock? Why are you babbling about American police procedures?"

Ignoring the pain, I grasped the Webley the Americans had recommended I keep strapped to my calf. I only took it off before bed. Thick leather bands held it in place and allowed me to slide it out quickly.

Lying on my back, I fired one shot.

She stared at the hole that appeared above her heart. A thin line of blood trickled down her dress. She dropped her pistol and collapsed.

"You had a gun? You could have… " Her voice grew weak.

"Killed you at any time? Yes, but I couldn't believe what you were telling me."

Her head fell forward, and she looked as lifeless as a rag doll. Downstairs, the sound of a door breaking told me that Cullen had heard the shot.

I lay back and kept pressure on my wound. It had taken me a decade, but the case of Jacqueline the Ripper was solved. Now I had to live long enough to convince the Chief Constable that I wasn't mad.

* * *

Editor's note: The identity of the notorious 19th-Century London serial killer, Jack the Ripper, has never been definitively established, although numerous theories have been advanced. The Ripper killed and mutilated five women in the Whitechapel neighborhood of London in the fall of 1888, and may have murdered as many as eleven.

Art for Art's Sake
by Carson Demmans

The artist sat in his studio, staring hard at his canvas. He had painted scenes of blood, death, gore and violence on it. His artwork was habitually bleak and full of despair.

He sighed. It was the same as it always was. He needed something new, something different.

He peeked around the edge of his canvas at his model. Again, he looked as hard as he could. He studied it intently for close to an hour, not moving. Somewhere, deep inside his model, he had to find some new horror that not only had he never seen before, but that the *world* had never seen before.

There was never a lack of inspiration when it came to the horrors of death, but the trick was showing it in a different way from how it was usually depicted. He took comfort in the fact that he never lacked inspiration as long as he had a model, and the fact that he would never lack such a model.

He went back to his canvas with a new plan. He left the focal point of the piece the same:

A death's head skull growing out of a rose bush, while the other roses had human faces sporting looks of terror. However, he now began adding frantically to the background. He had left it blank until he had finished the focal point in the foreground, but now he added Grim Reapers approaching similar rosebushes, harvesting them by cutting off screaming human-headed flowers that dripped blood. He couldn't show great detail, but with a few carefully placed drops of crimson red paint, he could suggest the agony of the victims.

He liked the effect. Normally he hinted at nothing. He showed death, pain, suffering and agony in as much detail as he could. The art store clerks wondered why he went through so much red paint. He never explained that he needed it for the gore his model showed him. People never understood such things, so he had stopped trying to explain it.

His art reflected the reality he saw in his studio when he peeked around his canvas to get the inspiration for his next work. It was not his fault that his reality wasn't the same as that of other people. Maybe one day the rest of the world would see life and death the same way he did.

He didn't spend much time thinking about such things, though. He didn't care. If he had to, he'd reshape the world to fit his vision.

The artist looked at his palette and then his paint tubes. He was out of red.

Again.

He was running low on black too. Too many Grim Reapers recently.

Normally, his face was emotionless. Now he grimaced, but not at his art. He grimaced at the world and the fact that he had to go out into it.

Still, he was nothing if not logical. Sometimes he had to go out into the world. He had to get art supplies. He also had to go to school. In some ways, the art supply store and school were the same. The art supply store gave him the tools he needed for his art. School gave him the tools he needed to reshape the world, at least one day.

The artist left his studio and began walking to the art supply store. The lone clerk acted like she wished she wasn't alone with him when he came in. He said little, but she plainly wanted him to talk more. Maybe then she wouldn't notice the way he looked at her. She was an attractive girl, and she told him once that she didn't like the way male customers gawked at her, but she preferred being undressed by men's eyes far more than the way he looked at her. He gawked at her as well, but in the way a raven might gawk at fresh roadkill.

After making his purchases, he was about to return to his studio as he always did, but he stopped in thought for a moment, and then turned, walking in the opposite direction. He would go see his friend. No, friend wasn't the right word. They actually didn't know each other that well, but the man was one of the few people who encouraged his art, and therefore encouraged his lifelong plan, which was only a reflection of his art, which was a reflection of how he saw the world and what he wanted the world to look like.

Patron. That was the right word. He was going to see his patron at the community center downtown.

* * *

The professor stared at the absurdity of a painting of a headless corpse sitting at a dinner table, a knife in one hand and a fork in the other. Perfectly plated in front of it was a dinner consisting of its own head with an apple stuffed in its mouth. Blood gushed from the stump of a neck where the head presumably used to be attached. Behind him, a Roman gladiator wrestled with the body. Why was he doing it? Was the body somehow still alive?

Two thoughts filled the professor's mind. The first was: How can I be seeing an unimaginable terror? *If I can see it, why did I never imagine it?*

The second was *Beautiful.*

The professor closed his eyes, trying to forget what he had just seen. He wanted his mind to be blank before he reopened them. It took several seconds, but his mind was as dark as the inside of his eyelids before he looked at what was now before him. A flower grew through the eye socket of a skull. The skull was bleached white but still had a tongue. Was it a fresh corpse or had it lain there for weeks unattended as the flower, full of life pushed its way through to sunlight? Or was the kill fresh and a lucky throw had somehow landed the skull perfectly over the flower like some kind of hellish ring toss? Did they have carnival games in Hell? Broken bones lay beside the skull, and behind it a tree screamed. What would that sound like? What was so horrible that made it scream?

All of these thoughts flooded the professor's mind at once. He was at once horrified and sickened but also fascinated, not only by the scene before him, but his surprise at how fascinated he was.

He closed his eyes and reopened them, this time much faster than before. In the next painting, three giant rabbits pulled the head of a dying man from a giant easter egg. One of them held a halo over the head, while another controlled the motions of the head with a marionette stick in the shape of a cross. *Was it blasphemous? Or, more likely, was it so absurd and horrific as to be too shocking to be blasphemous?*

The professor repeated this ritual until he had seen every painting in the room. He would look at one, close his eyes and step to his right until he thought he was in front of the next painting. He'd stare at a painting for seconds or minutes before moving on, and when he had finally seen them all he repeated the process in the opposite direction. Somehow, they were all new and shocking again, even when he knew what he would see next. Acid filled his stomach. He thought he might throw up.

He hadn't been that happy in years. He had been dragged to Pontiac, Michigan by coworkers for a conference that had nothing to do with him or anything he was interested in, but someone had canceled, and the administration didn't want the plane ticket to go to waste. Far better that his time be wasted than it appear the department wasted money on a plane ticket. He had asked at the conference about the nearest art gallery and was directed to this small show at a community center. The location was as mind-boggling as the art.

"Where is the security?" he asked the bored clerk sitting at the information desk near the front door of the center.

"For what?" the clerk asked, almost as puzzled as he was bored.

"For the art show, you fool! It's the finest collection of German fatalism I've seen in years! I'm unfamiliar with the artist, but the collection must be worth thousands of dollars."

"He's Armenian, not German."

"Armenian? Interesting. Perhaps the genocide influenced his outlook."

"Maybe of his parents, not him. They're immigrants but he was born right here in Pontiac. Good kid. Smart. Taught himself German, Russian, Greek, Japanese.

Taught himself to paint, too. I was the one who got him the show here. It's weird but good, know what I mean?"

"No, I don't" the professor snapped. "It's horrible but beautiful, a celebration of death that's full of life and energy!"

"Well, I'd call that weird, wouldn't you? Anyway, I like the guy. Doesn't have many friends, you know, but he has always come here with his parents for cultural stuff and we have a little library attached, and we had to bring in books from different branches after he read all the ones we had here. Read all the ones in his school, too."

"He's a child?"

"No, I don't think Johnny was ever a child. He's just young. There's a difference. Anyway, he's 17, done with high school, and going off to university. Wants to be a doctor, which means I'll probably never see him again. We're not friends, but I'll miss him, you know?"

A slim boy entered the building. He didn't seem to blink. The clerk waved him over.

"Johnny! A guy here looked at your paintings! I think he liked them."

"My name's not Johnny" he said in a flat voice. While the clerk's tone held affection for the boy, there didn't seem to be any for the clerk in return.

"Well, you go by Jack, so Johnny's pretty close. Consider it a nickname. It may be the best one you ever have. Anyway, talk to the man."

The professor stared into the youth's unblinking eyes. He understood what the clerk meant. This artist wasn't an adult, but he had never been a child.

"Do you like my art?"

"It's amazing! You're a genius."

"Yes."

"You're so young! How do you know so much about death?"

"I don't. Death is infinite. Life has a beginning and an end. It doesn't. We know far more about life than we do death and what comes after it, if anything."

"You're going to university to study art?"

The artist shrugged.

"I don't think so. I already know how to paint. I think I'll study medicine."

"Medicine? That's about saving lives?"

"It's about helping people, not necessarily saving them. Look at my paintings again."

The professor nodded. He had spent his life studying art and artists, something most people didn't understand. Studying art didn't mean looking at paintings, although he loved that part of it. The hardest part, and usually the most important, was to study the artist as well.

Another artist could look at a painting and reproduce it, and even if every brush stroke was exactly the same as the original, it would look nothing like the original. The artist producing the copy only had the original to look at, whereas the original painter was looking at the entire world when he produced the original. That was the key to art, in his opinion. One had to look at not only the painting, and what the painting showed, but what the artist saw the world as when he painted it.

The artist he had just met was too young to have seen the genocide that his parents saw, lived through, and escaped. They only escaped the scene of the genocide; the memories of it traveled with them against their will. Even if they had never told their son in words what they had seen, they had told him with every action and reaction he had ever seen them perform. Their experiences had shaped them, and even if their son had not lived through those horrors firsthand, he had relived them with his parents every day of his life.

The stranger was staring at the artist with great intent. People often stared at the artist, but not in this way. The stranger, the professor, was trying to understand him in the sense that he was fascinated, not appalled.

* * *

The clerk smiled. The two people standing in front of him were odd by any definition of the word, which was in his opinion a good thing. Odd meant different. Too many people that he saw go by him were trying to be the same as whatever idol they currently worshipped; the idol might be an athlete or a fashion model or a neighbor or classmate who was trying to look like a fashion model or athlete. The clerk preferred the type of person he was looking at now: two people trying to understand and not judge. In their own way, each was trying to shape the world and themselves, and not reshape themselves to look like someone else.

* * *

The professor nodded slowly and thanked the artist for his time and his art. He then returned to the gallery. Instead of sidestepping from painting to painting as he had done before, he stood in the center of the room and widened his eyes so he could see as many paintings as possible at once instead of focusing on them one at a time. He then started turning himself slowly on an invisible vertical axis, seeing the artist's world as a whole, the way the artist did. His rotation eventually brought the door to the gallery into view, and through it the clerk and the artist. The clerk smiled broadly, and the artist looked grim, yet somehow happy in his own way.

That in turn made the professor happy in his own way. He saw the artist, in that moment, as an artist should be seen: as part of his art and not the producer of it. The artist was himself one of his own creations.

The professor continued rotating and when his view had shifted from them, the clerk smiled directly at the artist.

"What do you think, Johnny? Are you glad now people are seeing your paintings?" the clerk asked.

"Has anyone else liked them?

"That doesn't matter. I asked how it made you feel that other people saw them? That they know about you?"

* * *

The artist nodded his head. He'd never admit it, but he was glad. His patron, the clerk, was not his friend, but he was very important in his life. Maybe sometime in the future he'd repay the favor to the clerk and be important in the clerk's death.

The artist left the community center and walked faster back to his studio than he had left it. He needed to paint. More importantly, he needed to look at his model. He rushed into his studio and didn't even bother taking off his coat. He took out his new paint and began mixing it on his palette. He would be out of red paint again soon. He peeked past his canvas and looked at his model, which was the only model he had ever used. He saw death. Other people may have seen horror, but they would have been wrong.

The artist looked intently at the mirror hanging on a wall a few feet from his canvas and easel. He stared intently at what he called his model and what others called his reflection. He returned to his canvas and began painting with fury. He would need more red paint very soon.

The clerk had been wrong about some things about Johnny, but very correct on one point.

To a lot of people, Johnny was the most complimentary nickname that Murad Jacob "Jack" Kevorkian, later known as "Dr. Death," would ever have applied to him.

* * *

Editor's note: A monster to some, a hero to others, Jack "Dr. Death" Kevorkian assisted in the suicides of an estimated 130 people. Only about sixty percent were terminally ill. He was convicted of second-degree murder after administering a lethal injection, by consent, to a patient with Lou Gehrig's Disease/ALS. A lifelong advocate of physician-assisted suicide, Kevorkian served eight years in a Michigan prison after the verdict, before receiving a mercy pardon due to health problems which led to his eventual death in 2011. His bizarre paintings showed a preoccupation with death and violence from an early age.

What the Forest Showed
by Trev Hill

The young, German traffic officer was a little surprised to find that the abandoned car was in such good condition. Normally, dumped vehicles were either torched or stripped within a few hours, yet this one, a rather nice Audi no less, was untouched, despite having been there a few days, according to witnesses.

The officer approached it casually; thinking that probably the owner had broken down or run out of fuel and, unable to phone for assistance because of the surrounding forest, had had to hitch-hike or walk to the nearest village. Still, it was puzzling that someone who could afford such a car wouldn't have arranged a quick recovery, which made the officer wonder if it was in fact stolen.

Even so, a lonely, asphalt turn-out on a main road seemed a strange place to dump it. Perhaps this was a rendezvous point for a delivery or they met further down the small forest dirt-road leading through the trees. He smiled to himself at the thought of apprehending drug-dealing gangsters or international mafia, it would certainly make a change to the mundane traffic cop routine.

Several meters from the car, the smell became obvious. He slowed his pace, feeling his mouth begin to water with the approaching nausea. Cautiously, he edged towards the trunk of the vehicle, thinking with a sudden, sinking feeling of the so-called Munsterland Murders that had been bedeviling this part of Germany for several years. The young, female hitchhikers, strangled and then left to rot in odd places. A prostitute had been reported missing and the cop had heard fears that she was another victim of the Munsterland killer.

* * *

The driver saw her as he approached the turn-out. It had been a long drive, perhaps he deserved to have a little "refreshment," and she certainly looked like she might be refreshing. He had been planning his latest display and how to pose his newest "models," perhaps she could give him some ideas. Unusually for roadside prostitutes or hitchhikers, she was sitting in a tree, with her naked, barefooted legs dangling from the branch and her light, wispy dress gently waving with the soft summer breeze. Normally, he would not have bothered, but there was something intriguing about this one; the girlish, almost innocent grin she wore, as well as the quaint, rural clothes, a world apart from the emotionless, businesslike faces and revealing skirts and fishnets most of the sluts who sold themselves by the roadside wore.

He pondered for a moment before pulling over. He was already busy, driving elsewhere to conclude the job he had started earlier that day. Still, the novelty of this one was appealing and perhaps a little dessert would make the main course even better. He eased the Audi over, noting that, like most of the trading places, there was a small forest road which meant a certain privacy was available for transactions. He and the girl would definitely be making use of it.

He stopped opposite the girl and wound the window down. Once more, he was surprised by her giggling face and the flush of excitement in her cheeks, as she swung her leg coquettishly and combed her fingers through her long hair, twirling a lock around her forefinger.

His gaze began to move down her legs towards her bare feet, but she tucked them up under the branch and giggled again.

"Do you want to see something?" she lilted, tilting her head to one side. He was confused by this behavior, so unlike the others. He paused for a second and, raising her shoulder to her cheek to give an expression mixed between childish innocence and nymphal teasing, she repeated, "Do you want to see something?"

"What do you want to show me?" he asked, with a slight smile, returning the playfulness in a way he never normally did.

"Come and see!" she sang in reply.

He climbed out of the car and having shut the door, he turned to find she had somehow got down from the branch and was standing almost in front of him, giggling and caressing her face with her light brown locks, while shifting from one foot to another in a restless, almost nervous impatience.

He stepped back slightly, shocked at the apparent speed of her approach.

He surmised that she had jumped down from the branch, suggesting her girlishness belied an athleticism that excited him. This little morsel might struggle a bit, which always made it more fun. He regained his composure and reciprocated the playfulness.

"So, what do you want to show me?" he asked, raising his eyebrow conspiratorially.

She squealed in excitement, raising her shoulders and rubbing her hands together in glee. She took a few tiny steps backwards down the forest path, beckoning with her hand.

"You'll have to come see!" she cried, as she danced backwards behind a tree, peeping around the trunk and smiling. He took a few steps towards her and she skipped backwards down the path a short way, luring and enticing him to follow. He understood. They normally had to walk to a place a little off the road for privacy; he had made use of them before, after all, but this one was using it as part of the service. It was certainly original! He just hoped, for convenience's sake, that it wasn't too far from his car.

He strode down the path towards her but each time, she skipped back and stopped, beckoning or widening her eyes and giving a broad smile or a pout if he slowed down. He decided not to run but to enjoy the pretend chase. He wondered for a second whether this was genuine playfulness or a unique form of marketing she had and whether there was a heftier price tag at the end, although there certainly would be this time, for her. Oh yes, he would definitely enjoy this and might even remember it amongst all the others.

The chase continued into the forest, but suddenly she skipped from the path and began darting between the trees, always facing him, never letting him from her sight, looking straight into his eyes. She skipped and giggled, singing little snatches of song, and he followed, lost to the game. Without warning, she stopped and peeped at him from behind a silver birch, her arms hugging it and her head on one side.

"We're here!" she crooned.

For the first time since they had left the road, he felt able to take in his surroundings.

So transfixed had he been by her gaze, that he failed to notice how deep into the forest she was leading him. But now he could see they were in a clearing—old, maybe ancient birches stood erect on either side and soft mossy ground lay below his feet. The forest canopy created an eerie green aura around the space, here and there sliced by the shafts of sunlight which managed to penetrate through the occasional gap in the branches and came to rest on the small algae-coated lake nearby.

As the man looked around, his mind suddenly shot back to his car. How deep had they come and what of his work which lay in the car's trunk, not to mention his tools? It would be problematic to have to go back to fetch them. As if to snatch him back to the place and moment, the girl leaned back against a slanting tree and lifted her knee, enticingly. "What would you like me to show you now?"

He stood, surveying the offered delights. His breath changed from the puffing of exertion, to controlled, yet shivering breaths of excitement and anticipation. The tools might not be necessary, after he had enjoyed the struggle and forced her to do as all the others had done, one of the nearby rocks would suffice, smashed on top of her head as she performed her final act of submission and degradation. And afterwards? Perhaps he could just leave her there rather than drag her back to the car to be filed with his other work. He chuckled; her private place would now ensure her an eternity of privacy.

She was still lying against the tree, lilting something which sounded like a folk tune, but now slowly writhing against the birch bark, like a cat laying its scent. He began to approach, squelching across the mossy ground. Ah, now he knew why she was bare-footed! He kicked his shoes and socks off, promising himself to remember to retrieve them when he came back alone.

The moistness of the ground oozed between his toes as he made his way towards her.

He found it sensual, stimulating—the moistness—the squelching softness caressing his bare skin, almost like a premonition of what was to come. He felt his excitement rising with the anticipation. Still, she fixed him with her smiling, unblinking eyes as her body pulsated to the quickening rhythm of the tune she was singing.

He was still trying to decide whether to play his usual game, the beating and pleading first, but her own game was having an enchanting effect on him. Perhaps, he smiled, as she seemed willing, he would first let her reveal what she had before showing her his hand.

He stopped a few feet from her and she rose, moving, writhing to her tune. She stepped towards him and stopped, bolt upright, her eyes shining with some form of raw energy. He waited, uncertain, until she reached forward and seized his elbows in a way which made him replicate the hold, squeezing her softness through her sleeves.

He felt spasms of excitement running through her as the lilting quickened. She began slowly to circle him, making him step with her around, and around again. The tempo of her singing and the steps of her dance seemed to channel from her hands—her suddenly, surprisingly, vice-like hands—into his arms and through his body.

His feet, shuffling and dragging at first, began to move with hers. The scenery around them began to blur as the pace quickened. Her eyes held his, making the space about them disappear as they spun on the spot, faster and faster, her pupils dilating with the thrill of the dance.

Her singing gave way to a wild undulating and frenzied whoops or ecstatic joy. His breathing became faster until it began to labor, his chest tightened as he gasped, retching for air. The rising panic forced him to snap his head to the side, breaking their eye-contact.

Without the fixed hold of her dilated pupils, his eyes embraced the spinning landscape and he became nauseous from the flashing imagery. The dizziness overtook him and he lost control of his steps, his feet tripping over themselves until he stumbled and crashed to the ground as the girl pirouetted above him. He lay gasping as she slowed her dancing down until she had stopped. Then darkness found him.

He came to with a jolt to find her kneeling beside him, gently tickling him and cradling his head whilst humming softly. She saw the alarm in his eyes and giggled again, her face still flushed and her eyes still bright.

"Not for you, too old!" she chuckled. "I shall show you something else," she whispered, softly massaging her neck with his long fingers. He found the sensation strangely invigorating and struggled to sit upright. She stroked his head and crooned, "Let me show you something!"

He was angry now, with himself and her. He had allowed her to take control and she had taken it. He was no longer the one in charge; he had allowed her to overpower him and none of them had ever done that. It was time for him to regain control.

"Maybe it is time for me to show you something," he smiled, reaching out to touch her face. She drew back coaxingly but grinned in delight. He motioned towards the tree where she had been resting against earlier, before the dance. "Maybe you want to lie down, against the tree again and I'll show you something really special." She nodded, still holding him with her gaze, and edged back towards the tree, lying along the length of the bent bough and straddling it with her long legs.

"Show me!"

He strolled over towards her, undoing his belt in readiness. He pulled it from the belt loops and caressed it in his hands. She glanced towards it and smiled, raising an eyebrow.

"Touch me!" he ordered.

"Come to me," she replied, "Show me you want this."

He straddled her, as she lay against the tree and pushed her shoulders down. In a blur he had the belt across her throat, determined to see the fright and pleading in her eyes, instead he saw her excitement.

Before he realized it, her hands were at his head and pulling him towards her mouth. Alarmed at her strength, he pulled backwards, only for her to ride with the motion and spring to her feet, spin him around and press him up against the tree.

He felt her fingers move across the back of his head, as if growing longer, and intertwining, gripping him fast as they pulled his mouth towards hers.

A shiver of fear went through him and he felt a new sensation, a sensual excitement.

He instantly felt compelled to follow this fear, to enjoy this moment of domination before taking back the advantage. Then he would make her suffer, he would make it last, he would make her pay for humiliating him.

Her lips touched his face and he gasped as he felt, for the first time. the cold sliminess of her skin. The shock made him drop the belt, his only tool, and his eyes widened in fright as he saw the glistening film which coated her skin. He threw his arms around her, hoping to wrestle her to the ground, but felt a warm wetness where her back was, or should have been.

He fought to understand this familiar feeling, so out of place yet so well known, like squelching mud between his toes or the texture of human organs in his bare hands. He tried to release a scream, only to find his lips enclosed in hers and the fetid stench of her breath pushing into his mouth. She jerked her hips upwards, wrapping her legs around his trunk. He imagined her interlocking her elongated toes, clasping him to her, and then she pushed the two of them away from the tree and rolled them over so that they fell—together—into the algae-coated lake.

As they sank into the blackness, she began to inhale, drawing the breath from his lungs. He kicked and wriggled weakly, but to no avail. Just before the last traces of sunlight lost their reach, she pulled her mouth from his.

He gulped, hoping for air, but tasted only the stagnant water of the pool. In his last moment of sight, he saw her eyes staring at him and her smile of predatory victory. As his life slipped away, his last thought was whether he had locked his car. Then, as so many of his own victims before, he gladly embraced the darkness of death.

* * *

The traffic officer wretched as the full stench hit him. The open trunk revealed its secrets and the putrid remains of the driver's work lay open to the summer air. The officer dropped to his knees as his stomach ejected its contents. Eventually he rose unsteadily and staggered away from the car. He wiped his mouth and shakily reached for his radio. The mundane routine of the traffic cop had been rudely interrupted and he realized he may have just found the young prostitute who had been reported missing a few days previously further up this stretch of road.

He cursed as he remembered the unreliable radio contact in this area, and he dropped his radio in despair. He began to walk towards the car, hoping to close the trunk and restrict the foul odor which was wafting across the turnout. Girding his stomach, he slammed it shut and turned and sank his face into his hands. When he eventually raised his head, he gasped at what he saw. He looked up in disbelief at the bare-legged girl sitting in the tree.

"Do you want to see something?"

* * *

The Munsterland Killer, or Munsterlandmorderer in German, has never been apprehended. The killer is thought to have committed four unsolved murders, near the German towns of Munster and Bentheim, from 1971 to 1974. The victims were all young, female hitchhikers, whose strangled corpses were found posed in peculiar positions near the roadside.

Hell of a Deal
by Dave Davis

The cattle driving business wasn't the easiest trade, but for a poor, ranch-hand drifter from Texas, there weren't a whole lot of choices in the cursed year of 1892. At least that enterprise could feed a Southern man well, and be downright lucrative, if you were willin' and able enough to endure the long cattle drives.

Hell, a steer worth two bucks down in the great Lone Star State would fetch ya forty buckaroos up yonder in Chicago! That would be my longest stint yet, but the World's Columbian Exposition was organized to take place up there the next year, and I figured my herd of beasts would sell out lickiddy split. And, for the highest bids possible, what with all the extra demand, and folks being in their jovial spirits and such. So that was my plan; to make one final big run, with me as the boss this time, makin' all the loot; then, retiring from the rough and dusty—not to mention dangerous as all get out— vocation.

After many long hard years ridin' along with other rustlers, I had saved enough money up to acquire my own decent sized herd of beef cattle. A supreme variety at that. I lucked into discovering the newer Angus breed during one of my treks through the other states, and came to learn how much better they could be for my purposes. They tolerated the heat well, had low birthing difficulties, were absent of horns, and produced a well-muscled carcass.

I reckoned a huge profit would come out of this, and set me up for a gravy train retirement, sippin' tequila with the senoritas down Mexico way, once I returned, that is.

Dang it all to hell, though, I hated them throngs of people up in the crowded streets of Chicago when my drive got there! It sure wasn't nothin' like the peaceful open ranges of the wild country.

Most of the folks seemed downright strange to me. I was the foreigner for sure; ain't no doubt about that. I did enjoy perusing the myriad pretty ladies though. They had all kinda fancy get-ups; the likes I ain't never seen before. The men folk were parading around in their slick attire too, but I didn't much care for the styles. Definitely wasn't aiming to acquire me none of that horseshit; not with my hard-earned green backs, no how. No siree, my cattle rustlin' digs suited me just fine and dandy.

You see, I had some time to kill. That's how I came about moseyin' through the streets. Seems like just about every rancher in the country got the same gumption as me. The stockyards were chalk full up!

The director of the stockyard told me it would take a few days to sort out all the sales. Told me just to go enjoy myself, since it would be a while. Go check out the big Expo he said. So, I figured what the hell? Couldn't just hang with the steers. Might as well take in the sights; treats 'n eats and all. I definitely partook in some of that, but it just wasn't my kinda scene. I was lookin' to book it back to Texas. I didn't come up there for no vacation, experience, or what have ya. All I wanted was to collect a fat paycheck, and split.

So, I got the bright idea to seek out a faster transaction. Drum up my own business. What? With nothing but time on my hands? I sure as hell wasn't gonna go blow the little funds I had currently on me—or even worse—develop some debts to settle before leaving this territory. Not that my accompanying cowboys weren't falling into that trap. They just couldn't resist all them glorious vices, especially while having to wait for me to pay 'em up with the profits. So, I left them to the saloons and brothels, and ventured out to some proprietors' establishments, askin' around to be pointed in the direction of some wealthy entrepreneurs that might be lookin' to acquire themselves some stockpiles of prime beef.

* * *

"Dr. Holmes, I presume?!" The well-dressed gentleman, sporting a thick mustache and a bowler, sauntered into the foyer, as I breached the threshold of his three-story hotel.

He briefly scanned me up and down. "You here to pick up the delivery for the medical school?"

After pulling off my silver-belly cowboy hat, I replied, "No-sir-ee. I was told you might have an interest in a private purchase. You got any need for superior Texas cattle?"

His eyes lit up, and I could tell I must've piqued his interest. "Well!... we may just both be in luck. My guests would surely splendor in the indulgence of an excellent steak dinner during their visits. And the myriad spare anatomical parts would serve my surgical studies quite well, as an added bonus. Human cadavers are… not so easy to come by," he sneered, as he finished his response.

The hotel seemed kinda deserted, but I wasn't about to look a gift horse in the mouth. We discussed the particulars, and came to an agreement. He didn't quip much. The good doctor was obliged to purchase the entire herd. Said he had one of them fancy vapor compression refrigeration systems (which I've heard of, but never seen) set up near the kitchen, so a grazing pasture wasn't necessary, and he could have the cattle processed immediately, without concern for spoilage. All he asked for was a little price break from what I was hoping for from the stockyard auctions. I was definitely agreeable to that, seeing as how he was facilitating a guaranteed, instantaneous, comprehensive sale! The way I saw it, he was saving me a whole bunch of trouble and wasted time, with the potential for my lot being portioned out, and dragging on the whole process; never mind the pre-existing delay to initiate the dealings for at least a couple of days, to begin with. Even fears of the livestock suffering injuries, or taking to sickness whilst cooped-up, crossed my mind.

After shaking on the deal, he asked to retain my stockyard slip, so that I wouldn't be tempted to sell the herd out from under him, and followed up with a promise to fulfill his debt upon delivery of the lot. I'd be lyin' if I said I wasn't hesitant, but I ultimately convinced myself that he was not only good for the money (seeing as how he operated that lodging establishment), but that he wouldn't risk ruining his reputation (being a physician and such). With an amused disposition, Dr. H. H. Holmes even offered to have me and the boys stay at his hotel, free of charge, after driving the Angus herd over to the pens behind his glass-bending factory just up the way. He invited us to take a load off, and enjoy the fineries of his establishment while waiting for him to raise the funds we were to be disbursed. The doctor wanted to process the meat as soon as possible, and he also wanted us to be comfortable, and have an enjoyable experience, before departing Chicago. This was turning out to be one helluva trip. I inwardly congratulated myself on the perfect transition into retirement, *you lucky ol' goat*!

Hurriedly, I vacated the dormant hotel lobby, being that most of the afternoon remained, and rushed over to the vice emporium where I'd left my employees earlier. *Why put off till tomorrow, what you can do today?*

I asked the Madame of the establishment to round up my boys, as we had some business to attend to. She remarked on how satisfied she was, with the amount of business they had provided her with, apparently, so didn't dilly-dally with hustlin' the rustlers out. I guess she figured the house had taken them for all they were worth, in a day anyway. We mounted our trusty steeds, and shot over to the stockyards, where my herd was secured. All the way there, I had to listen to them yawping on about their spectacular escapades.

"Hell, one of 'em was even from the Far East!" exclaimed Tom, my longest-running colleague.

I couldn't help crackin' with, "Shit, Tom, the way you're goin'… yer pecker's gonna quit workin' before you do!" The gang got a hoot outta that one.

After closing in the last of my prize Angus in the makeshift pens at Dr. Holmes's factory, where he had arrived prior to us, I asked him for a quick peek inside the place. Don't run across any facilities like that where I hang my hat, afterall.

While admiring the humongous brick furnace inside the glass factory, something curious caught my eye, protruding slightly from an immense pile of ashes. The starchy white, slightly porous item had an unmistakable geometry. With the doctor attending me, helping myself to fondling it was out of the question, not just out of proper respect for his property, but I'll be damned if I was about to screw up the deal after getting this far along, by possibly offending the strange man. I would tolerate his idiosyncrasies until all the cold, hard cash was in my grasp.

"That looks like a leg bone!"

"Ah… yes, good eye, my man. A femur, to be exact! Technically, a thigh bone. Since the factory hasn't become operational yet, I've been using the furnace to dispose of some excess rubbish from the hotel. We've gone through a plethora of livestock to satisfy the guests, as you can imagine. Even some of the specimens that I no longer need for anatomical studies end up in there," he stated coyly.

Now, I thought, I ain't no doctor, like ol' H. H. there, but I've butchered and chowed on my fair share of bovine, considerin' my craft, and plenty of other species in my time, for that matter. Even though I could only get a partial glimpse of it, it sure didn't look like any creature I'd barbequed before.

Best I could figure, it kinda looked like that of a man's! Like I said before, I was just gonna mind my own business. Shoot, he could've done away with some old medical models, for all I knew.

We returned to the hotel just as darkness was looming. I was tuckered out, and pretty sure my fellow cowboys were even more depleted, *in several ways*, I chuckled to myself. Partaking of a hot meal, hard whiskey, and soft bed sounded heavenly to me (especially since a chunky paycheck, and freedom from arduous toiling, was impending).

Dr. Holmes addressed us flamboyantly, "My associate will see you to your rooms. My services are needed elsewhere. Good evening, gentlemen!"

I couldn't quite put my finger on it, but something was really off about the doctor, not that I made it a habit to hang around too many city-folk, or physicians for that matter. Escaping his company for good, was a welcome thought.

While keeping an eye out for our host's concierge to present themselves, I couldn't resist nosing around the eclectic premises a bit. Within earshot of the lobby's threshold, some vigorous sawing caught my attention. My curiosity demanded satisfaction, as I seemingly rode as an unwilling passenger to my automated legs, which pulled me down the darkened corridor. A barely cracked double-door ended the terminal, allowing my gaze to fall upon the source of the industrious labors which so ardently drew me.

As my uninvited viewing began, all that could be made out after hearing the hacksaw clang onto the table, was the backside of a person wearing a lab coat, hunched over and digging at something feverishly. Oddly, scattered across a table more immediately, was an assortment of women's belongings: corsets, undergarments, dresses, jewelry, satchels, and the like. The nearest rightward wall supported a rack with dangling metal implements of myriad geometries, harboring a kaleidoscope of patina, blood smear, and gristle, along with a couple grimy aprons as well. In the distant recesses, infinite liquid-filled glassware displayed floating organs and tissues of all manner, arranged on numerous shelving units. Scanning more of the cluttered den was cut short, for as the figure turned and assumed an erect posture, to my astonishment, it was the doctor, admiring at arm's length, some type of grody viscera.

Holmes was crimson-dipped from finger to elbow tips; while the accompanying drips dangling from mustache tips didn't disturb a visage of determined pleasure. Now, like I've stated before, I ain't foreign to large animal disembowelment, but I never had been privy to the innards of a lady, which was obviously the subject of the good doctor's dissection, as I could unmistakably make out mammaries on the supine specimen, beyond the mutilated cavern between her widespread legs. Best I could figure, H. H. must've been examining her womb.

Again, I ain't no doctor, but from clear across the room, it sure looked more like savage butchery than pristine extraction to me; but hey, maybe he only needed that single organ from that region, and had other, more meticulous designs and procedures, for the more cephalad components. The peep show creeped me out. That lair's atmosphere in totality didn't sit right; however, my rational mind quieted any rebellion, with justifications. I didn't know how doctors like him came into possession of cadavers for medical craft. But it was none of my damn business; and I sure as hell wasn't concerned enough to ruin my own concerns because of it. *Keep your nose to the grind stone.* I eased back into the darkened hallway, away from the gore circus, before its conductor made eye contact with its sole spectator, returning to the commons area just in time to be greeted.

As the pretty and petite, fair-haired maiden of the hotel's employ directed us to our assigned rooms, under the doctor's auspices, I reflected back on my brief conversation with the bordello orchestrator, which I faintly heard (as I was in a rush, and preoccupied with grandiose thoughts) while waiting for the rustlers to don their skivvies and make their way downstairs for rendezvous. When the Madame learned of our destination, she let slip a little gossip.

She whispered about how some of her customers checked in to Dr. Holmes's hotel and never turned up again. Vanished without a trace; never to see the light of day once more. I dismissed it as balderdash at the time.

After spectating the first few of my cowboys enter, and then close the doors to the rooms they were ushered into by the sweet hotel hostess, Tom, myself, and Sam were led around a sharp corner to another small hallway, leading to the final three rooms that we were given. The kind lady bid us farewell, and scurried outta sight. We glanced at each other, mutually grinned and simultaneously shrugged, then shot directly into our individual, private quarters. I guess we were all tickled pink to get such unshared elegant respite, complimentary at that.

As soon as I finished pushing the door completely to the frame, I nearly jumped outta my boots, when a solid bolting sound emanated from the hallway beyond. Instantly, I gripped and ripped at the doorknob, only to find it unmovable.

Surprised at the peculiarity of what just transpired, I turned from the gateway of dismay, to inspect the room that had now turned into my prison. I soon spied a ragged hole in the adjoining wall to my left, approximately a good foot in width.

Approaching it hesitantly, for ignoring it was out of the question, a malodorous, no, putrid stench accosted my nostrils and palate. *Good God*! Powering through the revolting olfactory and gustatory assault, next my vision was given a reality test. My mind was sent reeling, as it interpreted the unbelievable optical input. Peering back at me from just below the wall's compromise, the remnants of a gelatinous, necrotic human eye floated atop a menagerie of purulent ichor and miasma; the vestiges of some poor soul's assorted, accompanying body parts.

"What the hell?!" clearly penetrated the wall adjacent to mine, escaping Sam's big maw.

"Sam… ?! You locked in there too?" I hollered back in his direction.

"Arrggghhhhhhhhh…." My stomach dropped, and my blood ran cold, as I heard only a mortified, rapidly dampening scream sounding from his room. My mind was flooded with the visual of a terrorized man falling into a fathomless well.

Before I could recover my equilibrium enough to investigate Tom's situation in the room on the other side of me, cacophonous coughing bellowed beyond our shared wall.

"Tom, godammit?! What's goin' on in there?" Through raspy broken phrases, interspersed with hideous hacking and labored breaths, Tom choked out: "Some kind of gasses are pourin' into my confines faster and faster-like… through some fancy ductwork around the corners of the ceiling."

With my ear pressed to the wall, the short interaction with Tom abruptly ended as a solid thud sounded from the floor, immediately followed by silence.

Feeling faint, in total disbelief and abject terror towards my predicament within Dr. Holmes's horror hotel, I did the only thing I could at that point… I sat down and waited. I didn't know what kind of sick games the good doctor had cooked up for me, but I'm fairly certain now what his talk about medical school deliveries was all about.

Oh, and my name… well, that doesn't matter none, since I know it won't be included on my anatomical specimen's exhibition plaque, anyhow.

* * *

Editor's note: Dr. Henry Howard "H. H." Holmes was the pseudonym of Herman Webster Mudgett of New Hampshire. Holmes was infamous for building his so-called "Murder Castle," a three-story hotel he operated in Chicago during the World Columbian Exhibition of 1893. He confessed to killing up to 27 people, many of whom were guests or employees of his hotel. He was convicted and hanged for just one murder—that of his business partner–but is suspected to have killed up to 133 people.

Alphonse
by Mord McGhee

You won't believe this. I barely do and I lived it. I mean, most people don't expect to be attacked in broad daylight the way I was attacked. Definitely not at the place where they work.

That's precisely what occurred, though. These events took place when I was serving at a diner on the corner of Third Avenue and West 15th, Staten Island, Erestina Grove. Quaint, quiet, and friendly; that's the way our small town was back then.

There wasn't even much there except the diner itself, a post office situated inside a little shed down the block, one rowhome of four units two stories high, a non-descript hardware/drugstore, and a boarding house. Every day I'd take the morning train in from New York City, walk about a mile, then take a ride back later in the day from a farmer who was kind enough to offer an empty seat in his pickup truck. I'd done it a thousand times. At the time, my biggest fear was failing, until one day I met a violent criminal.

The year was 1929. I remember the date: February 16th. Why can I be so specific?

Because it was shortly after Saint Valentine's Day. I'd been hoping the farmer might be sweet on me, but instead the only attention I got came from someone else: a middle-aged man, who was small, quiet, and unassuming, and had a face that blended in with any crowd, and who walked with the help of a cane, dressed in shabby clothes with a shabby, ill-fitting hat. The man acted like a pervert, with uninvited attention directed at me, peeking down my blouse while I refilled his coffee.

He smiled, and said, "Aren't you a delicious little thing? So young, so pretty. Must be wonderful to be you."

I left so quickly his mug spun around. It was strange, what he said. I didn't like him right then. The whole time he was in the diner, I kept catching him leering at me like I was a piece of meat hanging in a butcher's shop. I was glad we had other customers, because I didn't want to be alone with him. He gave me terrible shivers.

I mentioned this to my cook in the kitchen, and he said he would talk to the man if he gave me a reason to. He promised to throw him out on his ear and tell him to never come back.

It eased my worries. The cook was twice the little man's size, while I was the kind of woman often told by everyone who knew her that she looks like a baby doll, at just four-and-a-half feet tall.

But as it was, the middle-aged man finished his cup, wrapped himself in a gray trench coat, dropped the derby onto his bald scalp, and winked at me as he slipped out the door. I sighed, relieved, and sat down, studying the soiled mug. The cook, whose name was *Mr. Cook*, though everyone else just called him "cook"—funny on some level perhaps yet I did not laugh–called out from the back, "Everything okay?"

It was. I told him I was thankful that the man left without another word. I'd not ever seen the man before then and had no clue he would soon return to the diner looking specifically for me. And it was two days later when that happened.

That day the cook was late for work, and I was managing the diner by myself. The middle-aged man came in and sat, taking the same table as his prior visit. He flipped his dishes right-side up, and carefully set the mug in a place not easily reached by me. With a grumble I took the coffee pot to him, approaching with a pasted-on friendliness.

"Hello," I told him. "Kitchen's behind—can't take a food order just yet."

I sensed something off about him but wasn't sure what it was. His mouth curled; his voice was soft in a tone one might use to speak to a child. "That's fine," he said. "I was in here the other day."

"Yes," I said. "I remember."

He removed his hat. "Albert Budd," he said.

I replied without thinking. "Budd? Like the missing girl from Brooklyn, the one in the newspapers last year? Everyone here was talking about her. I think she ran away and will come home soon, and there's been some unlucky mistake."

He stared at me, his expression revealing naught of what he was thinking. It was then I noticed what was wrong about him: his finely groomed mustache had dark splotches stuck in it. I offered a napkin.

"You've got something right here," I said.

He accepted the cloth and said, "That child was my niece."

"Oh, God, Mr. Budd! I'm really sorry. I didn't mean anything…"

He wiped his mustache. He tried to hide it, but the cloth was streaked red.

"Are you okay?" I asked. I saw no injuries, yet it was clearly blood. He curled a finger at me and leaned forward. Not wanting to be rude, I listened reluctantly.

"There is no part of a woman's body upon which I won't indulge," he whispered, and when I reared back his eyes twinkled with some secret amusement. I froze. He laid the napkin down. "Coffee," he said, his eyes tracing my breasts–which, though covered–felt violated. And he then slid the mug closer to me. I filled it and slipped into the back.

Ten minutes passed and still no cook. I checked our stores and returned to Albert Budd.

He flashed yellow teeth at my approach. "Is the kitchen open yet?" he asked. "I'm famished."

"I can make eggs and toast," I offered. "Anything else you'll have to wait."

"Are you alone?" he perked up.

"The cook hasn't shown up yet," I said. "It happens sometimes. He's got children."

"I like children," Albert smiled. "Do you have any?"

"No."

He looked around and reached inside his suitcoat. His smile was infectious, and I caught myself doing the same. I saw he'd produced a box of matches and set them upon the table. "This is for you," he said, and before he could say anything more, the front door opened. I expected the cook, but it wasn't him.

A burly man in a dark blue suit and matching fedora, stepped inside, then stomped his feet–covered in shiny, brown dress shoes–to knock off the snow he'd brought in. He unraveled a scarf to reveal a chin marked with black stubble; thick, sweeping eyebrows; and a visible scar drawn across his face. The scent of cigar smoke and perfume arrived with him. He looked at me, then at Albert Budd. Turning back to me, he said, "Room for me?" and smiled.

"Sit anywhere you like," I told him, noticing Albert putting the matchbox back into his pocket. The newcomer took the next booth and removed his hat and coat. He began to turn the dishes over and I filled the mug with coffee and said, "All I have is eggs and toast."

"I'll have it," he said, gazing out through the window behind our painted storefront letters.

I hurried through the swinging door into the kitchen, took out a half-dozen eggs and set them up next to the stove. I opened a breadbox and laid out a stack. "You better get in soon, Mr. Cook," I mumbled, when a voice made me jump out of my skin.

"You didn't take my order," said Albert Budd, standing inside the kitchen behind me. He again took out the matchbox and held it in his palm. "And this, it's for you, my dear."

I turned to face him. "You can't be back here, Mr. Budd."

"No?" he asked.

"No," I told him, less cordially. "And I don't need matches. Go have a seat and I'll bring what I can in a minute."

He smiled wanly. "My dear, you misunderstand me. You're such a small thing. So pretty, like a little girl." He slid a foot against the swinging door, blocking it so it wouldn't push inward.

His lips curled into a sallow grin. "It's the box that's for you. You see, I'm going to cut you into tiny pieces and stuff you inside it."

I had no words.

Albert Budd removed his coat and dropped it on the floor, then he pulled a knife and jammed it into the doorframe, locking the swinging door as he tore off his pants. My mouth opened. I meant to scream but the sound caught in my throat. It was then that Albert Budd came at me, half-naked, teeth bared, growling like an animal.

"Took me nine days to eat her," he hissed through clenched teeth, lunging at me. I grabbed a frying pan but missed striking him, and his hand scraped against mine. "Not my niece, but she was delectable." And I swatted again, making space between us for a second of time. His tongue flicked over his lips. What he said didn't quite register just then. It was like a roll of distant thunder, just at the edge of hearing.

A glistening line of drool slid from the corner of his lips, and my chest collapsed; the frying pan dropped out of my hands. Albert's face wrinkled as his eyes followed the clatter to the floor, then darted back to my own rings of fire. At once he shoved me to the ground and dashed past, kicking through the backdoor.

An instant later I heard a voice from the front tables.

"Are you alright, missy?"

I croaked, unable to form words. Until finally, "Help!" escaped from my mouth. The swinging door smashed ajar with such force the knife splintered the wood and skittered across the floor and then the scarred man was there. He looked at me, then glanced at the pile of clothing on the floor. "What the hell's going on back here?" his lower lip puffed forming a thick sneer.

I jumped into his arms and hugged a perfect stranger like I've never hugged anyone in my life. "Thank God!" I cried into his shoulder, sobbing uncontrollably. "He… he…"

"Who?" he said, peeling me off and walking towards the back door.

"There was a man," I sputtered, one trembling hand showing the discarded suit.

The scarred man knocked the door open, and somehow a revolver appeared in one large fist. I saw footprints in the snow on the ground behind the diner. Wherever he went, the impressions crossed the road until they disappeared at a patch shoveled outside the boarding house.

The scarred man stepped outside, swinging the pistol side to side. Then, with a shrug and a laugh, he returned to me. "What did that codger do?" he snarled, popping a cigar into his mouth with a beefy hand, and somehow the gun was gone again. The back door opened, and I jumped and squealed, but it wasn't the return of Albert Budd. It was the cook, at last, and he looked at the scarred man and the color drained from his face.

"Janey?" he said, raising his hands as if we were being robbed at gunpoint.

I quickly explained how the scarred man had saved my life, and the cook made breakfast while I did all I could to stop trembling and crying. A little after that, I heard Mr. Cook thank the man and send him off. He returned to me in the kitchen and said, "I thought you were in real trouble there. Do you know who that was?"

"What?" I asked. "Didn't you listen? He took off his clothes and attacked me!"

"Janey," Mr. Cook said. "Did you not hear about the St. Valentine's killing? It's been all over the papers. That man, that was him, the man who did the massacre! One of them. The papers said he'd been spotted down at Nifty's. Not ten miles from here!"

* * *

And it was him. The cook was absolutely correct. I met Alphonse Capone, the notorious mobster and the man whom police believed orchestrated one of the most infamous killing sprees in modern times. It was in all the newspapers, just like the cook said. And later, I read everything I could find about Alphonse. If he was such a monster, why had he not done anything bad to me? Why had he saved me? And I laughed, a nervous, disingenuous sound, and thought it was over. My brush with fame.

But it wasn't.

Alphonse didn't come back to the diner, but it wasn't Capone who returned to my life. The man he rescued me from, who attacked me that day, did come back. But not in person. You see, I began to study the newspapers regularly, a new thing in my life, and it was some years later when I saw the familiar face, the carefully groomed mustache, and the beady eyes staring back at me from the front page. In the photograph, he was aged a bit, but it was him.

Albert Budd wasn't his real name. It was, instead, Albert Fish. And the article started off by saying: *"Investigators tracked down the suspect, Albert Fish of New York, at a boarding house and after questioning, he was arrested after admitting to several killings of children in and around New York City, plus assault, three kidnappings; and much more. Fish used multiple aliases and law enforcement continues to investigate related crimes, including that of a well-known case relating to a child's disappearance in Brooklyn."*

And the prosecutor, too, supplied a short quote. He said, "New York can sleep safely knowing a cold-blooded killer is behind bars. A hearing is scheduled to figure out if Fish is sane enough to stand trial."

As I read on past, my encounter with Albert came back. The terror of the moment revisited me, remembering how he took off his clothing, then stretched out his hands like bear claws towards me. A lump formed in my throat. I read the testimonial words of Albert Fish—

my Albert—and I retched, tears welling in the corners of my eye, and as I was choking, they soon rolled down my cheek, splashing onto the newspaper, where reporting said he had owned up to strangling the children and desecrating their corpses in random abandoned homes.

I imagined him saying to the poor Brooklyn child, "A delicious little thing. So young, so pretty" —exactly what he told me, in those first, seemingly cordial pleasantries. I remembered his hairless body, bony and pale, and the serpent's hiss issuing from his bared teeth. Brown, bloodied teeth.

Breath caught in my throat.

His eyes…

Looking down my shirt.

Penetrating and burning.

What had he been trying to do… what had he done to that poor child? Then, I read on and found the dreaded truth. "Strangled her. Dismembered her remains. Cooked and consumed them." I dropped the newspaper as those dark seconds flooded my mind, and I sobbed uncontrollably.

A horrible, awful, disgusting realization rose in my gorge again. Of Albert Budd, notorious cannibal killer arrested under the name of Albert Fish, and words I had nearly forgotten, spoken in a voice I can only describe as pure evil: *"I think I'll start with your fingers."*

* * *

Editor's note: Albert Fish was captured and convicted of the murder of a child in 1935, after sending an anonymous letter to the child's mother detailing how he had killed her and eaten parts of her body. He confessed to killing three children, but was strongly suspected in a total of ten child murders. However, he may have killed up to 100 children and teens, having hinted that he had "had a child in every state." Fish was executed by the State of New York in 1936.

So Simple
by Ethan K. Lee

Alice agreed—suburban life was all dull. No, she wouldn't have preferred (as her mother so often reminded her) to be living back in a Brooklyn tenement or, as her mother had done as a child, in a car while her father searched for work.

But still, comparisons aside, there was a dreariness to the middle-class ease of suburban New York. Did she really long for the wild, morally abandoned thrills she saw happening in California? No. No, that would be uncouth and ungrateful.

Still, a part of her agreed with her neighbor, Waneta. "It's just," Waneta was saying, "not what I expected." She leaned over Alice's kitchen island, martini in one hand and the other flipping idly through a magazine on the countertop. Her brown hair was done in a bouffant, which managed to frame her face pleasantly. On Waneta's pointed nose sat a pair of stylish glasses.

Outside, Alice could hear the two women's husbands discussing the Yankees' chances that year. Frank, Alice's husband, was saying something about the future of baseball lying in the Caribbean islands, and Waneta's Tom laughed.

The two men stood on the back porch, polos tucked into gray shorts, clinking glasses as they surveyed Alice and Frank's perfectly manicured lawn. "No, I guess it's not perfect," said Alice. She spoke in a low voice, not wanting to commit too fully to what felt like blasphemy.

Waneta scoffed. "Not perfect? No. It's far from it. I thought there'd be a little more adventure, but no, we can't even have a good war to talk about," she said. Waneta did not sound shrill, only bored, perhaps exacerbated.

It was, Alice had to admit, quite frustrating. They lived in the bosom of freedom and affluence in the wealthiest nation that had ever existed, and yet, strangely, it was utterly unfulfilling.

Of course, women like Waneta had more to complain about—at least she did not sound so utterly blasphemous, given what had happened.

Poor Waneta. Four children dead from SIDS. What a tragedy. What a disgusting vile joke—it was the type of thing that Alice had raged about at St. Mary's School for Girls. Every time the nuns mentioned the Good Lord's overpowering love and goodness, Alice had to bite down on her tongue until she bled, thinking of all the horrors He let happen. Weren't we now learning what had happened to the Jews in Germany? And what about the Communists in Russia and China? Dear Lord in Heaven, hadn't the nuns read about the gulags?

Those things, though, were perhaps too large for most people to fully comprehend. But the death of four children? That was something that everyone could understand; that was the type of horror that would turn anyone against the church.

"And the babies. Mary Mother, he always wants another," said Waneta. "Is Frank the same way?"

Alice smiled. "Well, you know, Frank's a good Catholic boy."

"Jesus, you'll end up with a whole football team, won't you? What does he want, nine, ten?" asked Waneta.

This made Alice laugh. "Three. Just three," she said. As if on cue, the baby—her nine-month-old first-born son, James—began to cry from his nursery.

Waneta's hand shook. She almost dropped the martini glass. Was she grimacing? No.

Well, maybe. Would it be so weird for a woman with her trauma to grimace at the sound of a baby crying?

With a quick, muttered apology, Alice rushed off to her son's room. James lay in his crib, his face red and scrunched, wailing. His diaper did not need to be changed, nor was the child hungry. It seemed, instead, to just be one of those ineffable moments where an infant cries out in anguish.

This is silly, Alice thought. If the child could be given a moment of rational deliberation, he'd see how foolish he was being. Honestly, this behavior was ungrateful, bordering on idiotic.

Alice laughed at herself. "No, not idiotic," she said aloud, holding her son to her chest. The preciousness of the life in her hands soothed all of Alice's discontent. James's cries quieted against his mother's heartbeat.

When Alice returned to the kitchen, Waneta was standing by the new television set. A fresh martini was in her hand, and an olive dangled from her mouth. Noticing Alice's return, she said, "I don't know how you do it."

"Do what?" asked Alice.

Waneta raised her martini glass to indicate the nursery. "That shrill screaming. It's just—" and her voice trailed off.

Crossing to the liquor cabinet, Alice considered what to say. She wanted to be gentle—the woman had lost four children.

Good Lord, the thought of that horror made Alice's blood run cold.

"Oh. It's alright. This is how it is, isn't it?" said Alice.

Waneta turned from the television. Her face looked disapproving, as if Alice had been on the verge of some sort of great esoteric discovery and then had disappointed Waneta by floundering about in the muck of mundanity. "I suppose," she whispered.

Alice let the conversation drop, and seeing as James did not cry for the rest of the afternoon, Waneta's comments and disapproving stare slowly faded from her mind. The rest of the day went along pleasantly. They had pot roast and mashed potatoes for dinner, with a Jell-O mold that Waneta had made for dessert.

The men knew each other from one of the local clubs—Rotary, Elks, Masonic—Alice couldn't keep track. She was grateful that they kept talk of their shared hobbies to a minimum, instead keeping the discussion focused on local politics, which later turned to neighborhood gossip as the alcohol started to flow more freely.

Tom held up three fingers. "Jim just had his third boy. Incredible," he said, his voice a bit slurred.

"Almost got himself a basketball team," said Frank.

"Must be a nightmare," said Waneta.

Alice was pleased to notice that Frank laughed, and that he didn't take the poor woman's outburst too seriously.

For his part, Tom put an arm around his wife's shoulder. "Come on, honey, our hosts don't want to hear that type of talk," he said.

In response, Waneta drained her glass and then held it out to Alice, smiling. "Oh, I think they might. Let's be real. It's not all rainbows and sunshine. Is it, Alice?"

This was what Alice had been dreading all evening— the idea of being drawn into a debate, in front of her husband, about the joys and follies of motherhood was a bit too much to bear.

Alcohol, though, seemed to provide the necessary courage to at least engage in the conversation.

Putting on her best vaudeville-style smile, the one her mother had trained her to have, Alice said, "Well, you have to admit, it's not all perfect." Something about Alice's smiling face made the men laugh. With her high cheekbones and button nose, Alice guessed her own doubts regarding the wonders of motherhood were more palpable.

"Honestly, I do sometimes feel like our mothers lied to us. Right, Waneta?" asked Alice.

Waneta's eyes narrowed. "Definitely," she said.

"I mean the constant crying."

"Screaming."

"Being woken at night."

"Endless."

"But you love it, don't you?" Frank said, interjecting.

There was a longer-than-normal pause, and then Alice leaned over and kissed her husband on the lips. His breath tasted like cheap beer. "Of course," she said.

* * *

Dinner carried on normally from that point, and as the time stretched towards midnight, Tom said that they should get going. Frank yawned his agreement.

Alice was beginning to slump on the couch. She hadn't drunk like this since before she was pregnant. The thought of the vicious hangover awaiting her tomorrow started to make her feel remorse.

And the baby. Lord, could she handle its incessant crying with her head pounding from a hangover? If Frank was too lazy to get out of bed, she might just stab him. The thought made her giggle.

"What's funny? I want to laugh," asked Waneta.

Alice held her hand to her mouth. "Nothing, nothing, a weird thought just popped into my head," Alice answered.

Waneta seemed unimpressed by this answer. She kept her eyes on Alice for a second too long. Finally, she announced that before she and Tom left, it was imperative that she use the bathroom.

"No, no, I can manage," Waneta said as Alice offered to show her the way. With a sinking feeling, Alice watched Waneta teeter on her heels up the three stairs and down along the carpeted hallway.

The men returned to their conversation about Lyndon Johnson and whether, as Frank's cousins down in Texas insisted, the Box 13 Scandal was legitimate.

Alice barely listened. She stared down the darkened hallway where Waneta had gone to the bathroom. There was no reason to feel so anxious. What could possibly make her heart thud so hard? Did she really think Waneta was going to do something nefarious in the bathroom?

No.

Not the bathroom.

Alice got to her feet unsteadily. The men barely noticed, and Alice made an excuse about checking on Waneta. Her head felt heavy with alcohol. Alice's vision swam as she stumbled forward, suddenly feeling desperate. Her tongue tasted of copper. Ash burned in her nostrils.

What was wrong? What was wrong? The question pounded through her head, mixing with the throbbing of her heart, which now thundered so loudly in her ears that she could hear nothing—nothing except a sharp buzzing that made her teeth ache.

James's nursery door was open.

She'd closed it. Alice knew she'd closed it when she put him to sleep, but there it was, open wide. Unable to breathe, Alice crept the last few feet down the hallway, until she stood in her son's doorway.

Alice's breath caught in her throat. "It's easy," Waneta whispered.

She was standing next to the crib, James nestled in her arms. Alice's stomach lurched at the sight of those thin fingers enclosed around her son. Waneta's nails, which earlier had seemed so well-kept, were now reminiscent of talons, of the vicious, biting grip of some ancient predatory beast, a monster haunting every mother's most primitive dreams.

Yes, a small voice spoke in the back of Alice's mind, the most ancient primordial monster—the child thief; the strangling silence in the night.

Alice wanted to scream, but, pathetically, she couldn't find her voice.

Waneta turned her head. "It's so easy," she said. "Doctors don't really want to discuss it, you know. They just call it SIDS and move on with the day. It's horrible, right? Who would want to talk about dead babies?"

One of those sharp talons came to James's nose. He gurgled, and Waneta pinched at his nostrils. Alice gulped, steadying herself against the doorframe. "I'm afraid I just don't—" she stammered.

"No?" asked Waneta.

Her mouth was dry. She thought of screaming for Frank, but for what? Because Waneta was holding their baby? Because this poor woman who'd lost four of her own children was taking a moment to cuddle their newborn?

Alice straightened up. "I'd prefer we let him sleep," she said.

There was no immediate response from Waneta. She pinched James's nose harder. The baby gurgled, then began to struggle, thrashing out with his tiny fists. "So simple," Waneta whispered. "Nobody asks any questions."

"Please put him down," Waneta said. Her voice was so small—so frail and without conviction. There was a secret here, a sacred mystery that went unspoken between mother and daughter, a path to freedom so heinous that it could not be conveyed through words.

A tense moment passed when Alice wasn't sure Waneta had heard. The other woman tightened her grip on James's nose, her knuckles growing white with the strain. The baby coughed. Waneta's jaw was clenched, and Alice thought she could hear the bones grinding.

"You'll never feel more relief," Waneta whispered.

She held her teeth so tight together that Alice couldn't tell if she'd really spoken. For a brief second, Alice had to suppress a laugh, imagining Waneta as a ventriloquist's doll—a large, life-size female dummy, her strings pulled by a malevolent unseen master.

It was the tension making her think these crazy thoughts. Yet, what was there to be afraid of? Even when she asked herself this question, she knew the answer. There was something deeply wrong here, something inherently wrong with the way Waneta eyed the young child.

Worse, there was something disturbing about Alice's own inaction.

Would it be so bad really? asked a voice Alice could not recognize. If the child just drifted away—no pain, no agony, just a simple sleep from which it would never awake.

Waneta licked her lips. "Two-hundred and ten seconds," she whispered, then turned her eyes to Alice. "That's all it takes, if you do it yourself. A bit longer if you put the baby's face in a pillow."

Before Alice understood, she was standing beside Waneta, her fingers caressing James's cheeks. It would be so simple, so very easy to place a hand over his mouth.

Waneta's voice came from far away. "It's freeing. I promise. I'll teach you how to look grieving at the funeral, but that's nothing," she said.

Now, Alice rested her fingers on James's nose. She pinched lightly, testing the way the barely formed cartilage collapsed beneath her fingers. Alice felt her son's tiny breath against her skin.

What would Frank think? Externally, he'd be devastated of course, but what if he came home to an Alice who was no longer tired and worn down by childcare? What if, as at the start of their marriage, Frank came home from work to a wife bubbling with excitement, willing to give all her attention to a single male entity?

She could give up the child for that, couldn't she? They could always make another if Frank asked.

Another child.

Her child.

Alice suddenly snapped to attention from her place of frozen trepidation. With trembling hands, Alice reached for her son. "Let me do it," she said.

Waneta's eyes widened. The lips curled into a smile at the edges, letting her cigarette-stained teeth show. Handing the child over, she spoke so low that Alice strained to hear. "Just a hand over his face, darling," she said.

James nestled into his mother's arms, his tiny fists moving in circles. Waneta continued to stare, her pupils dilated, her breathing heavy as she watched with desperate fascination. For a brief moment, Alice's hand caressed her son's face. She tickled his nose. Lightly, she pinched the nostrils closed.

Beside her, Waneta's breath came in slow, raspy gasps. Her excitement was palpable as Alice practiced closing her son's lips together, but suddenly and calmly, she placed the child back in the crib. With a swiftness her husband would've found shocking, but that the girls at St. Mary's would've recognized, she slapped Waneta hard against the face.

Glasses askew, Waneta dropped to her knees, gripping her face. She bit her lip until it bled, apparently to keep from screaming.

James didn't cry. The house was quiet. Alice could hear nothing but the thumping of blood in her ears until Tom called, "Honey, it's time to go."

Wordlessly, Waneta left the room, and Alice did not allow herself to breathe until she could hear the wheels of her dinner guests' car turning on the gravel driveway.

* * *

Editor's note: Waneta Nixon Hoyt of Newark Valley, New York was convicted of killing all of her biological children as infants or toddlers, during the period between 1965 to 1971, via suffocation. The children were originally thought to have died of Sudden Infant Death Syndrome (SIDS) until more than two decades after the last death. In 1994, an out-of-state forensic pathologist working on a similar case studied the Hoyt files and concluded strongly that the deaths were homicides. She tipped off local authorities, who wangled a confession out of Waneta that she killed the children. In 1995, she was sentenced to 75 years in prison for five second-degree murders, but died of pancreatic cancer soon after.

Death Trap
by Damon Nomad

Rudy was quietly singing along with *Rock the Bo*at when he heard Carl shout from the front. "Turn off the radio and come up here."

Rudy finished tightening the drain plug and wiped down the oil pan. He shouted back, "Just a minute. Finishing up the Buick." He lowered the lift and took off his gloves; then washed his hands in the dirty sink in the corner. He turned the radio off and headed toward the office area and the front counter. Rudy saw the corner closet door was half open, and he pushed it shut as he walked past. "Why do I have to keep closing this?" He looked at Carl.

Carl held his hands up in mock surrender. "Don't say it. I know. Everything has a place and everything should be in its place. You keep this garage neater than a country church on Sunday."

Rudy snorted a laugh as he sat on a stool a few feet away from Carl, who was sitting in his beloved black vinyl chair. The chair was parked in the usual spot, beside the desk that stood behind the counter. Styled to look like an expensive leather office chair, the chair had been in the garage longer than Rudy, and he figured it was ugly the day Carl bought it in some second-hand store. Now it was tattered and worn from too many years in the garage. "What do you need?"

Carl smiled with a nod. "Never seen such a neat and orderly mechanic and such clean hands. Only one I know who always wears gloves." He leaned back in his seat. "Anyway, I want to catch up on some business." He gestured to the clock up on the wall. "It's Friday and I'll be heading home early."

It was just a few minutes after four. Carl had been going home early every day now for nearly the last five years. Fridays and Saturdays, he left even a little earlier. He was sixty-two and could not put in the hours he did years ago. Rudy was trusted to lock up the garage and close out the cash register to the safe before leaving. Carl's Auto Parts and Repair was open ten to seven, six days a week.

Rudy shrugged. "Something specific?"

Carl waved a hand with a sweeping motion. "The future of this place. Have you been thinking about it?"

Rudy stared at the floor. "You said that was not for another three years." He shook his head. "Besides, I won't have the money to buy the business from you Carl. You need to find someone else. Tell them that I'll work for them. I've got a reputation as a good mechanic and that helps for repeat business. That means something, right?"

"You're a great mechanic and that does mean something. That's not the point. You're thirty-one years old and the work is easy for you now. You don't want to be climbing under cars when you are fifty years old. You've been working for me for twelve years. I pay you a good wage and let you have after-hours business for your own pocket. You must have money saved. You don't live a fancy life. We can set up a payment schedule."

Rudy continued to look down. "It's my momma, she's got no insurance and I've been paying her medical bills." He looked up. "Let's talk about this later." He tugged on his baseball cap.

Carl rubbed his chin as he nodded his understanding. They both went quiet for a few moments. Carl tapped on the newspaper lying on the desk. "What kind of world are we living in? These missing girls and the one killed earlier this year near campus. There's an article about some psychiatrist who says it might be the same monster." He shook his head. "So much violence now. My brother lives in Chicago. Do you know how many murders they had last year?"

Rudy shrugged. "I know it's a lot."

"More than eight hundred and it might top a thousand this year." He paused a moment.

"Seattle's not like that, but the idea that some psycho is hunting young women here." He frowned as he slowly shook his head. He waved a finger at Rudy. "Two businesses on this block have been robbed just this month. One of them roughed up Felix—you know, at the fruit and vegetable bodega."

"Yeah, I heard about that." Rudy winced, with a nod. "Why don't we talk about something else?"

Carl leaned back in his seat as he slowly nodded his head. He gestured at Rudy's ball cap. "How about those Oakland A's of yours? Red Sox beat them good yesterday, at home." He chuckled.

Rudy took off the cap and ran a hand over his closely trimmed Afro. He put the hat back on. "My man Vida is pitching tomorrow; it will be a different story."

They jostled back and forth about the baseball season for nearly twenty minutes. Carl glanced at the clock as he got up out of his seat. "Let's see how your team does tomorrow." He headed for the door. "Don't work too late and keep the door locked after I leave. You can't always hear that bell on the door when you're working in the shop, especially if you're using power tools. Let them use the buzzer. Somebody can come up on you from behind at a workbench or even worse while you're on a dolly under a car."

He paused at the door. "Keep that lead-filled baseball bat close at hand; you can take down a man with a knife with one swing of old Hickory."

Rudy nodded with a shrug. "I try to leave by nine and I'm careful. Old Hickory is in the corner of the shop. See you tomorrow." He smiled as he watched the gray-haired man shuffle out the door. Carl was a short, stocky, white man of Irish descent and Rudy was a tall, slim black man. They didn't look like family, but Carl treated Rudy like a favorite nephew. That's how Rudy thought of Carl like an uncle. He didn't have any real uncles or much of any family for that matter.

Rudy headed back to the shop and slipped on a clean pair of thin white cotton gloves. He always cleaned up the shop late on Fridays. He organized things, made sure important tools were in proper working order, and calibrated some of the test equipment. He switched the radio back on and turned the dial to a news channel before he sat down at the large workbench. He heard the tail end of the weather. He smiled. Nice weather again tomorrow, the Red Sox are gonna take it on the chin.

He adjusted a set screw on a caliber for measuring brake pads as the radio news moved onto politics. "President Gerald Ford refused to answer reporters' questions today about a pardon for former President Richard Nixon." The radio news faded into the background as he focused his attention on his work.

He heard the jingle of the front door, the door closing and then a man's voice. "Anyone here? Can someone help me out?"

Rudy glanced up at the old, white-faced electric clock on the wall of the shop; it was five minutes after seven and he had not locked the door. He took off the gloves and found a thin white man about his age, standing just inside the front door. The guy was a few inches shorter than Rudy and was dressed casually in blue jeans, a short-sleeved tennis shirt, and sneakers.

Rudy gestured to the man. "We're closed for the day."

The man flashed a toothy smile as he moved toward the counter. "I live nearby on Twelfth Avenue." He gestured at Rudy. "Could you help out a fellow A's fan?"

Rudy folded his arms across his chest. "Really? Who's your favorite player?"

The man eyed Rudy with a hint of a smirk. "Hmm... you think I might be conning you?"

He paused for a moment. "I guess I could say Reggie, but everyone has heard of him. I don't really have a favorite, but you gotta love a team with a pitcher named Catfish and another named Blue Moon." He waggled a finger at Rudy. "They will do it again this year, three World Series in a row."

He shrugged. "Could you take a look at my engine? I'm driving to Utah at the end of the month and its sputtering badly when it idles. Maybe I can do you a favor someday. I'm in law school, maybe some free legal advice." He paused with a grin. "Please, sir."

Rudy chuckled. "I don't get called sir often. What ya driving?"

"Sixty-eight VW Beetle."

"Could just be the plugs or a stuck needle valve. Those would be quick fixes, but I got some more shop cleanup to take care of before I can get to it."

"I kind of need it tonight."

"There's a twenty-four-hour coffee shop, half a block down on the right. Go ahead and pull it in and come back between nine and nine-thirty. I'll see what I can do."

The man parked his VW in the open bay of the garage and grabbed a thick law book and legal pad from the back seat. They went to the front of the shop and the man laid the keys down on the front counter. "Thanks so much." He held out his hand. "I'm Ted."

Rudy shook his hand. "Sure thing; name's Rudy." He gestured to the book. "That's a thick book, what subject?"

"Criminal procedure. It's good to know the rules they play by." He shrugged with a mischievous grin. "Thanks, Rudy." He headed out the door.

Rudy stared at the door for a moment. Rules *they* play by? Rudy printed out the daily summary from the cash register, counted the cash, and wrote the balance down on the summary.

He locked everything in the floor safe and headed back to the shop.

No reason to lock up at the front. *I'll be fine.*

Rudy quickly finished up the routine shop cleanup and was ready to work on the VW Beetle. He shook his head as he stared at the small car that didn't weigh much over two thousand pounds. *Darn thing is a death trap*, he thought. He went to the front and retrieved the keys lying on the counter. He opened the driver's side door.

He muttered aloud, "What the heck?" The front passenger seat was missing. He saw it lying on the rear seat. He studied the mounting hardware for a few moments. Nothing looks broken. He noticed that the inside door handle on the passenger side was missing. He frowned and mused about his new customer. *Does he make everyone sit in the back? How do they get out?*

Rudy sat in the driver's seat, cranked the engine, and listened to it sputter as it struggled to idle. Dirty or worn-out spark plugs. He got out, returned the keys to the front counter, and grabbed the service and parts manual. He shuffled back into the shop area and sat down on the stool at the smaller workbench. He opened the thick book to find the plug type and gap distance for the '68 VW beetle.

The radio caught his attention as it shifted to a special report. "We have as a guest, psychiatric doctor Frederick Ballard, who is consulting with the Seattle Police Department. He recently published an article titled *The Mind of a Serial Murderer.* Doctor Ballard, what does this term serial murderer mean?"

"This is an evolving area of study and somewhat controversial, but my definition is someone who has killed at least three people over a period of time, not in one spree. These killers are not killing for money or any of the classic motives for murder. They kill because of some sort of psychological compulsion. I use the Boston Strangler as a case study in my article."

Rudy felt a chill as the psychiatrist began to describe the crimes and the postulated psycho-sexual motivations of the Boston Strangler. He brought his attention back to the manual and found the specifications for the spark plugs. It didn't take long to get the four plugs out.

He started cleaning them and checking the gaps as he sat at the large workbench.

His attention came back to the radio announcer as he was putting the last of the newly cleaned plugs back into the engine. "Dr. Ballard, you have summarized two infamous cases. The Zodiac Killer in Northern California in the late 60s and the Boston Strangler in the early 60s.

Why are you consulting for the Seattle Police? Is there a serial murderer in Seattle?"

Rudy paused his work as he waited to hear the answer. "I believe an emerging serial murderer is hunting in the Seattle area. That is my opinion and not the official position of the Seattle Police Department." Rudy slowly finished connecting the cable to the last plug as he focused on the radio.

The announcer pushed for more details, "What do you think this person is like?"

"Eyewitness accounts provide a foundation for a basic behavioral portrait. Witnesses who were at Lake Sammamish when the two women went missing and three other women. The three women were approached on separate occasions by a man who had his arm in a sling and he requested their assistance. The three are physically very similar—younger women, all in college.

Witnesses from Lake Sammamish describe a man of similar physical appearance, also with an arm in a sling, approaching young women for assistance."

Rudy slipped off the cotton gloves and sat on a stool at the large workbench, nearly in a trance as he listened to the radio. The announcer queried, "What do these accounts tell you about this potential serial murderer?"

"They described a physically fit, Caucasian man of average height, approximately thirty.

They say he was handsome and well-mannered. He dressed casually and was confident in approaching them. I believe he is intelligent and likely well-educated. He understands human behavior and might have education or training in psychology."

Rudy thought he heard a tinkle of the bell on the front door, but it stopped and he didn't hear the door being closed. He glanced up at the clock; it was fifteen till nine.

He shouted out, "Is that you Ted? I'm in the shop with your car."

There was no answer.

Rudy scurried over to the open door that led to the front of the shop and looked around.

Nobody there. He was too focused on the radio to pay attention to the corner closet or other places where an intruder could conceal themselves. He sat back down on the stool in the shop as the psychiatrist continued, "He's using the sling and the need for physical assistance as a ruse to lure women to a vehicle. Preying on their sympathy and making it appear he is not a threat. He can easily overpower them when he has them alone and then immobilizes or restrains them. Then he drives away with them inside and hidden from view. These two women have been missing for nearly a month, and I fear the worst. A serial murderer will continue to kill until someone stops them."

"What should people be on the lookout for?"

"There was a sketch in the newspaper this morning, a composite from the witnesses at Lake Sammamish. These witnesses and the other three women all said the man used the name Ted and he drove a tan or brown VW Beetle."

Rudy's eyes flew wide open. *Ted driving a Beetle.*

The psychiatrist continued, "Contact the Seattle Police Department if you think you know who this is, do not confront this man. He will kill anyone who gets in his way, with little more thought than he would for a pesky insect buzzing about his face. He will seem to be normal and even friendly, but that is a mask covering the dark soul of a predator and a master manipulator."

Rudy turned off the radio and walked quickly to the front of the shop and sat down at Carl's desk. He opened the newspaper and stared at the sketch for a few moments. Could be him.

He bolted up off the seat when a car honked its horn on the street outside. He chuckled and muttered quietly, "Could be a lot of Teds who drive VW Beetles." Dude didn't seem dangerous.

He slowly walked back through the door into the shop area. He was focused on the car as he moved closer. At one point, he was vaguely aware of a quiet squeak from the front of the shop that resembled the opening of a door or a heavy lid, but he put it down to the frequent settling of the old building the shop was in.

Rudy stared at the passenger seat lying in the back of the Beetle, and saw a partially open satchel on the floorboard. He opened the car door and pulled the satchel closer. He looked inside. He saw an ice pick, handcuffs, rope, and a ski mask. He looked closer at the floor under where the front passenger seat was supposed to be. Several long brown hairs were caught in one of the slider tracks. He felt the hairs on the back of his neck stand up.

This is a death trap, he thought for the second time that evening. Rudy sat down in the driver's seat and opened the glove compartment and found the registration. *Theodore Robert Bundy.* He put the registration back and closed the glove box. He was startled by a voice.

"You figure out what's wrong?" Ted Bundy was standing in the doorway to the shop area. He was wearing the same relaxed expression he had when he'd dropped the car off.

Rudy was confused; he had not heard the front door jingle or the door being closed. He stammered as he got out of the car. "Ahh… Um… Yeah, just dirty plugs. You're all set."

Bundy moved a few steps into the shop. He gestured to the radio. "You like to listen to music while you work?"

His eyes narrowed and his mouth tightened into a thin frown.

Rudy's throat went dry as he tugged on the bill of his ball cap. "Yeah." *Calm down, he doesn't know that you suspect him.*

Bundy smirked as he moved a few steps closer. "Or maybe the news, this time of night."

Rudy inched toward the lead-filled baseball bat leaning in a corner. "I'm not much for the news." He glanced at the corner to make sure old Hickory was there.

Did he hear me listening to his description on the radio? Rudy's heart started to race.

Ted said in a sarcastic tone: "Really? I saw the newspaper open on the front desk." He sneered, "You believe someone could hunt people like that? Murder just for the pleasure of killing?" He moved closer to the car and the bat in the corner. They were each about six feet away from Old Hickory.

Rudy tugged on his ball cap again. "Don't know nothing about that." His mind was a jumble of tense thoughts. *Can I make a run for it?*

Bundy pointed at the car. "What were you doing inside? Not testing the engine. The keys are on the counter." He fixed his glare on Rudy. "You get a look at my tools, in my satchel?"

Rudy's blood ran cold from the icy stare; Ted Bundy seemed to have transformed into a different person. He knew he had to make his move. Just two big steps to grab old Hickory and whack Bundy. He bolted quickly but felt a kick to the side of his knee as he planted his right foot. He tumbled headlong onto the floor and struggled to sit up. Everything went black before he could turn around.

* * *

The next morning, Carl stared at Rudy's body on the floor as the police detective talked to the police sergeant. "Got the drop on him from behind with that big old bat. Cracked his skull pretty good, but strangled him with something that we can't find. Wiped the blood off the bat, we aren't gonna get any prints. We will wait for the medical examiner for the cause of death."

He turned to look at Carl. "Anything missing or out of place?"

Carl looked away from the body. "No. I already checked. They didn't get any money.

Rudy must have closed the register and transferred the day's take to the safe before they got here. The only car we had for work is that Buick parked in the first bay. Like I explained, he does clean up on Fridays."

The detective gestured at the doorway. "Let's go to the front, the medical examiner will be here soon."

They followed behind as Carl shuffled to the front and sat down in his chair. "Why would they kill him? You think it's the same guys hitting the other neighborhood shops?"

The detective shrugged. "Doesn't really fit their pattern, they haven't killed anyone. Maybe things got out of hand; hit him harder than they intended. Maybe they wanted him to open the safe and he refused, who knows?"

Carl gestured at the corner closet with its door opened a crack. "That's strange, Rudy wouldn't leave that door open. Always getting on me for not closing it."

The detective opened the door fully and glanced inside. "Just some office supplies in the corner and a few jackets and coats on hangers. Nothing in here of any value." He pushed the door closed. "Not like someone is gonna hide in a closet before robbing someone in the shop." He winced. "We don't have much of anything to go on. This case is probably going to stay open for quite a while."

* * *

Editor's Note: Theodore Robert "Ted" Bundy confessed to thirty murders committed in seven states between 1974 and 1978. Authorities believe he may have killed far more than the total he confessed to. He was executed in 1989 by the State of Florida after being found guilty of killing two women at a sorority house and a twelve-year-old girl.

I Wonder if God Will Be Watching
by Charles Reis

Melissa wore her thin green Adidas tracksuit, but the running kept her warm on this November afternoon in 1983. Vapor burst from her mouth and her feet crushed dead leaves. The yellow headband captured her sweat, and she kept her long blonde hair tied into a ponytail.

The recently turned eighteen-year-old inherited her running passion from her father, a former track-and-field star back in college. Their mutual love of it made her a daddy's girl, especially after the death of her mother three years ago.

Pine and oak trees stretched up to the horizon, with the branches of the oak stripped bare. The cold, pleasant smell of pine filled her nostrils. In the last half hour running on a country road in Plainfield, Connecticut, only a single blue Toyota drove by.

Kids in America by Kim Wilde played on her Sony Walkman. She shouted out the main chorus, pumping herself up in the process. With the sun in front of her, she pretended to race against it. She stared as the same blue Toyota passed by again.

Hmm, the driver must be lost.

From the corner of her eye, she spotted a teenage girl standing in the woods among the thick brush. She had short blonde hair and wore a white dress. Melissa turned her head to get a better look, but the girl was gone. She stopped and stood there looking around. *I swear to God, someone was there!* She shook her head and smirked. *Maybe she was a ghost!* After rolling her eyes, Melissa jogged in place for several seconds and then ran on.

Five minutes passed. She saw the same Toyota on the side of the road as she ran in the direction it was parked. When she got closer, she saw an older male kneeling by the lower-left tire with a jack and another tire next to him. She paid no attention while running by him.

The man shouted, "Excuse me?" After grunting, she stopped but jogged in place.

She sighed and pulled off her headphones.

The man, who looked to be in his twenties, wore red-rimmed glasses and a gray three-piece business suit. He reminded her of Matthew Broderick in the movie *WarGames* that she saw back in June: slightly geeky yet harmless. She stopped running and took several deep breaths.

"Yes?"

He smiled. "Hi. I tried to find a shortcut but got lost, and then I got a flat tire. It's fixed now, but I'm still lost. Do you know the way to Preston?"

"Yes, I do."

"Oh thank you! Let me grab a pen and my map, and you can mark it down for me." He opened the back door and bent over to rummage through junk on the seats.

After a few seconds, he stood back up and handed her a wrinkled-up map and Bic roller pen.

He held his hand out. "I'm Michael Ross."

Her parental upbringing made sure that she shook his hand. "Nice to meet you. I'm Melissa."

Using the hood of his car as a desk, she traced the best way toward Preston.

While doing so, Melissa paused for a moment. How did he get lost? It's so easy to get there. Regardless, she traced the correct route.

After she handed him the map, Michael grinned. "Thank you for your help, Melissa. You're a good person." Melissa noticed that when he took the map, he kept one hand behind his back. Although she found it strange, she saw him as a teddy bear.

She smiled back.

"You're welcome, sir." Melissa put on her headphones, took a few deep breaths, and jogged in place. *Total Eclipse of the Heart* by Bonnie Tyler played and aided her in getting back into running mode. She waved and then turned around to return to her course.

Like a snake attacking its prey, Michael rushed up from behind and held a hunting knife to her throat. She thought this was a joke, but that notion left her mind when the cold knife pressed against her skin. She froze and broadly opened her eyes and her heart throbbed against her chest.

"Don't scream, just do what I say... and you won't be harmed," he said and she nodded. "Put your hands behind your back."

A glint of tears formed in her blue eyes. She complied, but made a silent prayer.

God, please help me!

He tied her arms behind her back with rope, doing it so tight that it slowed the blood flow to her hands. Next, he placed duct tape over her mouth.

He pushed her to the back of his car. Michael opened the trunk and shoved her into it like a dog into a kennel. She landed on her stomach; her face smacked the rough trunk liner. He grabbed her legs and quickly roped them. Before she knew it, he slammed the trunk shut and trapped her in this dark coffin. She cried out as loud as her lungs allowed.

* * *

Melissa knew some time had passed. Her mind raced with horrible thoughts.

Tears dirtied her face and the bondage made her limbs numb. A sharp pain pulsed through her spine. Cold sweat poured over her face and her body trembled. Several times, she tried to free her arms and legs, but the ropes tightened. Trapped in darkness for so long, her eyes played tricks, as she imagined shadow figures moving inside the trunk.

The car bounced while the song *Runnin' With the Devil* by Van Halen blasted on the radio. When the car stopped and the engine turned off, she closed her eyes. As the door clicked open and then slammed shut, she prayed again. *Heavenly Father, protect me.*

The unholy jingle of keys sounded and then the trunk lid leaped open. He turned her bound form over onto her back. Minor pain inflicted her wrists and elbows from the weight of her body. She twitched open her eyes, witnessing the stars and a half-moon glowing from behind the ominous silhouette of Michael.

He wore black gloves and held the hunting knife in his hand. He went back and forth from grinding his teeth like a dog to licking his lips. His eyes stared at her with such vigor that her skin crawled.

He caressed her hair with his hand. "You're beautiful," he said in a soft voice.

The knife got closer. She twitched and cried, believing he would stab her, but he cut the ropes around her legs. After placing the blade in a leather holster located under his jacket, Michael grabbed her under the armpits and pulled her out of the trunk. The side of her head hit the edge of it as he did so. When he tried to get her to stand, she fumbled and spun her head around. Despite that, she looked around to find a way to escape.

The car was parked on an isolated dirt road that cut through a small grassy field that stretched to the front of a darkened building. The moonlight illuminated a white wooden building with two floors and a black pyramid-shaped roof. Three large arch-top windows lined the second floor, while the first floor had a small window on each side of the black, arched double doors. Michael retrieved his knife and pointed with it.

"This way."

As they walked towards the building, Melissa knew she had to escape. It was now or never. With all of her strength, she kicked his foot. He moaned and lost his grip; she ran but with her hands restrained, she couldn't sprint the way she usually could. He grabbed her arms, pulled her close to him, and pressed the knife to her throat so hard she felt its sting.

"Don't do that again, or I'll slice your fuckin' throat!" A wave of repulsion went through every vein and muscle in her body. She looked at him with tears in her eyes. After he took a deep breath, Michael pushed her along.

Upon getting closer, she spotted a sign on the building to the right of the doors that read "The Holy Trinity Church, 1771." Melissa felt his warm breath on her ear as he whispered, "I wonder if God will be watching?"

She shivered; tears streamed down her cheeks, and she cried through the duct tape. *God, please listen to me! I pray to you every night, please listen to me now!*

He pushed her towards the left side of the church, where a cemetery rested.

Despite the moonlight, Melissa stared into the pits of the abyss with shadows and voids everywhere. The cemetery resembled a desolate city with monuments, monoliths, and tombstones of assorted sizes and shapes. Many stones were in various stages of decay.

Her eyes opened wide and her body shook when he forced her into this realm of the dead. Mucus dripped from her nose.

A young woman stood at the border where the cemetery and the forest met. She didn't move; instead, she remained still, like a statue. Melissa believed that Michael couldn't see the woman, so she screamed in hopes of gaining her attention. When she got closer,

Melissa shook her head and her muscles tensed up. *No, this can't be!*

She couldn't believe it, but the figure looked just like the teenage girl she'd seen earlier, with the same hairstyle and dress. A few seconds later, the girl vanished like smoke in the wind. Melissa wondered if her mind had bent so much that it snapped.

Michael shoved her body down to the ground in front of a tombstone. She hit the cold, wet dirt so hard that pain pulsated through her head and her vision blurred.

Lying face down, she felt him undoing her ponytail and spreading out her hair. "I love your hair. When I saw you running, I had to choose you."

She fantasized that her dad would run out from behind the church yelling, "Get away from my daughter, you motherfucker!" and beat the man's brains in with a baseball bat. He then would hug her and tell her she was safe. She hoped that maybe if she imagined hard enough, it would happen.

A strong, cold sensation pulsated through her body. Although still on the ground, she shifted her face to look left. A tall oak tree with bare branches stretched into the sky a few yards away. The moonlight illuminated only this tree in that area. A long thick branch stretched to the left and a brown owl perched on it. It was twice as large as a normal owl, and its big yellow eyes seemed to glow. It stared at her, acting like a spectator of her terror.

I can't stand this! I want this all to end!

Michael lifted her shirt. She felt his fingers caress her from the neck down to her lower back. Goosebumps covered her back from his cold touch.

He pulled her sweatpants and underwear down, and then whispered into her ear,

"It will all be over soon... I'll let you go after... I promise."

She knew that was a lie. While she didn't fear death, she feared his plans for her while alive. He groped her behind; Melissa groaned and her body squirmed. When he unbuckled his belt and unzipped his pants, she squeezed her eyes and mouth shut.

Why have you left me, God?

As she gave in to despair, a gentle, warm sensation covered her body and drove the cold away. When Melissa looked towards the tombstone, she saw the same teenage girl standing next to it. *Wha-what's she doing here?* The fact that Michael didn't react to the teenager's presence added to the confusion.

The girl looked familiar. After a few seconds, she remembered this girl from the news. Her name was Heidi

O'Conner, a sixteen-year-old who went missing from Brooklyn, Connecticut last year.

Heidi knelt and touched Melissa's head. Freezing energy entered Melissa's body and knowledge of Michael's true nature filled her brain. After suffering years of abuse from his mother, he developed an impulse to stalk and kill women. Although he resisted for years, he recently gave in to his desire. Michael both enjoyed and hated the monster that lurked within. Heidi wasn't the first, nor his last, victim. He planned to add Melissa to his kill list.

Bright white light entered her vision, but it didn't hurt her eyes. Seconds later, it dissipated. She found herself standing in a sunny meadow. She touched her face and discovered she no longer had duct tape on her mouth.

Wearing a white dress, she spun around. The grass reached up to her knees as a gentle breeze made it dance. She felt warmth over her skin from the sun up in the lively blue sky with many fluffy clouds.

Is this Heaven? While her body remained in the cemetery, her soul resided in this spiritual place. She looked to her left; the owl and the oak stood several feet away.

The animal looked larger and more malicious than before. It stared at her with uncaring eyes that pierced into her heart. She balled her hands into fists and took a few steps back.

Feeling another presence from behind, she turned around. Another large oak tree grew in the meadow. An eagle sat on a long branch that stretched to the right. It looked like a golden eagle, but twice as large and with glowing yellow eyes.

"God?" There were so many questions floating in her mind. *Why are you an eagle? Why are you allowing Michael to kill me? Are you here to save me?*

She stood in between these two trees while looking back and forth. She noticed the tree with the owl had colored leaves and some empty branches, while the other grew small green leaves and buds. Both fowls glanced at her; neither blinked.

Michael's voice echoed through the air, "I'm sorry, but I'm going to have to kill you now." She heard his heavy breathing and felt pressure around her neck as if someone grabbed her from behind. The pressure grew stronger and her breathing got shallower. Her heart throbbed louder, but it slowed down. Darkness formed in the corner of her eyes and crept inward towards the center. As Michael strangled her in the real world, it affected her spirit here, in the heaven-like meadow.

"Why won't you save me!" she shouted while looking at the eagle. He just stared back at her with unsympathetic eyes.

She fell to the ground, with weakness taking over her muscles. Darkness fully overtook her as she laid her head on the ground. Lub-dub! Lub-dub! Her heart throbbed louder, but it slowed down with each throb. Lub-dub! Lub... dub! Lub... dub! Her heart completed its last beat. Lub... Dub.

Slowly, her consciousness moved from this abyss to the real world. As her vision recovered, light and shapes appeared. Moments later, she found herself standing back in the cemetery. As everything became clear, she noticed she didn't feel the cold on her skin nor the beating of her heart. Her body felt like air; her only senses working were sight and hearing. She looked at herself and saw she still wore the white dress.

So, this is what it's like to be a ghost.

Nearby, her half-nude lifeless body lay on the ground. Large black bruises covered the neck. The body looked like a mannequin in a surreal site. Although she sobbed, no glint of tears appeared.

Michael stood near the church with his back facing Melissa. She screamed; he turned and rapidly looked around with confused eyes. He stood motionless for a few seconds, but then shrugged his shoulders. With a knife in his hand, he turned back towards the church and carved on its wall.

When her killer walked away from the church, she gasped and shook her head.

On the wall, he carved the phrase "I like little girls."

I could kill you! She balled her hands. She knew that if it were possible for a ghost to kill, the other girl would have done it to Michael.

The other girl, Heidi, stood to her left. Melissa hoped to see her mother welcoming her, but she got no such gift. Her hopes of angels, music, and the love of God didn't materialize.

She looked up at the sky, with the stars scattered like sand on dark glass. She questioned the years of going to church and all of her prayers.

I guess it was all for nothing.

She clenched her jaw. The more she looked at Michael, the harder she bit down.

Melissa didn't understand why God allowed him to live, while she had to die. *This isn't fair!* She hoped her killer would face justice, but she didn't know if such hope existed.

Michael looked at the body. He tilted his head and his eyes focused on the corpse. After several moments, he slapped his face and walked back to his car.

Melissa pounded her fist against her hips. God damn you! Her new friend took her hands; they were like sisters now. Melissa looked over at the oak tree. The owl stared back for a few seconds, and then it took flight. Flying high towards the trees, its eyes glowed, looking like fireflies. The flapping of its wings overtook all sounds, but it grew softer. The bird vanished into the dark.

Gazing down with drooping eyelids, she thought about her dad. She would never run, laugh, or smile with him again. She hated the idea of the pain he faced and prayed that one day they would reunite in the afterlife.

The girls held hands while walking towards the woods. They entered the forest, and slowly faded away. As they exited this plane of existence, Melissa said to herself, "Don't forget me, Dad."

* * *

Twenty-two years had passed, and not a day went by that Melissa's father, Craig, didn't think of her. When his daughter's body was found a day after Melissa went jogging in the woods by the cemetery's groundskeeper, Craig spent days in his room, crying and drinking for hours. He almost approached the abyss of despair, but he sobered up in time. It took several weeks; still he made it, and then vowed he wouldn't rest until he got justice for his daughter.

He did many interviews on television programs, like Donahue.

It took a while, but he received his justice.

Michael Ross, who became known years later as The Roadside Strangler, was captured in 1984. During his time, he murdered eight women, from ages fourteen to twenty-five, in Connecticut and New York. After confessing to the killings, he was sentenced to death on July of 1987, which was fulfilled on May 10, 2005.

On that day, Craig was there to witness the execution.

As was Melissa, still in her white dress.

Her arrival at Osborn Correctional Institution marked the first time she returned to the physical world. For a while, she was plagued with sorrow. The pain of seeing her loved ones would had been too great, so she stayed in the afterlife, where she eventually found her mom after a lot of searching.

While she loved her mom dearly, she missed her dad. A day never went by that she didn't think of him. With time, she grew to accept her situation and embraced Heaven.

She vowed never to return to the physical world and would wait for her dad to join her.

Once word that Michael's execution was near, she broke that vow. Entering the prison wasn't a frightening experience for her, as she had been through a lot worse. The loud humming of prisoners and numerous guards didn't deter her from her mission. The chatter around the facility concerned the upcoming death of a serial killer. She followed a group of reporters to her destination.

As she entered the viewing area of the execution chamber, she walked around with crossed arms. Everything was brightly lit and clean with grayish-white walls and floors. Shaking her head, she believed people like Michael deserved something dark, gloomy, and dirty to represent their souls. He should be made to suffer. Slowly removing his skin with a dull knife, for instance. But that wasn't in the cards for Michael.

Still, he had a big surprise waiting for him.

She stood behind the two small rows of viewing seats. Despite it being around two in the morning, not a seat remained empty. Several others stood. Everyone was dressed in formal clothes; suits and dresses. A few that represented the media held writing pads. She didn't care for them—only for the person who sat in the back row. Her father.

Although his brown hair had thinned and grayed while his body had a small gut, he still looked familiar. Ghosts couldn't cry, but the inner hurt still bubbled inside and made her feel like large boulders were weighing her down.

She turned that pain into hate that burned through her energy like a firestorm.

With her hands balled, she stared through the viewing window at Michael Ross, dressed in a jumpsuit, strapped down to a table. He lay there motionless as another man checked the tubing that went into Michael's arms.

This is a merciful death.

But, he would die today. As she watched, a kind of cheer flowed through her like a gentle brook. She wanted to clap with glee, but wouldn't do it. Even though no one would hear or see, this wasn't the place for that kind of joy. At least that was what the angels told her, so she had to behave.

"Do you have any final words?" An unseen man said over an intercom.

"No, thank you," Michael said, as he kept his eyes closed.

The process began. Melissa focused her eyes, erasing her surroundings to create a solitary image. It was just her and Michael. If she was alive, Melissa would have felt sweat pouring down her face and her heart throbbing. Now, the only feeling she had was the rage that fired her up.

A machine setup on the wall had four long IV tubing sets that stretched across the room and attached to Michael's arm. One by one, the tubing releases the chemicals.

While Melissa didn't understand the entire process, she saw this as a cure for a social disease. The drugs were a pleasant end to him in this world, but with a large smile, she knew what waited for him in the next one.

Not once did Michael open his eyes. As the drugs flowed into his veins, he became still like a rock. The poison ate away at his life as his journey into death neared its end. The event lasted about nine or ten minutes, but Melissa didn't keep track of time. She only watched. A husky man wearing glasses leaned over Michael and used a stethoscope to listen to the heart. After a few seconds, he called out the time of the man's passing.

Death was the bridge between planes of existence, and Michael just crossed it. A new path waited for him. Unlike what happened to most others who died, his soul didn't appear near his body. Melissa knew there would be no mourning for him, just celebrations.

Although he didn't show it, she knew her father wanted to cheer.

As people got up to leave, her father bowed his head and closed his eyes. Melissa focused on him, as she remembered their times together. All the time running around the track at her high school. Going to see Prince together during the Controversy Tour.

Craig giving her a Spyder Bike when she turned twelve and then the two of them riding together. So many memories. She placed her hand on his shoulder.

He glanced over and looked at his shoulder. Melissa knew he didn't see her, but instead, he felt the cold sensation that happened whenever a ghost touched a living person. Some living people could sense that the cold was a deceased loved one. An instinct told them that. Most dismissed it, but her dad smiled and tears formed in his blue eyes. If she had the ability, she would let the tears flow down her face, reflecting the mixture of sadness and happiness that was swirling in her spirit.

* * *

He's here.

A female voice vibrated through her spirit, in a way that was similar to the effects of standing in front of a large speaker as music blasted through her body. It came from an individual she knew very well, who remained in the afterlife. Even when in the world of the living, a soul was always anchored to the spiritual world. It was a connection that could never be severed. Communications between souls in both realms happened using a form of telepathy. Melissa used it with ease, but still didn't understand how it worked.

She took her hand off her dad's shoulder. *I love you*, she said silently. Keeping her head low, she walked away. If she could, she would call for him, but that couldn't happen today.

She wanted to stay longer with him, but she had another priority. A tingling sensation covered every inch of her spirit. A white light overtook her vision. It kept getting brighter, eventually it glared like a large star. After several seconds, the light and the tingling sensation dissipated.

Before her lay the meadow with its tall grass and gentle breeze. The sun forever glaring down from the blue sky with many clouds. Here was the Fields of Elysium, a spiritual limbo where souls resided before heading to Heaven or Hell. She had already been sent to Heaven, but she was back here due to the arrival of a new soul.

A few yards away, a group of seven women, ages fourteen to twenty-five, stood surrounding someone. As she approached, Heidi turned around. Her friend carried a baseball bat in each hand. Barbed wire was wrapped around the bat's barrel.

"We've waited for you," said Heidi.

"Thank you," Melissa said. Heidi handed her a bat, and Melissa gripped the handle. She joined the others in the circle and spotted the person she waited years to arrive here.

Michael.

He wore the same jumper from the prison. Souls damned to Hell wear the same clothes in which they died. His hands were bound behind his back with steel chains. His mouth was gagged with a black bandana. His eyes were wide and his body shivered.

Melissa smiled, seeing his fear. Michael became a devout Catholic after his arrest, even meeting up with two priests often. But his good deeds, from translating documents into Braille to being a mentor to other inmates, didn't erase his sins.

Besides, he never truly repented, so now it was time for his punishment.

She looked up towards the horizon. Several yards away, the familiar large oak trees were there; on one perched an owl, the Devil, while on the other rested the eagle, God.

The eternal spectators were prepared for the next event.

"Who gets the first swing?" asked Heidi.

Another person spoke, "Let's just start swinging on the count of three."

Like a pack of wolves, the women surrounded Michael, who rapidly darted his head. As he whimpered, Michael obviously knew he was trapped and wouldn't be able to escape.

"One," said Heidi.

Melissa couldn't be happier as she wanted to jump for joy. Instead, she gripped the bat and stared at his face. She planned to smash her bat against his cheek, ripping the flesh off.

"Two!" another girl said.

The rules for spirits were different in Elysium, something Melissa learned after her second return to the afterlife. While spirits couldn't feel physical pain on Earth or in Heaven, they could in Elysium and Hell. It was part of God's and the Devil's rules to allow victims to enact justice. This time, these women were allowed to beat Michael for as long as they wanted. For Melissa, this was more about revenge than justice. She wasn't happy with God, and maybe never would be, but she was grateful for this.

"Three!" another girl said.

In unison, the swinging began. Cracking bones and splashings of blood accompanied the women's cheering and Michael's screaming. God and the Devil watched in their stoic manner.

Time meant nothing to spirits, so this could last a long time. Melissa didn't care if it took an hour, a day, or a year. She just wanted to inflict as much pain as possible.

My sweet revenge!

* * *

Editor's note: A native of Connecticut, Michael Ross confessed to the murders of eight women and young girls in Connecticut and New York in the years between 1981 and 1984; he also raped most of his victims. He was convicted and sentenced to die by lethal injection by the State of Connecticut. Ross spent eighteen years on death row before his execution.

Missing Lula
by Ann O'Mara Heyward

My first real job for real pay (if you can call it that) was as a motel maid at one of the joints lining Route 42. Which one? It doesn't matter. They were similar in clientele; truckers from the interstate, noon trysters from local businesses, high school kids like me, upgrading from the back of someone's car for a couple of hours. People drifting. Some were long term, pay-by-the-week lodgers with nowhere else to go. There was Murphy's Motel; the Starlite; and the Drop Inn with its Spin-a-Night-Free gimmick. All gone now.

I'd put in my application at the motel a few weeks before the end of the school year, and my graduation from high school. The boss called and offered me the job, starting the first Sunday that June. As it happens, my mom had planned my graduation party for that same day.

I mentioned this to the boss. "Do you want the job, or not?" he said, and waited.

"Yes, sir," I said. There wasn't much available in the way of work. Especially if you didn't have much experience. And I needed every cent for college if I wanted to go that fall.

I hung up and went to tell my mom. Luckily, she hadn't bought the food for the party yet. Truth be told, it wasn't going to be that big. We had planned to have my cousins, my aunt and uncle, a few neighbors, a couple of friends from school. I didn't have that many. Friends, that is.

It had always been that way. Because of "the incidents," as they were referred to in annual parent/teacher conferences. When it comes to a long memory, an elephant has nothing on your average suburban school system. It began with my kindergarten teacher, Miss Krepps, whose hand I had innocently grasped on the way in from the playground. I didn't really remember it clearly, but my mom said I started crying inconsolably and couldn't stop.

The school nurse called her to pick me up. A week later, the school principal introduced a new teacher to our class and explained that Miss Krepps was very sick and would be out the rest of the year. It was leukemia.

Mikey, my fourth-grade crush whom I'd happily chased and caught by the shirt on the playground—*tag, you're It!*—turned and punched me when I said without even thinking that his dad needed to stop stealing or he was going to get caught. His dad's conviction for embezzlement made the newspaper.

My first "best" friend in eighth grade was giving me a manicure when I begged her to please stop cutting herself under her clothes where it didn't show. Her mom stood by in shock as my no-longer-friend literally chased me from the house, screaming at me to get out.

There were other incidents, most less consequential, but enough to mark me as an oddity among my peers. My mom sat down with me after one of the early ones and explained matter-of-factly that the women in our family had this happen from time to time. It wasn't something to be ashamed or afraid of, she said; it was a talent, like being able to draw or having perfect pitch.

"Katie, your grandmother had it; your Aunt Ruthie has it; I have it. Your grandma said it goes all the way back to Ireland, hundreds of years ago."

But I would rather have been born with a talent to predict the Lotto numbers. Not feeling these sad, hidden things sometimes when I touched someone or something.

It only took a few phone calls to "postpone Katie's party," my mom told everyone, "We'll have it later in the summer, before she starts college."

As it happened, we didn't, but it's just as well. Things were tight that year. She never would have said so, but at least part of Mom's calculus going into the party was whether any inflow of congratulatory checks to help me with college would balance the outflow on fried chicken, potato salad, beer, and the obligatory sheet cake. I didn't think so.

I met Lula, the other maid, that first Sunday. She was a compact, wiry woman in her thirties. I liked her immediately. On her side, she took a protective interest in me. Part of it was her women-gotta-stick-together nature; part of it was self-preservation. She had a vested interest in keeping me on the job. Until I showed up, she'd been cleaning thirty rooms on her own after the other maid had ridden off with one of the truckers.

There were no uniforms; the owner didn't want to spend any money he didn't have to. That first day, Lula cast a critical eye over my jeans and baggy T-shirt. "Good choice on your clothes, Katie," she said matter-of-factly. "Don't wear anything tight. No short shorts. Nothing too bare, no matter how hot it gets. Some of these guys will try anyway, but you're not advertising." I held myself back from commenting that I should be able to do the job naked as a jaybird if I wanted to, without fear; but both Lula and I were realists.

"One thing though," she said as she rummaged in her cleaning cart. "You need gloves." With that, she pulled out a yellow pair of Playtex's finest. I tried to turn them down, being polite, but she insisted. "Not kidding, now," she said. "You're going to be scrubbing out sinks, tubs and toilets. Aside from the wear and tear on your hands, even the nicest, cleanest person in the world spits in the sink when they brush their teeth, and sometimes their gums bleed. Sometimes they pee in the sink, you can smell it. Sometimes people have sex and wash up in the sink after, instead of the shower." She paused. "My own ex-husband washed up in the sink afterwards, and I knew where he'd been. Can't say the same for the guests here. I used to be a nursing assistant, so glove up, honey."

By then, I not only wanted the gloves; I felt like going home for my raincoat, too.

The job was, of course, a grind. Sheer drudgery. After a week, I understood completely why maids were referred to as "drudges" in some of the novels we'd read in English class.

Having shadowed Lula through a couple of room cleanings the first day, I had it down to an efficient routine that I moved through on autopilot. Strip-the-bed-gather-up-the-towels-scrub-the-sink-scrub-the-tub-throw-out-the-used-soap-swish-out-the-toilet-and-flush-put-a-new-roll-on-the-holder-if-it-needs-it-put-out-new-soap-quick-mop-the-bathroom-floor.   Empty-the-wastebaskets-dust-the-nightstands-and-the-TV-wipe-down-the-remote-vacuum-the-carpet.   Put-fresh-sheets-on-the-bed-fluff-the-pillows-pull-up-the-spread-over-them-put-fresh-towels-in-the-bathroom-lock-the door-behind-you.

One room after another. Sometimes, someone would leave a tip, a few dollars on the night table or the bed; more often, they didn't. Lula and I split whatever we found. I joined the vast class of working folk who shower after the day's work, not before.

You can tell a lot about a person by how they keep their surroundings, especially when someone else is cleaning up after them. The vast majority were no messier than you or I are at home (unavoidable body fluids in the sink included). The outliers fell into two extremes on the bell curve of mess. Some left their rooms so shipshape I wondered if they'd even actually slept there; I always tried to figure out if they were ex-military, or just neat freaks. Invariably, the neatniks left a tip.

Others seemed to take a vicious glee in the knowledge that they weren't cleaning up and took it as license to be as disgusting as possible. Invariably, the pigs did not tip.

Lula and I had fun comparing notes on the guests as we passed each other on our rounds. The motel was cinder block, its rooms stretching in two long, single-story rows like open arms framing a square, black-topped parking lot, big enough to hold truck semis as well as cars.

The office, the cleaning supply, and the linen closets were in the corner where the two "arms" met. One arm was "A" and the other arm was "B." So 1A and 1B flanked the office, and 15A and 15B were at opposite corners of the parking lot. Lula would take the A's one day, and I would take the B's, then we'd switch the next day.

Anything to relieve the monotony.

Looking back on that summer, I would give anything now if it had just stayed the same boring routine, day after hot day under the Ohio summer sun. But it didn't.

Sam Little checked into room 12B and stayed for a week.

He was a nondescript man. Stocky build, balding, close-cropped Afro, dark mustache, skin the color of coffee with just a little bit of milk in it. Not especially tall, a couple inches taller than me. He'd nod and smile pleasantly to me or Lula if he saw us; he usually left in his car in the late afternoon.

My shift ended at three, so I never knew when he came back. He never asked for anything. By the time he left, I was scared to death of him. And I didn't want to even touch his room. Because of the drawings. And because of Lula.

As luck would have it, I got to clean his room first; it was my day for the B's. It wasn't especially messy. When I came into the room, I noticed some papers scattered across the bedspread, but I didn't pay much attention. I just got going on cleaning the bathroom.

I didn't touch the papers until I started changing the bed. I picked them up to move them aside to the night table so I could change the sheets. The sheaf of papers was in my hands when my throat closed up and I couldn't breathe.

I'd never had asthma or anything like it in my life. When I was little, I had almost choked on an ice cube once. It was like that. I was choking. But choking on nothing. I'd eaten the sandwich I'd brought for lunch hours before, washing it down with a soda, without incident.

I dropped the papers on the floor and staggered to the open doorway. I couldn't call out to Lula for help; I couldn't get any air to speak.

Just outside the doorway to the room, I fell on my hands and knees on the concrete walkway. Finally, I was able to draw a whooping, sobbing breath.

Lula was just coming out of 11A when she saw me across the parking lot and came running. She squatted beside me, while I was still sucking in breaths on my hands and knees, and held my hair out of my face. She must have thought I was going to throw up.

You know what a good friend is? Someone who'll hold your hair out of your face when you're about to puke.

Lula waited to ask any questions. Finally I felt able to talk. And promptly started crying. She waited some more and rubbed my back. "Katie-girl, I'm not going to ask you if you're OK, because that would be stupid." She handed me a tissue, and I blew my nose. "I don't know what happened," I told her. "All of a sudden, I was choking and couldn't breathe."

"Did you spray any room freshener or anything? It gets me sometimes. Maybe you're allergic?" I remembered she'd been a nurse's aide. "No, nothing, I was just starting to make the bed. I moved some papers and then this choking thing started."

Recovering, I was starting to feel like a complete idiot. I got up and dusted off the knees of my jeans. "I still have to finish the room," I said, and turned toward the door. "I'll come in with you," Lula said.

I bent to pick up the papers that had landed on the floor when I had lost the ability to breathe. At first I thought there was nothing on them. Then Lula said quietly, "Wow. Look at these."

She had picked one up and turned it over. I did the same with the papers in my hands. They were portraits. Of women. One after another. Lula and I laid out each one on the bedspread. I didn't count them. Brunette hair; blond hair. Black, white, brown skin.

Green eyes, brown eyes, blue eyes. A little crudely drawn, but each one had an intensity that held your gaze.

You couldn't stop looking at them. At their eyes, especially.

"You said these were on the bed?" Lula asked me, and her eyes narrowed. I nodded. "They were face down. They fell on the floor when I started choking."

Lula pulled them into a stack and turned them face down on the night table.

"Rule number one is gloves," she said. "Rule number two is never mess in a guest's business. Those drawings have a really bad vibe. I'll help you make the bed, and we'll just put them back where you found them."

Later that week Mr. Little spoke to me for the first time, as he was heading toward his car. "Hey, little girl," he said. "Thanks for cleaning my room." I forced myself to reply. "You're welcome," I said, and scuttled (hate to admit that I moved like that, but as my mom would say, tell the truth and shame the Devil) into the next room I was cleaning.

Lula and I always ate our lunches sitting on upturned buckets in the cleaning supply room. I remember that day, I was telling her about my plans for the fall. I was going to the local community college. My mom and I, usually allies, had a battle royal, months earlier, over my wanting to leave home for college, and her wanting me to stay home. The compromise was going to a community college, at least for my first year. I guess I must have still sounded resentful; even now, years later, I'm embarrassed to think what an entitled little snot I must have sounded like to Lula.

Something she said that day has haunted me ever since. She looked straight at me and said, "At least you have someone who'd miss you." She got to her feet, wadded up her lunch bag, and went back to work without another word.

The next day, I started to apologize, but Lula brushed it away with a comment about the unusually stinky trucker in 5A, wondering out loud if he'd take the hint if she left one of the little bars of motel soap on his pillow.

"Nope," I said, "He'll probably think it's a mint, and eat it." It was a completely lame joke, but for some reason it cracked us both up. I think it was relief that things were OK between us, again.

The next day, I saw Sam Little talking to Lula. She was smaller than I was and had to tip her head back to look up at him. I watched as she reached up to her neck to touch the cross she wore on a chain. It was unlike the take-no-shit-from-anyone Lula I knew; she looked distinctly nervous. After he left, I asked her what he'd said.

"He talked about those damn drawings in his room," she said. "He asked if I'd sit for a portrait sometime before he leaves. I told him I couldn't, the boss'd kill me."

This was a bald-faced lie, as we both knew. The boss never budged from behind the desk, except to go to the bathroom or to leave when the night clerk arrived. I'd barely seen him all summer.

"You know what creeped me out the most?" she asked. I shook my head. "He kept commenting on how pretty he thought my neck was," she said, and touched the cross on its chain again.

"When does he check out?" I asked. Hoping it was very soon. *Like immediately, that day.*

No such luck. Lula sneaked a peek at the register in the office while the boss was on one of his bathroom breaks. Little was checking out the next morning. At least it was soon. I knew both of us would be happier than usual to see this particular guest get on his way. By now we both had the willies.

Lula didn't show up for work the next morning. I started on my rooms; at first I thought she was just late. Maybe her car broke down or something. But she was never late. And she hadn't missed a single day all summer since I had been there. Mr. Little's car was still in the lot. Between room cleanings, I was watching for him to come out. Check out time was eleven.

My stomach turned to ice water when he came out of his room, saw me watching, and beckoned me over. I put most of my cleaning supplies back on the cart, but I kept the spray bottle of tub-and-tile cleaner clutched in my right hand. Just in case.

"Hey, little girl," he said again. "I'm on my way today." He reached into his trouser pocket, pulled out a ten, and held it out to me. I reached out for it, although I didn't want to touch it. "I wanted to give you this tip," he said, "toward your college." I was startled. I'd never so much as mentioned my school plans to him. Ever. I'd barely spoken to him, once.

"I wanted to give you another tip, little college girl," he said. And smiled. "Stay away from men like me."

With that, he walked to his car, and drove off. That was the last time I saw him.

Until the news program years later.

Lula never did turn up for work that day. I finished the rooms myself and ended the day tired and at least a little mad at her for sticking me with the whole job. The next day, when she didn't show up again, I got seriously worried. I braved the office and asked the boss if she was all right.

"I don't know and I don't care," he said. "She didn't call. As far as I'm concerned, she quit." He didn't even look up from his paperwork.

By now I was starting to get pissed, boss or no boss. "You're not worried about her?" I asked. The naivete of eighteen. When you still believe most people actually care one way or the other.

"Look," he began, looking at me directly for the first time, clearly irritated. "She probably started using again. She tell you she used to be a nurses' aide?" I nodded. "She got busted and did some time for trying to steal drugs off a med cart, and I have a little arrangement with the county social services people to hire graduates of their system and get part of their pay covered by the taxpayer. The parole deal includes maintaining a good work record, so she blew that too."

I decided I didn't need the job, after all. I hadn't missed the snide crack about graduation. The sarcastic sonofabitch. Fuck him.

I left the office and finished the room I'd started. Whatever Lula was, she was a professional, and she would never have left a room half-cleaned for a guest. When I was done, I put my supplies back on the cleaning cart, locked the room door, then hung my key ring neatly on its hook on the cleaning cart. Then I got in the rusty little bucket I'd bought with my baby-sitting money and drove away. I kept the yellow gloves Lula had given me.

Years later, the authorities caught Sam Little in Kentucky, after they linked his DNA to some murders of women in the 1980s. In 2018, a Texas Ranger got him talking. And talking. And drawing. Portraits of so many women. He choked most of them; drowned at least one.

I made the mistake of watching a video of his confession to the Texas officer on a TV news program. He laughed about choosing women nobody would look for. "Plucking a grape off the vine," I think, is how he put it. He had a sexual obsession with women's necks that had started in his boyhood when a teacher had touched her own neck, and it turned him on.

Later, choking them to death also got his motor running. They think he killed more than ninety people.

I remembered Lula's conversation with him, then ran to the bathroom and vomited.

She hadn't walked off the job. She had fucking disappeared. And no one, including me, had looked for her.

In the years after that summer, I thought of her. More often than you might think. There were more crap jobs while I worked my way through undergrad, then grad school. I would remember Lula then. She had lightened my days that summer and I never got to thank her. I hope, somewhere, she knows that I miss her.

And I hope they find her.

* * *

Editor's note: Samuel Little confessed to murdering 93 women between 1970 and 2005. He evaded law enforcement for many years. He was only charged and convicted of killing eight women. The FBI has confirmed Little's involvement in at least 60 of the 93 confessed murders, the largest number of confirmed victims for any serial killer in American history. He was serving a life sentence in a California State Correctional Facility when he died of natural causes at age 80.

Definitely Not Your Mother's Book Club
by D.W. Milton

The counselor read the sign aloud again to the newest member of the group. "What is the worst thing you have ever done?"

The young man was mute, refusing to meet her eyes; instead, he retreated further under the hood of his dark sweatshirt, avoiding the accusatory stares from the motley group of people sitting in a circle of loosely arranged chairs.

"Kevin?" the woman counselor prodded, "I have been patient with you, but you will need to begin contributing to *the group* and I think," the counselor wheedled, "today would be a great day to start."

The youth in the hoodie remained mute.

"Maybe he likes clowns," the portly man sitting across from the teen said with a smile. "Do you like clowns?"

The counselor frowned, "John, please. Your teasing is not helping things."

"I am just saying, everybody likes clowns. What weirdo doesn't like clowns?" The man smoothed his moustache and rocked in his seat while his generous middle section jiggled with laughter.

"Ugh… why don't you just shut the fuck up, clown man!" cried a female voice. She flashed an ugly grin and flipped her stringy blonde hair in exasperation. "Nobody gives a shit about your side business." The woman sat, on the defensive as usual, with legs crossed and both arms folded as armor.

In this small, poorly ventilated room that reeked of body odor and sulfur, Kevin reverted to a childhood habit of chewing a finger. He gnawed, drawing blood. The smell of the ferrous metal from the blood comforted him, even if it was his own.

Peering out from the hole of the cloth covering his head, he wondered about one of the members. There was only one other woman in the circle besides the counselor and Aileen, the lady with the crazy eyes and crooked teeth. Something about the third woman was wrong.

The woman sat with her hips so far away from the handsome man next to her that she was almost in the lap of the impish man wearing a funny hat sitting on her other side. Kevin watched as she tried to maintain her Victorian-like composure, but failed, miserably.

Kevin was also mesmerized by her disgust at the good-looking man's silent advances. He seemed fascinated with the lace on her long skirts. Touching it. Fingering it. Weighing its sheerness.

Lace Lady spoke with a soft, anachronistic New England drawl, "If the young gentleman does not feel he is ready to share, then we must respect that."

The attractive dark-haired man, wearing a prison jumpsuit, leaned closer in to her. "Come on honey," he coaxed, "maybe he needs a little motherly lovin'. I know I could use some."

The imp in the plaid cap bristled, visibly pained, "Let's leave the mothers out of this."

"Now, now," the counselor said, as she regained control of the discussion. "I need not remind everyone that this is a safe space. "However," she continued, in her pursuit of Kevin, "participation is required under the terms of each of your arrangements." Her gaze lingered on him.

The nice-looking man in the jumpsuit ignored the counselor, preferring to focus on the strange, Victorian-dressed Lace Lady.

Noticing the rebuke from the Lace Lady, the counselor decided on a different approach. Wanting to distract everyone, she gestured toward her and said, "Lizzie, why don't you begin today's meeting."

Groans of protest filled the room. Kevin felt the temperature of the already-overheated room surge. He began to sweat in his hoodie.

Lizzie nodded. "Very well. I would like to begin today's meeting with a prayer." She began, head bowed, hands clasped, "Our Father…"

"Oh fuck me!" exclaimed a scruffy, bearded man across from Lizzie. "How many times I got to tell you woman, He does not want to hear you babbling and slobbering out in His name."

The man began to move erratically in his chair, pointing at the air as if he were swatting hallucinatory flies. "Here we are in this bottomless pit, and you think He even cares about you and your homicidal ass?"

Lizzie stopped. For a moment, Kevin thought she looked as if the man slapped her but she quickly recovered. Holding her head, chin raised, she proclaimed, "I, unlike the rest of you sinners, was acquitted."

The disheveled man continued to gesture wildly, humming and drumming on his chair in a familiar rhythm. *Tat-tat-tat.* Even though the man appeared untamed, Kevin had spotted something underneath. This joker had a slyness that hinted that all his craziness might be an act.

The man kept humming and tapping. After a few beats, he started singing in a hoarse but melodic voice, "You may be a lover but you ain't no dancer, *Da-da-duh-da-duh.*"

Kevin remembered his mom playing that song on the record player. Some kind of hippyBritish bullshit, although he did like the song. He preferred the Mötley Crüe's version however.

He frowned at the memory. He had stolen that album from his older brother Kenny and played it to death. It echoed what he was into anyway. He listened to the music of Deicide and Mayhem on heavy rotation no matter how much his mom bitched.

Kevin closed his eyes; thoughts of his family, especially his brother, vexed him. He bit harder on his finger.

Handsome Man reached out to touch the fabric that accidentally brushed his ankle when Lizzie moved. "Innocent, huh? Forget the prayer, what's the worst thing you have ever done, sweetheart?" His brown eyes met hers. Getting bolder now, he moved his hand from the hem of her skirt to the outline of her buried knee.

"You mean with or without an axe?" Aileen burst out laughing, a husky smoker's guffaw that hitched itself into a phlegmy coughing fit.

Lizzie smacked the groping hand away, her eyes boring across the room into Aileen. "I am a good Christian woman." Lizzie crossed herself, almost stabbing at the four points. "Something you would obviously know nothing about."

"I seriously doubt your father and stepmother would agree."

Kevin stared at the man who spoke. Since Kevin joined the group, he, like Kevin, had also stayed silent—until now. The man pushed his glasses back up the bridge of his nose. "Can we get a move on things, counselor? I'm getting hungry."

The elf in the ball cap stood and shouted, "I told you to leave the mothers out of this!"

The counselor felt her control slip. She looked at the man with the glasses, "Now Jeffrey, Lizzie will confide in us when she is ready. And lunch is at the usual time—you know that."

She turned to address the small man in the tartan hat. "Ed, we will get to you, but you must let others speak about their concerns, too. We cannot censure here. I promise you this is a safe space."

Ed would not sit. The counselor attempted to redirect. "Please sit, Ed. Let us all take a deep breath in… " the counselor inhaled and exhaled audibly, "… and out." She looked around the room attempting to engage the members of her group. "Again, in… and out."

Despite himself, Kevin took a deep breath and nearly choked on the fumes. The heat intensified the vapors. Others were uncomfortable, too. Aileen kept coughing. Searching for relief, she stepped away to the ancient coffee maker. She poured the thick, overdone sludge from the crusty glass pot into a paper cup. Somehow, she managed to swallow the liquid.

John sat, sweating profusely, with beads of perspiration lingering in his moustache. The quiet man that the counselor called Jeffrey repeatedly returned his glasses to the bridge of his nose, his face shiny with oil.

Even the twitching, pseudo-crazy man wiped his brow, in between drumbeats with his fingers. Only the good-looking man in the jumpsuit sat cool as a cucumber, seeming to revel in everyone else's discomfort—both physical and psychological.

"Can't we get some damn air-conditioning in here?" Aileen barked, as she threw away her used cup. Instead of returning to her seat, Kevin saw her finger the faded flyers on the corkboard hung above the table with the coffeemaker. "It's hotter than a church basement."

The group's labored breathing only made the stale air in the room worse. Ed finally sat down, looking exhausted.

"Lizzie, Lizzie, Lizzie," Handsome Man said while shaking his head, "Just answer the question."

"I do not have to answer you." Lizzie turned her back on him. He grinned, a predator circling in for the kill, absolutely loving the effect he had on her.

Fascinated, Kevin watched these two members of the group. Their script reminded him of his mother's soap operas. Since he was small, she would drop herself in her recliner with a box of cheap chocolates and a two-liter bottle of Tab diet cola diluted with bargain brand whiskey, and waste away the afternoon. Kevin and Kenny would wind up fending for themselves for dinner. That was until Kenny started middle school, leaving Kevin, four years his junior, alone with her.

Kevin concentrated on Lizzie, reinforcing his thoughts that there was something wrong about her. Artificial—meaning false or fake—was the word that came to his mind.

He had missed that word on his last vocab test. It was as if she was not real or real in this place. Teaching Sunday school or cleaning a church rectory was where she looked like she belonged.

Kevin figured Handsome Man caught on to it, as well—her falseness. One of the other questions he missed on the multiple-choice vocab test was insincere. A synonym for artificial. Kevin decided *insincere* fit better for her.

The longer he studied Lizzie, the more he struggled to place her… and then it came to him. That woman Aileen and her comment about the axe! *That was funny!*

"So wait a moment." The freckled-face youth finally spoke from inside the fabric of his hoodie. Kevin pulled his hoodie down and temporarily removed his finger from his mouth to speak. "You're Lizzie, Lizzie *Borden*?" The kid laughed at that, almost tipping his chair over.

Lizzie's head snapped around in order to look at Kevin. "Yes, so what of it?" *Defiant* was another word that came to Kevin's mind.

The bearded man squealed. He had stopped his drumming. "*Lizzie Borden took an axe. She gave her mother forty whacks. When she saw what she had done. She gave her father forty-one!*"

"Enough with the mothers," Ed muttered.

"Why am I even here?" Lizzie's voice stayed high. "I don't deserve to be here! I haven't done anything!"

"How long have you been here, Lizzie?" Handsome Man caressed her sleeve. "From the look of your dress, you have been here for at least a century. Isn't that right, counselor?"

The counselor sat shocked. Kevin's comment about Lizzie was the first time she had heard his voice. She seemed to think that this was the opportunity she was waiting for, a possible breakthrough, and she needed to keep Kevin talking. But in order to do that, she plainly needed Ted to shut up.

"Yes, Ted," she addressed Handsome Man, "all of us here know that admitting responsibility is the first step. It can be the hardest and it does take some of us longer than others."

"You mean like Charlie over there." Aileen lit a cigarette and blew the smoke out of her pursed lips towards the bearded, erratic man.

Charles Manson snarled, "Bitch, I am the most famous human being that has ever lived!"

"Exactly," Aileen took a drag.

"Aileen, there is no smoking in the therapy room. Please put that out." The counselor faced Kevin, "This will be Lizzie's burden, as are all the burdens we carry." She gestured at Lizzie. "No matter how long it takes."

Ted Bundy never stopped touching Lizzie's sleeve. "So what's the worst of the worst things you have ever done, Lizzie Borden?"

Indignant, she said in a shrill voice: "I never killed a soul! Not like any of you!" Lizzie's anger focused on Kevin, ignoring Ted's strokes. "I don't even know why I am here with you!"

John giggled, further irritating the room. "Look at the fucked-up Florence Nightingale over there. Obviously, you did something bad to be sitting here, too."

"Are you going to judge me? Judge *him*!" Lizzie pointed at the hooded teen. "His heart is as black as night. Look at his garment! Symbol of the Devil and he is calling me a bad person?"

"No one is here to judge, Lizzie," the counselor reassured.

"*Where* is *here*?" Kevin finally asked.

As long as Kevin had been here, in this room, he did not recognize it. The room was ordinary. The chair he was sitting on reminded him of a high school assembly. He remembered high school. The bullying. The anger. The helplessness. He remembered Kenny and Kenny's friends out in the woods. Kevin remembered the ceremony and how, afterwards, he no longer felt powerless. He was no longer afraid of his tormentors. Kenny was right. The Dark Lord saved him.

"Come on, tell us what is the worst of the worst things you have done in your horrible miserable life?" Ted's petting had stopped.

Lizzie scowled at Ted, murder in her eyes.

The counselor caught it. She looked like she wanted to engage Kevin some more, but realized that she still had seven other group members to manage.

"No, Lizzie, look at me."

Lizzie glared at Ted; Ted glared back. Tension thick, the counselor tried again. "Lizzie, look at me."

"She can't," said Kevin. Lizzie's eyes flashed to the youth, who nibbled his finger absentmindedly.

"What the fuck do you know about anything, you little shit?" Lizzie stood. Her Victorian façade gone, she was tiny, lost in the folds of her skirts. Kevin had a hard time picturing her swinging an axe.

He kept chewing, drawing blood, "I know that you are here because you won't come to terms with what you did. You still think that you can chop up your parents with an axe and get away with it. Why did you do it?"

Lizzie sucked in her breath, "I was acquitted!" she screamed.

Kevin never faltered, "But you are still guilty."

Lizzie stood, "You self-righteous scab! I ought to- "

The rest of the group sat mute. Even Charlie was still.

Everyone was tense now, even the woman counselor. All watched her as she seemed to realize that she had completely lost control.

"Wouldn't matter," Kevin replied calmly, "I am already dead."

Lizzie took a step forward, her arms outstretched for Kevin's neck.

Kevin continued, "And so are you."

Lizzie's shoulders slumped, her hands fell, deflated.

Aileen's breath caught. Her cigarette burned, ash teetering, ready to fall.

Seizing the opportunity, the counselor stood and took Lizzie by the shoulders and led her from the center of the circle back to the empty chair next to Ted. Lizzie sat, defeated.

"You're a big man now, aren't you? Figured it all out?" John smirked at Kevin.

"Shut up!" Lizzie's scream reverberated off the walls, but the fight had drained from her.

The rest of the group looked at their hands or their feet, except for the counselor. She could not look away from the teen-ager.

The counselor took a chance, "How does that make you feel, Kevin?" This was the most the boy had ever spoken.

"I deserve to be here." There was blood on his lip from the mutilated finger.

"Go on," the counselor coaxed.

"I made choices and decisions and now I am paying the consequences." He shrugged his narrow shoulders.

Ed mumbled something but the counselor let it go; she continued to focus on Kevin. Lizzie's narrow eyes switched from the counselor to Kevin and then back to the counselor; a taut stare.

"Why Kevin, why did you make those choices?"

"I wanted to see what would happen."

"Yeah," Jeffrey Dahmer mumbled "And your dumb ass got caught. Can we go eat now?"

The counselor frowned. "Jeffrey, please don't interrupt." She refocused on Kevin.

Lizzie could not look away from the boy as if she needed to know, wanted to know but was terrified of the answer.

Kevin shrugged again, "I needed help. No one else would help me, so I made a deal with the Devil. Signed the blood pact. It was better, for a while; then it wasn't. In the end, I guess I was just curious. I wanted to know, I needed to know."

"You wanted to know what, Kevin?" The counselor licked her lips.

Kevin pulled his hoodie up back over his head, retreating from the room, with its dark heat, its unnatural fumes, its subversive despair. "I wanted to see if I would go to hell."

"Oh dear!" Lizzie crossed herself again. Jeffrey groaned, shifting his legs, looking hungry.

"Well you certainly found out, didn't you?" laughed John.

Kevin's cold eyes met his.

Challenged with the truth, John looked down, guilty.

The counselor leaned forward, almost dropping her pen, "What do you mean?"

Tears of realization coated Lizzie's eyes and rolled down her cheeks. "I was acquitted," she mumbled.

Kevin had resumed chewing his finger.

The group sat awkwardly.

"Kevin?" The counselor persisted.

Kevin spoke through his fingers, "My mom was just like you." He pointed with his other hand at Lizzie. "We went to church every Sunday."

It was Ted's turn to groan. "Yeah, buddy, I blame my mother, too. Just like the Norman Bates Psycho, Ed Gein, over there."

Gein whimpered.

Kevin's stare returned, chilling and malevolent. "No, I am saying that it is God's fault."

John chuckled, "Oh that's a gas! Hey Satan, I confess. God made me kill and bury those boys in the crawlspace under my house, can I go now?" His laughter mutated into a sick giggle; it was an eerie sound.

Lizzie twittered at the mention of the name.

Kevin's steely eyes fixated on John Wayne Gacy, but Gacy, truly engulfed in his own joke, failed to notice.

"John please!" The counselor was irritated. "But God gave man free will," she challenged, careful of her footing, so near the edge.

Kevin's attention was restored. "Yes," he conceded, "but supposedly He made man in His own image." Kevin spit bloodied skin onto the floor as a thin stream of crimson slid down his hand, soaking into the torn sleeve of his hoodie.

"Go on," the counselor coaxed.

"And man is weak. Satan has nothing to do with it." He spit another bloodied fragment of flesh on the floor. "Satan is only our babysitter."

"No!" Lizzie screeched. She stood and stomped her feet like a tantrum-bound child. "Stop it! Stop it! Stop it!" Tears streamed down her reddened face.

"Hush, Lizzie," the counselor commanded. "Sit back down and be still."

Kevin did not stop. "Your egos got you here and it is what keeps you all here." He looked at each member of the group. Finally, his eyes rested on the counselor. "You are the worst of all."

"What!" Vague exclamations bounced throughout the room. Disbelief rained and relinquished into outright anger. "You are supposed to be helping us!"

The atmosphere deteriorated into wails and cries of hopelessness and futility, yet Kevin and the counselor were not distracted. Their eyes locked in a showdown.

A hideously fanged grin spread across the counselor's face. "Go on," she sneered. Lizzie Borden never saw it, unlike the others who did see the counselor transform; Lizzie's own guilt finally consumed her as she burst into flames.

"As long as I," Kevin began, then corrected himself, "we." He stopped, glancing at each member of the group. "We continue to believe in outside influences, skirting the possibility that we can and do make decisions that have horrible, devastating and far-reaching outcomes, we will remain here. I will remain here, in hell."

The counselor nodded, enraptured. She ignored the chaos of the room, which was now aflame with rage and denial and for the first time in their lives, fear.

Kevin looked at his ravaged finger. "I deserve to be here after what I have done."

The counselor's face, horrifically transformed, was now naked and true. A set of Baphometian horns had grown from her temples, blood dripping as the growths emerged. The milky white, porcelain skin melted away, leaving a horribly deformed bare skull, and trailed drippings of flesh and fat on her silk blouse. The hideous countenance gleamed under the fluorescent lighting. Without a recognizable nose or lips, the hole of her former mouth moved over jagged, broken teeth.

"Why?" Reaching out a transformed talon in false sympathy, she pleaded, "Tell me why, Kevin?" Her eyes blackened in anticipation; she was so close now. She looked like she knew Her boss would be so pleased that she got Kevin to fulfill his end of the bargain.

"Because I am empty. I am a void. I have no feeling, nothing, no emotion or pain. Because here," Kevin spit again, replaced his finger in his mouth, now gnawing at the other side, "I am," he looked around the room. His eyes came to rest on the smoldering Lizzie Borden, "We are where we deserve to be. We are home."

* * *

Editor's note: We hope that Charles Manson, John Wayne Gacy, Lizzie Borden, Ted Bundy, Aileen Wuornos, Ed Gein, and Jeffrey Dahmer are currently participating in a group encounter session in hell just like this.

The Time Killer
by G.N. Anderson

Jenny wasn't looking for trouble when she met Ed Gein at a tavern near Pine Grove, Wisconsin. They'd connected in that way lonely people do when they observe each other long enough from across the room. Their almost telepathic connection allowed them to pick up on the "no one understands me" vibe in each other that initiated the spark.

Jenny was alone in a world that her grandmother would feel comfortable in, a world she was now doomed to live in unless she found a way back to her own time. It was overwhelming to think about, but she'd somehow traveled back to the 1950s while visiting the home of Sam, a strange man she'd connected with on the Tinder dating website. She'd woken up alone in a motel room bed in a small town in Wisconsin, and upon searching her surroundings, found the wallet, car keys and driver's license of a twenty-four-year-old woman from Chicago.

Jenny looked in the mirror and the face looking back at her was similar to her own, but it wasn't hers. Jenny looked around the room again for clues as to what year it was, given the driver's license future expiration date was 1959, but no luck. The woman's wallet only had two dollars in it. Jenny did what anyone finding themselves in a bind would do without any money or connections in a strange place: she went to the nearest watering hole to find new friends. Luckily, the other woman's car was parked in a space marked with the same number as her room, and Jenny found it easily. It was a huge, light-blue Chevrolet with many unfamiliar controls that felt like a tank to drive, and Jenny lurched uncertainly out of the motel parking lot, but eventually she got the hang of driving it.

At the tavern, Jenny initiated the conversation with Ed, but she instantly regretted it.

After introducing herself, he shook her hand way too hard. He appeared older than the guys she normally dated, and not exactly a man she'd normally find attractive. He was at least thirty-five years old, with salt-and-pepper hair, a brutish body type, and a face hardened by life. His hands revealed someone used to manual labor. He was very quiet and rarely spoke, except to respond to her questions or she to his.

"What's your name?" Jenny asked.

"Ed," he replied, twirling his bottle of beer on the table.

Jenny struggled with what people in the 1950s Midwest liked to talk about, and eventually, she chose the cinema.

"What do you do for fun, Ed? You know, in your free time. Do you like movies?" Jenny said.

Ed scratched his head and stared up into the ceiling. "Umm, I don't really watch movies.

I read the newspaper and crime magazines."

Jenny had hoped Ed would elaborate about his free time preferences, but clearly, she would have to pull it all out of him.

The closest she could relate to his interests was her own devotion to her favorite crime podcasts, so she pulled on that thread. "Oh, I like, uh, crime magazines too. Do you like reading about bank robberies or murders? It's all quite grim, but fascinating, don't you think?" Jenny said, repressing a side eye.

She studied his face more closely. He might pass as ruggedly handsome with a makeover, but his short stature and extremely introverted behavior would take some getting used to, not that she planned to do so. Comparatively speaking, he was not a bad-looking man, just not someone she'd normally want to get to know better in her own life. He was, however, the easiest mark, given her circumstances.

Where he was unfocused before, Ed trained his eyes on Jenny's. He rubbed the stubble on his face and gulped down a swig of beer. "Why do you ask?"

"No reason in particular. Just trying to keep the conversation going. You seem like a man with a lot on your mind." Jenny shrugged and sat back in her own chair. She let the silence hang between them. Sunset was approaching and her options for lodging were limited. She had all of a dollar in the woman's wallet.

Ed leaned in closer to her chair and whispered to her. "Do you want to come to my farm?

I'll show you some of my favorite magazines. Maybe make a hot meal for you."

Jenny considered the offer. She didn't have much to go on in the way of shelter. The motel manager had asked her what time she would check out so that he could turn over the room.

She wasn't quite comfortable around Ed upon their initial conversation, but he seemed like a solid person. Someone who might have empathy for her if she needed a warm bed to lay down her head.

Still, something about Ed's name rang a bell and made her feel uneasy. Jenny was frustrated about being stuck in a time with limited technology. She had no way of Googling his name or looking him up on social media. She had to go with her intuition on this one.

It was an odd situation she found herself in, but she needed time to think. She hadn't decided how far she'd go for that warm bed yet. She let down her guard and agreed to follow him to his home under one condition: he'd keep his hands to himself, unless she consented.

* * *

Ed stood in the middle of the parking lot outside the tavern next to Jenny's car. His eyes revealed a longing for her that she hadn't noticed earlier. He had kept his hands to himself throughout the entire night, though. "You can follow me in your car if it makes you feel more comfortable."

"Yes, I'd like that very much." Jenny intended to stall, but it looked like the sky was about to open up, pouring down hot summer rain. "How far do you live from here?"

"My farm is about fifteen minutes up the highway in Plainfield," Ed said.

Jenny wanted to shake out the details before she went all in. "Oh, I forgot to ask, do you live alone?" Ed hadn't revealed much about his personal life, but she needed to know exactly what kind of situation she'd be walking into.

Ed nodded and got into his car.

This is exactly the kind of situation that Jenny's roommate Jon would warn her against—going home with strange men. If she were back in her own house and time, Jon would make her promise that she'd text him if she found herself signing up for a one-night stand, something Jon was fond of doing himself.

When Jenny drove up to Ed's house, it was a two-story farm home, just like in a movie. The home was plain and reminded her of a quaint bed-and-breakfast in the middle of the woods. The door had lost its color long ago—it was just washed-out wood. The concrete steps leading up to the door were a dull gray. The place was screaming for some maintenance.

Ed got out of the car, walked up to the front door and beckoned Jenny to come and join him. His hooded eyes told her everything she needed to know about what he intended for the night.

Jenny couldn't lie. She was both repulsed by him and magnetically attracted to him. She couldn't explain it, but she was drawn to know more about him, about the place she landed, and to the promise of temporary security for the night. He looked so lonely and pitiful. A depth of her emotions she could relate to. She released the death grip on her car steering wheel and followed him into the house.

The house was in complete disrepair. None of the furniture or appliances were modern, even for the midcentury. The hardwood floors creaked under her feet, and there was a pungent odor in the house. She couldn't place what it smelled like.

Ed left her standing in the living room, staring at the time-worn couch. No place on the thing looked clean enough to sit on. As if things couldn't get any worse, the rain came down hard. There may have even been some hail. Great, Jenny thought, she was going to have to stay over longer than she expected. There was no way she was going to get pelted in the head with ice bullets.

Country music emanated from one of the rooms adjacent to the tiny kitchen. It was melancholy music from an era she didn't know even if she tried. Any music pre-Elvis was a mystery to her without using a mobile phone app to identify the tune. It blared, "*Gonna find me a bluebird.*"

Shortly after the music started, Ed emerged from the room carrying buckets. He knew exactly where to put them: one in the kitchen, one in the living room behind the dirty couch, and another one in a back room that was sectioned off by a floral curtain.

When Ed was done, he turned toward Jenny and started pawing at her sweater. Jenny wasn't sure if she was turned on or slightly freaked out that he hadn't uttered a word to her since they'd come into the house. She let it flow and allowed him to remove her gray sweater.

Ed kissed her shoulder and put his hand against her back before landing her roughly on the couch. Although the couch looked atrocious, it didn't smell bad after all. Ed pulled back and unbuttoned his pants. Yes, he wore pants with buttons instead of a zipper.

Jenny sat up and started unbuttoning her white blouse.

As she sat there, a flash or a vision teased at the edges of her mind. She ignored it for a second, but she began to feel dizzy. She had finally identified the smell. It was rot. The undeniable smell of something foul that died. Maybe a mouse or a cat? Jenny's stomach lurched and her hamburger came up for a peek at the back of her throat. She sat up on the couch and arched her back.

Ed frowned at her and got up to walk to the kitchen. "Do you want something to drink? I've got some beer."

"No, thanks. I'll be fine. I just get a little lightheaded sometimes," she lied. Suddenly, all of her senses were heightened. She heard the raindrops falling into the buckets. The drops started out slow and then they sped up. The buckets had to be nearly full by now.

Then the flash of the vision came back to her. It was of a young woman with a plastic bag over her head trying desperately to remove it, but someone held it down over her head. Jenny found herself being sucked into the woman's suffering. She got up off of the couch to disconnect from the vision. Or was it a *memory* from the woman whose body and time she now occupied?

She thought ruefully that she was now in almost the same situation she'd been in her own time, visiting her Tinder date Sam's home a few nights before.

His home gave her the same creepy vibe as Ed's. When Jenny had opened Sam's front door, a gust of wind slammed it shut in her face. When she turned around, Sam was gone, and the room had changed to the motel in Wisconsin, where she woke up in the 1950s.

Shit! In her hurry to disconnect from the disturbing vision, she had lost sight of Ed's presence in the room.

Ed hovered behind her, breathing in her scent. "Are you all right? Are you sure you don't want a drink to calm yourself down?"

Startled, Jenny eased herself away from him and began to close her blouse. "No, I'm fine.

I just need to use your bathroom and freshen up."

Ed looked confused and gave her directions to an outhouse and then suggested, "But with the rain, you may want to use one of these buckets and go in one of the rooms on the top floor."

"Oh, that's right. I almost forgot." Jenny cringed and took the bucket that he handed her.

Her mind raced to figure out an exit plan without being obvious. She took her purse, which had her keys in it, and went upstairs.

One of the rooms Jenny passed by had an especially putrid scent emanating from it. She cracked open the door and it was one of the only neat and clean rooms in the home. The room was dark, but Jenny thought she saw the back of someone's head sitting in a rocking chair. *What the hell? I thought he said that he lived alone!*

"Oh, I'm sorry, I didn't mean to disturb you," she sputtered.

Jenny got up close to the chair when the figure didn't respond and walked around to get a better look. It was difficult to see, so she turned on a nearby lamp. To her horror, the chair contained a skeletal head that was loosely propped up by a pole attached to a rotting corpse. She backed up away from the chair, but she couldn't look away.

Jenny found herself against a wall near a table with another shaded lamp on it. She pawed for the switch to turn it on, grazing the bottom of the shade with her hand. Something about this other lamp shade felt lumpy and uneven. She looked over and saw unmistakably human features on the tanned leather patches that stretched over the lamp. Jenny retched as silently as possible, overwhelmed by the macabre displays she saw in the room. She realized she had walked straight into a terrifying nightmare, and she tiptoed fearfully out of the chamber of horrors.

Her unease in Ed's home switched to full-on panic, but she couldn't let Ed know what she had seen. She didn't know the old house nearly as well as he would, and she needed to find an exit.

On her way out of the room with the skeleton, Jenny caught a glimpse of a waste basket, which, like the lampshade, was wrapped in a leatherlike covering that she felt certain was human skin.

Another dry heave threatened to send her into a tailspin and a full breakdown, but survival mode took over.

Jenny found another room and entered it to look for windows or an exit. A couple of the rooms had been boarded up, except for one with two windows above a tree right outside. She inspected a window and realized that the drop down would be far, but she might be able to hit the ground without injuring her legs or ankles.

The room only had a chair and a bed with a blanket on top of it.

Jenny cracked the window open with ease and a little creak. She had already been upstairs too long and feared Ed would sneak up on her, so she turned back, closed the room's door tight and propped the chair up against the handle. She'd have a fighting chance if there was at least a little barrier between the two of them.

Jenny looked down at the tree under the window. Given the winter season, there wasn't any foliage to latch onto. She threw the blanket atop the highest of the tree limbs, hoping to minimize bruising as she climbed down the prickly branches.

Jenny jumped and a few branches broke under her weight, but she was safely cradled in the blanket she had aimed to hit. She rolled off of the blanket and groped in the pitch blackness for a sturdy tree limb. She found one and then the next until she reached the trunk of the tree and shimmied down it. She touched ground and assessed the damage she thought her body may have sustained. No major scratches, but her skirt had snagged in the tree and a branch had left a couple of holes.

Jenny checked that her car keys had not fallen out of her purse after the climb down and then crept around the side of the house. She was careful not to be seen out of one of the first-floor windows. She needed to see where Ed was. She didn't want to be caught off-guard before she could reach her car.

Jenny peeked her head up just enough under one of the windows to the room where she found Ed inside. He stood at the base of the steps to the second floor, looking up with a shotgun in his hand.

He seemed to hesitate, then looked back her way. She ducked down quickly. When she heard his slow footsteps going up the steps, she felt around in her purse for the keys and made a run for her car.

Jenny got in the car without closing the door completely and lowered her head below the steering wheel. She fumbled a couple of the keys in the dark, before finally getting to the one that fit into the ignition. She turned it on, and the engine of the old light blue Chevrolet roared to life on the first try. Jenny said a silent prayer and closed the door shut. She backed out of the front yard in the mud. The car spun a couple of times, but thankfully didn't get stuck.

As she righted the car and headed back on the road to her freedom, she saw Ed in her rearview mirror standing on the porch. He aimed the gun at the car, but lowered it when she was out of view. He raised a fist at her in the air and she was relieved to see that he didn't follow her.

Jenny turned on the wipers to clear the windows of the pouring rain. After a safe distance from the house, she pulled over to catch a breath. The stress of escaping a madman who had surrounded himself with such macabre items had worn her out. Her mind raced in jumbled thoughts: who were his victims, and what kind of psycho could stomach fashioning human flesh into furniture? Ed looked so normal, living in such a normal part of

America, that she would have trouble believing herself if she had to recount the story later on.

The incident with Ed was the final straw. She trusted no one to help her. Everyone had a network and people talked in small towns. How would she explain her predicament? What if Ed had his own connections and told people that she was his runaway wife? One thing she was clear about was that the women's rights movement was barely a whisper in 1950s America.

Jenny closed her eyes and prayed for a pathway to somewhere safer than the town of Plainfield, Wisconsin. She didn't care where, she didn't care how, she just willed it with all of her heart for an escape, for a place where she could breathe and make a plan.

Hot, wet tears flowed down Jenny's face. She would never take for granted the warm embrace of her family and friends. She would never go out on random dates with anyone she hadn't thoroughly vetted ever again. Most important, she vowed to be on the lookout for vulnerable people in need of food and shelter and offer them her help.

Jenny had a deeper understanding of what it felt like to be abandoned and to fall prey to people who could sniff out someone in need and serve it to them with giant red flags. She understood how desperate people ignored all the signs of danger to find the most basic of needs.

Crime stories had a whole new angle for her now.

Jenny gripped the wheel of the car and leaned her head down, accidentally blaring the horn. She gasped for air in between crying and hysterical laughing. She had escaped death! But only to be lost again. How funny life can quickly turn from the mundane to the insane, she thought.

A warm light washed over her. Jenny looked up and the windows had fogged up. The swishing of the window wipers drowned out any other sound beyond the engine.

The light got brighter and closer to her. Was it a truck or another car driving too close to her side of the road?

Jenny shielded her eyes with her arm. She felt faint and sat back in her car seat as the light turned into complete darkness behind her eyelids.

* * *

Jenny woke up in an unfamiliar bed and looked down at herself under the covers. She was dressed in a man's t-shirt. Her date Sam emerged from what she assumed was his bathroom. He was drying his hair with a towel.

Jenny quickly gathered the covers over her chest and up to her chin. She blinked her eyes several times to make sure she wasn't seeing things. She looked at the Star Wars poster on Sam's bedroom wall and breathed a sigh of relief.

I've never been so happy to see a man-child's 21st Century bedroom wall in my life!

The only words Jenny uttered were, "Where are my things?"

Sam chuckled, "You're welcome and they're right over there."

She looked around for her belongings—in particular, her phone—to see her most recent texts from Sam the Tinder date.

Jenny only vaguely remembered Sam. She'd found him on Tinder and they'd connected on anime, then time-travel movies and books, and her all-time favorite pastime: watching horror flicks. Sam had seen all of the same movies that she'd seen.

Her memories came back to her more clearly. After chatting online for a couple of weeks, Jenny agreed to meet Sam for a movie—a horror movie, of course—at the local dinner-and-a -movie theater right next to the bowling alley. It was a slasher flick, but even a novel horror lover could appreciate the ending of the film—the final girl lives to fight another day, but not without some scars.

She turned back to the present. After reviewing her texts with Sam, Jenny felt somewhat comfortable that he was wasn't crazy. She asked, "So, did we... um, you know."

Sam flashed a wide-grinned smile. "No, I wouldn't do that. I'd make sure you were awake for that. This show is not one to be missed."

His response didn't make her any less uncomfortable around him. He seemed dangerous, wild even. Jenny had always been attracted to those men, and sometimes women, but this time she wanted to honor her instincts. She couldn't have another Ed Gein situation follow her into her own world.

Jenny didn't care to find out. She gathered her clothes while freedom was still an option and walked straight past Sam and out the door.

Sam yelled after her from his bedroom door. "So, it's like that, huh? Just waltz in here, faint and vomit all over my living room couch, pass out and then leave? Women today. Sheesh!"

Jenny got into her car and breathed a sigh of relief. The first thing she did was Google Ed Gein. She dropped the phone in horror at all of the articles on his murderous deeds. She was in the presence of pure evil and yet she somehow survived.

The second thing Jenny did was to honor the promise she'd made to herself when she had no hope left: called her roommate Jon and thanked him for being in her life.

Jon picked up the phone with absolute attitude. "Bitch, do you know how worried I was about you? Did you go home with a rando again?" He sucked his teeth.

Somehow being chastised by her best friend brought her comfort. Jenny laughed and responded, "You will never believe what just happened to me."

* * *

Editor's note: Edward Theodore "Ed" Gein confessed to killing two women near the Wisconsin town of Plainfield in the mid-1950s. He is thought to have been a long-time serial killer who murdered many more people than the ones he confessed to killing. His farmhouse became notorious when authorities searched it and found furniture and other items fashioned from human skin and bones, much of which he had retrieved by robbing local graves. Gein was tried for one murder and found not guilty by reason of insanity. He was committed to a mental institution and died there in 1984 at age 77.

The Babaylan
by James Musgrave

Recorded at Stateville Correctional Facility, Illinois, by Rose Aquino, R. N.:

For the record, it's 1998, August 4. The Administration gave me complete authority to do what I'm doing. They respected me as a nurse, working in their infirmary for years, and now they respect me as a shaman for my people. How could they refuse? All their prisoners have become walking zombies. They never talk, they never want to leave their cells, and it takes cattle prods to get them to shuffle in line to the cafeteria. Forget about work. They refuse.

When I talked to the warden, Joseph Fallen, he told me that other disturbing things were happening.

Unexplainable things. The lights in the Roundhouse, the circular structure containing the cells, will go out at least twice a day, for no reason the authorities can determine. The prisoners at those times will howl like werewolves, and then change their sounds to that of some kind of high-pitched buzzing noise.

One of his guards, Tommy Roberts, a beekeeper on his off days, told him it sounded like the noises his hives make when they expect a threat to their domain. I know I am now a threat to these prisoners and their domain.

As I work my way up the ladder to the first circle of cells in the Roundhouse, I look back at the central hub where the guards are watching me. I can see the barrels of their rifles pointed out the windows. Mickey and Roy, I know, are superb snipers and former Green Berets, so as I stand on the steps leading around the first rung of Dante's infernal circle, I begin to chant my black magic chants. These chants are meant to bring out the demon ghost or even the living demon of Richard Benjamin Speck, the killer of eight women that we know of, if he is still alive. What form he has taken, or has evolved into, is quite another matter. Either way, I doubt the guards will be any good to me at disposing of this phantom.

I didn't tell the Warden, but this is not the first time I've removed demons from a location.

I've done it three times in Manila. Once in a home, once inside a church, and another time down in a deserted bomb shelter from World War Two when the Japanese held the islands. Demons come in a variety of forms.

In the first instance, it was a simple case of possession, and I was able to exorcize the devil inhabiting a fourteen-year-old boy. The second occurrence came when the church demon entered the corpse of the deceased during a funeral Mass and caused cameras to explode, and the lid of the coffin to spring open and shut as if in a storm. The final demon was a bit more difficult, as he was the ghost of a Japanese soldier who refused to leave because of his patriotic allegiance to the emperor.

The first two were dispersed into the nether world by my chanting and black magic, and the last one flew back to Japan when I used an effigy of the emperor and cut off its head. Such are some of the strange ways we shamans must do our work.

Warden Fallen, I am certain, would not have been impressed. He is already doubtful I can do anything to help his own problem, but he has come to his wit's end, which is usually the case with these matters. I decide that the best way to approach this ghost or demon is to observe the convicts as I cast my spell upon them. If they are being controlled by the otherworldly entity, then its location can perhaps be revealed by getting clues from the prisoners.

I keep chanting and shaking my goat skull, my body swaying to the piercing yells I make as I move down each circular path of cells. I gaze into the cells and see the eyes of the prisoners.

They stare back at me in terror, covering their faces and making those buzzing noises again.

When I reach the fourth uppermost ring of cells, it begins to get very warm, and then, gradually, it's quite hot inside the rotunda.

I then feel the entire Roundhouse begin to shake, as if it were a quake from Hell, and I stagger, as I come to the far end of the last row. The noise of the prisoners buzzing in their cells is deafening, and then, just as quickly as it began, it stops. It is deathly silent, and I can hear the water pipes, and then, everything is thrown into pitch darkness!

* * *

I turn off my mother's recording. My name is Precious Aquino, Rose's daughter. What can be happening? I am in the same Roundhouse, now empty in 2023, on the anniversary of my mother's ghost hunt, I can hear the same buzzing that Rose was referring to in her audio. It is coming from the same cells, on each row, up to the top of the fourth row. *How can this be? Wasn't she able to rid this place of that ghost? How can I hear it?*

As the cells begin to vibrate and creak all around me, I can feel my stomach begin to warm.

I touch it, and it's my navel that is the hottest, almost as hot as adobo chicken in a frying pan.

When I see the long, flesh cord coming out of my navel, I scream, and I can hear the yell echo all around this deserted hell hole. I feel my hand being pulled by the cord back to my mother's phone recording, and I press play. But it's not me who presses it. It's the cord. What I hear freezes my body in place with horror.

***

I am here because of the bayanihan my people formed after the mass murder took place in Chicago, on July 14, 1966, by Richard Benjamin Speck, at the South Deering townhouse where his student nurse victims lived. A "bayanihan" is when a large and often patriotic group of Filipinos is formed to perform a specific goal or task. In this instance, it was to employ my mother, Rose Aquino, who, when she lived, was a shaman and nurse who worked at the prison. I am not a shaman, but I am a nurse.

Mother also wrote down her experiences inside the alleged haunted prison at Stateville and gave them to me on her deathbed two weeks ago. Mother explained that if any of the "religious people" ever found out about what she did, the spell would be broken. Yes, my mother could cast spells, and she could also communicate with the dead, including séances for groups. This specific story, however, does not include any group séance, except for the one she conducted at the Holy Innocents Catholic Church in our native country in 1992.

My mother was employed to find out if what the bayanihan believed was true about what happened after Speck's incarceration and alleged heart attack and death in 1991. They wanted my mother to see if Speck's spirit was haunting the prison, or if he might be alive, even though Rose was there when he died. They asked this because the lone survivor of the mass murder, who hid under the bed, and another nurse, who knocked on the door, said they have almost daily "visits" from Speck, in their dreams, and even while they are awake.

I am good friends with prison officials today, as they loved my mother for what she did inside that prison. It's not only the prisoners who are often forgotten by society, but so are the guards, staff, and families of all these people. I'll be streaming my mother's words as I take this final tour around the prison. It is a supernatural story, so I warn you of this, as a trigger warning, if you're afraid of strange apparitions and malevolent ghosts.

Sadly, we seem to be increasing mass murders these days, as well as the number of imprisoned humans, so who knows what can happen on any given day in the U.S.A.? My mother and I both believe that any social organization, whether it's a family, a town, a state or province, or a country, can become infected by greed, lust, and evil. We are, each of us, in other words, walking prisoners, or prospective prisoners, perhaps waiting for the cell doors to be shut if the right circumstances arise, as they do for many in this country, and that number is increasing.

* * *

I wasn't born when Rose, my mother, wrote this story. As I look up at the large building called "F-Block," the last one standing from the four that used to be here, I can understand how mother was so frightened that day in 1998.

The building resembles what one might call the Thunderdome in the *Mad Max* franchise films. The guards and inmates call it "the Roundhouse," and what the Panopticon shape means is "all-seeing eye." This eye is the big tower in the center of the arena where the guards stay, armed with tear gas canisters, grenades, and rifles. Above this tower, in a huge circle, are the four tiers of cells where the inmates live, when they aren't eating in the cafeteria, exercising in the yard, learning in class, or working in the welding and machine shops.

I always tear up when I read my mother's writing, as she was a very intelligent woman, a graduate of the University of Chicago, and she worked in the same South Chicago Community Hospital as the eight doomed nurses until she transferred to Stateville.

On that late night in July of 1966, all of them were taken into a back room, one by one, and stabbed and strangled to death. The last one was also raped. The one Filipina, who hid under a bed all night, survived, as she was a visitor and not a resident of the dorm's townhouse.

I will read this with as much emotion as I can, making certain to pronounce the words properly, so my mother would be proud of me. She wrote:

The bayanihan meeting took place inside the auditorium of the Holy Innocents Catholic Church and school in Manila. We knew the Monsignor, Father Perez, and he understood what the bayanihan meant. Our business was beyond what the church could do, so he allowed us to congregate so I could inform the group's leaders of my plans. It was not going to be reported to any newspapers or government entities, so we had a secure place to organize what had to be done.

I called our meeting the 'Born to Raise Hell' group, as this was what Richard Speck had tattooed on his left forearm and was how the ER doctor on duty recognized him. Speck had attempted suicide after the murders but was taken to the hospital and arrested there after being treated.

I knew that before I entered this prison where his ghost was supposed to be lurking, I must tell my people what to expect from me, as most had never seen my black magic performed. They knew that I was a shaman only because my mother had been one, and I had learned everything from her because I had the dream that every shaman must have had to be called forth to practice. Nobody else in our Aquino family of eight siblings, my two brothers and five sisters, had experienced the dream call. Just me.

I played a video promotion made in 1966 of Stateville to show my people what the public wanted to believe was going on there. As it played, I would freeze the frame to make comments.

For example, when the warden showed the journalist one of the many contraband weapons created by inmates over the years, I made a joke.

'This was a knife made from a bed spring. And this was a key that worked in the prison cell lock. But when I researched the records, there were no murders, and only one prisoner escaped from Stateville before 1966. So, one is to believe the officers stopped all the activities before they happened, correct?' I smiled, 'This was certainly a time when more money was being spent on prisons than it was in 1996, after government spending evaporated and the overcrowding began that continues to this day.'

I pointed to the screen again. 'See how the hundreds of prisoners are lined up at the same time, and proceed, in an orderly fashion, to circle around, and flow down, to journey across the cement walkways and into the cafeteria? They say there were no riots, and that this was the only place where prisoners could talk, in a quiet voice, like a church. No problems. Unless they ran out of beans, their favorite food!' I laughed, and my group laughed with me as I shut off the projector.

So, this was what Stateville was created to do. House prisoners who committed major and violent crimes like murder, rape, and robberies. But today, what happened? When I worked there, beginning in 1973, the system began to change drastically. After Congress and the states passed the Three Strikes Law and other harsher sentences for drugs, the prison population ballooned.

Strangely, wardens began allowing some gang leaders in the prisons to dress in their own clothes and wear jewelry and other decorations, including gang insignias spray-painted on their cells. Lockdowns didn't happen as much, and these prison leaders encouraged work and the education of inmates to succeed on the outside, but it proved to be just a cover for the illegal activities going on.

My mother was telling them how things gradually changed, obviously, as the money from the state to pay guards and staff dwindled, and another payment method began to control the entire prison system. The gangsters inside were running their drug business outside by intimidating and providing protection inside. Low-paid guards were being bribed by these gangland criminal enterprises, and so were their fronts of supporters in the communities with money for childcare, social activities, and education scholarships. Even the politicians believed this ruse for decades.

Inside the maximum-security prison at Stateville, and throughout the Illinois prison system, it was as if the biggest con job of all were succeeding. The inmates, especially the younger inmates, were being recruited into the many Chicago and other city gangs to ultimately earn over one hundred million dollars per year in the drug trade alone. This, in turn, helped finance the prison payoffs of guards and even higher administrators, to allow cocaine, marijuana, and other drugs to be smuggled inside. In addition, rules were relaxed so that visitors came more often, and picnics were held, as well as other special privileges such as movies.

My mother then explained what she believed happened in 1998, on the day she attempted to see why the strange changes had taken place inside Stateville after Richard Speck died from a heart attack inside her prison infirmary. It was what brought her to decide to use her shaman powers against a much more evil force at work that could not only kill the prison inmates and staff at the prison but also spread as a contagion throughout the entire world.

As I pass by these empty cells in 2023, row upon row of them, numbering over a thousand, I can't help but envision my mother dressed in her shaman outfit. She told me before she died that she was pregnant with me when she did this, which made it all much creepier. I know she won't describe her shaman dress in this recording, so I will do it for her.

She wore a giant black wig of kinky curls that exploded out from her head. In the center of this wig was the magic tassel of corn shucks that she used to dispel the evil curses inside any human she met. She also wore a full shawl made of the same husks, and it served as the shaman's dream cloak, whereupon she could fly in her trance to wherever it was she needed to go in this or other universes. Her body was adorned with black and white paint. First, in the form of a painted-on mask, with white vertical lines on her forehead, and the pitch-black, glistening coat encircled her eyes in two snake patterns, two inches wide, that met down her cheeks. Within these black snake forms were white inscriptions written in Tagalog.

The rest of her body repeated the snake's black and white pattern on her arms and wrists, with pitch-black dye fully covering the backs of her hands and bare feet. Held in front of her, as she proceeded down the rows of cells inside the Roundhouse, was the emblem of the Evil One, the King of Black Magic, in the form of a skull and horns from a goat's skeleton. It must be remembered that Black Magic spells will never work on those who are innocent. As for those under the power of this ghost or other curse, Rose would, hopefully, be able to cast out the evil force in the same way Jesus did in the Bible.

How my mother was able to convince the prison officials to allow her to perform her black magic will also be explained in her story. What eventually happened, I do not know, as I have never read her story out loud to anybody. This streamed audio will be received back home in

Manila and to all our bayanihan members on their cell phones. Again, this was not happening to you, only to my mother, Rose Aquino, and to the helpless victims of this haunted prison.

***

Rose speaks again in the recording:

My baby! I grab at my stomach, and I can feel the heat. Whatever has caused this darkness, I now understand, has come for my child! In the dark, I move

around, hoping to find something to bring light into this demonic darkness. Up ahead, I can see the lighted face of Warden Fallen.

He is grinning at me, with one of those smiles your brother gives you with the flashlight held under his chin on Halloween. I have no choice at this point. I move down the row toward him.

When I'm standing in front of him, I can feel the heat pouring out of his body. He laughs insanely, pointing down at my stomach.

His voice has that same buzzing vibrato that is coming from the prisoners.

'A rose, is a rose, is a rose. You were gettin' so close to it, weren't you? Thought you might call him from the darkness. We're all under the power of the Queen Bee now, and you were correct, little darlin'.' He needs a new life to continue. Why do you think I chose you? Because you're such a magician? With that Filipina shaman bullshit? No, my dear, we need a real female next time to spread the word, so to speak.'

I continue to chant, out of habit, but it isn't helping. All around me, the cells inside the Roundhouse are constricting into another shape. A shape I should have realized was from the source of this demon's power.

'Joe, what do you mean spread the word? Is this a hive of some kind?'

The idea came to me from the buzzing and the beekeeper guard, Tommy Roberts, and his reference to how his bees made the same noise to ward off predators. I am the predator, and my baby is, somehow, going to be the sacrifice!

'Oh, yeah, hive is good. See all those cells now?' He pointed his flashlight down the rows on each circle of the F-Block's layers. They were now in the form of wax bars, malleable, throbbing, and glowing red-hot. 'Funny thing.

I never told you, but when the Queen first came to us, in 1969, we called him Birdman, after that guy in Alcatraz,' cause he nursed a sparrow back to health. But you know what? Richard threw that sparrow into a fan. He said he was meant to be the Queen Bee around here. When the gangs took over in this place, that's when it all began.'

'What began? All this ... this insanity?' My heart is pounding, and I feel a new pain coming from my navel. It is the birthing pain of a new creation. Not my baby. A creature I can see coming at us from the darkness below. She finally stops and stands in the center of the circle, her arms raised, her ovular body spinning slowly under the tower floodlight one of the guards has shined on her. One of the prisoners pushes a huge leather chair under her bottom, and she collapses inside it.

She is huge, and she is human, except for the middle of her body. The foot-long eggs are coming out of her vagina, even as she does a courtship ritual with us. A dance in the chair. What would have once been an attractive woman, this person is now a stretched-out, voluminous, and ovulating flesh machine. She must weigh over six hundred pounds, and she is completely nude, as she splays her hairy, insect-like legs inside the big chair. Her giant abdomen is pulsating under the lights, and it is the most fascinatingly horrendous sight I have ever seen.

Her pink face is swollen with fat, the jowls hanging down in fleshy clumps, and her blond hair is matted in perspiration.

The oblong, dark-gray egg coming out of her three-foot wide vagina falls, with a plop, into a padded basket for collection. As I move my way down the stairs, closer to the inner circle, I watch a prisoner, as he pushes his way in a bee line to the natal basket. He gingerly picks up the leathery egg and carries it off, exiting toward another entrance to a cell in the back of the birthing room.

I assume this is the room where they keep the rest of the eggs for incubation. Directly ahead, I can finally see what is happening at the front of the ever-shuffling line of attending prisoners and guards. As each of the attendants reaches the innermost circle, he opens his fly and takes out his member, showing it to the queen, and then he lumbers around the circle until he relocates into another cell on each level of the roundhouse.

That can't be Richard Speck's ghost. She's a woman, obviously. Those drones who work for her are the prisoners and guards, however, so somebody is running this show. I can feel the pull again in my abdomen. I must save my baby! The magnetism forces me along the path, spiraling down into the center of the birthing circle.

'That's right, Rose, go on down. She just needs to get that out of your system. We changed Richard into what he always wanted to be, and now it's your turn to give us your child. We gave Richard a woman, and he changed her into our Queen Bee. But she's worn down. We need a new progenitor to give the eggs we need to plant in other prisons around the world. Your baby's just a parasite that needs a purpose, that's all. It will all be over very fast.' Warden Fallen begins to buzz and laugh, until the entire assemblage of thousands of guards and slave prisoners begin to do the same.

I hold my goat skull up and scream, but I keep getting pulled down. I drag my feet, kick, continue to scream, as this beast pulls me closer to her yawning vagina. I can smell her disgusting odor. It's as if all the criminals, the rapists, the murderers, the thieves, and the pedophiles are swarming around this one hive—this cursed Panopticon—the all-seeing eye of evil.

'Once we extract it, the Queen will rejuvenate your little fetus until it grows into our new ambassador. She will have wings. We know your baby is a girl, as I had you examined, Rose. We gave you the drug last night in your sleep. Did you have a strange dream? I know those other surviving nurses are having them!' His insane laugh echoes in my ears as I am pulled closer to this monstrous queen demon.

Help me, my child! Ignite this living hell and stop the power of Speck's demon ghost!

***

As I hear the recording, I can feel my phantom umbilical cord pull me down to the same spot my mother described in her panicked voice. Is it now up to me to stop what has happened in the past? Does this mean the past and present are fused together the way I was with the placenta connected to my mother inside the uterus? Is her womb being torn open right now? Past and present live together in the eternal now! Just as the Buddhists say it is and in Quantum Physics.

The pain in my stomach increases and burns like a thousand church candles against my flesh. I scream in the darkness, but I move on to the central tower where all the ammunition is kept.

I fling the door open and stagger inside. It's the only way! I pick up one of the grenades from a wooden box on a shelf. I open the door and rush back outside, as my stomach feels like it will explode at any moment. I scream again in excruciating pain. I pull the pin on the grenade and fling it back into the central guard tower. I slam the door shut behind me to form a firewall of protection.

As I run for the exit, *I trip!*

I pick myself up frantically and spring toward the exit door, as the explosions begin. I can see within the fire below all the figures of the enslaved men and the giant Queen Bee beast being devoured by flames. But my mother, Rose, is not among them. She must have survived. I was with her on her death bed in Manila.

Above, on the top floor of the cells, I do see Rose. She's being held by several prisoners from the past, and something dark looms in front of them all. It's the ghost of Richard Speck! I hold my stomach as I run up the stairs, as the first level flames lick at me from below. I struggle to the end of the top floor of the cells, until I reach my mother, who is still trapped in the corner near the exit.

"Ina!" I cough and shout the Tagalog word for mother, as the smoke is reaching the top level.

The dark form in front of Rose, the ghostly incarnation of Richard Speck, turns toward me. He is luminescent orange, and his face is pock-marked, and yet I can see the tattoo on his arm: "Born to Raise Hell." He grins, and I can see his skeletal frame pushing toward me.

"Mama's little baby girl!" His voice is deep and horrific, and I can feel his energy as he comes closer.

"Kamatayan sa diyablo! Death to the devil!" the ghost of Rose screams, and she waves her goat skull and strikes the demon Speck, and his form changes to flesh-and-blood. She apparently transformed the demon ghost into the corpse of the Richard she saw die in her hospital in 1991. He crumples to the catwalk, and the prisoners from the past fade out.

My mother's shaman form also fades, as I rush, coughing and wheezing to the exit, and push out the door, as the flames take over the entire Panopticon, creating a fiery tomb of destruction.

***

I make it down the outside stairs, stumbling and coughing, and up the grassy hill that encircles the Roundhouse. Across the divide, on another grassy hill, wavering in the sunshine, I can see Rose's iridescent form. Her body is radiant, glowing at me like Mother Mary, with a smile I'll never forget. Her pregnant belly holds me, her daughter, in the past, but I am here now, with my own child. I clutch my stomach. That's when I feel the implosion of her shamanistic gift enter me, and I begin to cry with joyous abandon. I, too, will have the gift of shamanistic magic to go with my nursing duties.

As I stand at the top of this hill and watch the last of the Roundhouse, as it comes crashing down into the burned rubble, I touch my navel. My child will be saved also, thanks to my mother and my own connection to her, which goes much deeper than anybody will ever know.

* * *

Editor's note: Richard Speck was a lifelong petty criminal who was convicted of murdering eight student nurses residing at a nurse's dormitory in the Chicago area in 1966. A ninth student nurse survived by hiding under a bed. He was sentenced to death in 1967, which was later commuted to more than a thousand years of prison time. In 1991, he died of a heart attack in a local hospital near the prison where he resided, Stateville Correctional Institute, Illinois.

One Order to Go
by Kevin Hopson

"I'd like thirteen cheeseburgers, please."

The man's request forced me to look up from my newspaper. I'd been reading about President Clinton's recent trip abroad, but now I was more interested in the customer. I sat in a window booth, finishing the last of my chicken sandwich, as I watched the scene unfold.

"Pardon?" Greg said. He was a teenager who worked behind the counter, and I only knew his name because of the tag on his shirt. I couldn't help but glance at it when I ordered earlier.

"Just what I said," the man replied. "I'd like thirteen cheeseburgers. Please."

Since his back was to me, I didn't get a good look at the man's face. But he was a burly guy with a neck as thick as a tree trunk.

Greg eyed a clock on the wall. "But we close in two minutes, sir."

"So?"

The boy pursed his lips and pondered. "Do you mind if I talk to my manager?"

The man shrugged.

Greg circled around the counter and walked toward the far corner of the restaurant, where a portly fellow stood with a broom in hand. The two of them conversed, but I couldn't make out any of the words. The manager handed the broom to Greg, then approached the customer.

"What can I do for you, sir?" the manager asked.

The man leaned forward, apparently reading the manager's name tag. "Well, Stanley. You can put in an order for thirteen cheeseburgers."

Stanley glanced at his wristwatch. "It's closing time, sir."

"That may be the case, but I was trying to place an order two minutes ago. When you were still open. If the boy had simply taken my order, there wouldn't be an issue now."

Stanley couldn't muster much of response, and I realized in his moment of hesitation that my mouth was agape. In fact, I was parched, so I raised the cup of coffee to my lips without shifting my gaze.

"Let me ask you something," the man said, breaking the silence. He looked my way and pointed. "That gentleman over there."

My eyes bulged. I was the only other customer in the restaurant, so he was obviously referring to me.

"He's still eating," the man continued. "Are you going to kick him out right now?"

Stanley shook his head. "That's not our policy. As long as customers are in the restaurant prior to closing, they can finish their meal."

"And if they step inside the restaurant before you close, they can also place an order," the man said.

"Whether it's a cup of coffee or thirteen cheeseburgers. Right?"

Stanley cleared his throat. "Technically, yes."

"Then what's the problem?"

The manager deliberated. "There's no problem. Well, sometimes we have to check to make sure we have enough supply to accommodate the customer. Being that it's the end of the day."

"Then go check," the man insisted. "Please."

"Yes, sir. Just give me a minute."

Stanley walked behind the counter and made his way into the kitchen. I couldn't see him as clearly because of the partition that separated the counter area and the kitchen, but I heard two voices.

"Are you kidding me?" a woman shouted.

I assumed she was one of the cooks.

"I know," Stanley said. "It stinks. But just do it, Renee."

The manager appeared again.

"I'm sorry for the delay, sir," Stanley said to the man. "I'll put your order in. Anything else besides the cheeseburgers?"

"Just a Diet Coke."

Stanley nodded. "For here or to go?"

"To go."

The man paid for his meal, and Stanley handed him his drink.

"It might be a few minutes," Stanley said.

"That's fine. I'll have a seat while I wait."

The man grabbed a straw from the condiments table and headed in my direction. I lowered my head and picked up what was left of my sandwich, taking a bite of it.

"The nerve of some people," the man said, stopping short of my booth and sitting at a table diagonal to me.

His coffee-colored eyes met my gaze. He also had short brown hair and a matching mustache.

A nervous chuckle escaped my lips. "Yeah."

"Sorry," he said. "I don't mean to bother you."

"It's okay."

"I'm Paul."

"Jeremy," I replied.

"It's nice to meet you, Jeremy."

I nodded.

"You ever have one of those days where you feel like killing someone?"

I swallowed, debating whether or not to answer. "Of course," I finally spit out. "Who doesn't?"

"Exactly. I mean, it's not as if I'm going to actually do it. But sometimes I wouldn't mind if certain people met a cruel demise."

I bobbed my head in agreement, but I did it more for show than anything.

Paul glanced over his shoulder and eyed the kitchen, then turned back to me.

I swallowed the last of my sandwich, nearly choking it down as Paul stared at me. The combination of silence and Paul's unflinching glare caused my stomach to churn, a bout of uneasiness washing over me.

We sat in silence for what seemed like an eternity, Paul refusing to look away the entire time. Despite being an introvert, I would sometimes create small talk when there was an uncomfortable pause in a conversation, so I decided to go that route.

"So," I stuttered. "What are you going to do with all of them?"

Paul's brow furrowed. "What?"

"Sorry. All of the cheeseburgers," I elaborated.

Paul's lips stretched into a grin. "I'll probably eat a couple of them and save the rest. I can eat them for days. Lunch and dinner. Even breakfast sometimes."

"Makes sense."

I took one last swig of coffee and rested the cup on my tray. Then I slid down the bench and got to my feet.

"Leaving?" Paul asked.

"Yeah. My shift starts at midnight, so I have to get going. It was nice meeting you."

I grabbed the food tray and walked past Paul on my way to the trash bin. A hand grasped my left arm from behind, startling me. The tray dropped to the floor. Paul relinquished his grip on me, and I took a step back.

"Sorry about that," he said. "Let me get it for you."

"No. It's okay."

"I insist."

Paul got up and collected the mess, depositing it in a nearby trash bin and leaving the tray on top. If he wasn't blocking the way, I would have hightailed it out of there.

Paul turned to me. "Sorry again. I didn't mean to alarm you. I was just curious about something."

"What's that?"

"I don't know many people who work a midnight shift. What do you do for a living?"

"I'm a security guard," I replied.

It was an exaggeration. I was more like a night watchman, but I wanted Paul to think I was someone who could handle himself in a fight. Just in case he had any ideas.

"Nice," Paul said.

"Sir," the manager shouted. "Your order is just about ready."

As Paul pivoted and approached the counter, I took the opportunity to bail. I pushed through the door of the restaurant, pulled a key from the pocket of my jeans, and got behind the wheel of my sedan.

I buckled my seatbelt and started the ignition. My car faced the front of the restaurant, so I could see Paul through the building's massive windows. I noticed Paul's hand slide along the back of his jacket. He lifted it and pulled something from the waistband of his jeans. My eyes went wide. It was a gun.

Paul aimed the barrel at Stanley's head, a loud pop immediately following. Stanley slumped to the floor. I couldn't believe it. Paul had just shot him execution style.

Greg stood only a few feet from where Stanley had just met his demise. Greg backed away with both hands in the air. If his moving lips and contorted face were any indication, the poor teen was pleading for his life.

Paul circled around the counter and raised the gun again. Greg retreated into a nook next to the drive-thru window and disappeared from view, but Paul quickly closed the gap, stepping over Stanley's body in the process. Paul didn't hesitate. Another blast came.

Paul then made his way into the kitchen. I couldn't see him behind the partition, but the sound of the third gun shot was obvious enough. All of it was surreal. I wasn't going to stick around any longer, so I put the car in drive and took off.

My heart pounded up into my throat and my breathing was labored, so much so that I feared passing out. Thankfully, I made it to a 7-11 a few miles away. I used a pay phone to call the police, stuttering the entire time as I reported the shootings I'd just witnessed.

I was too shaken to go to work, but at least my boss was sympathetic to the situation. He managed to find someone else to fill my shift. Plus, there were a couple of detectives who wanted to talk to me, so that took priority over my job.

I met the detectives at their precinct and told them everything I knew. I only had the shooter's first name, but I'll always remember that face. The rendering the sketch artist did was spot on, too.

The next time I saw Paul's face was on the television a few months later. His full name was Paul Dennis Reid, and he'd robbed three fast-food restaurants, killing seven people in the process. Known as The Fast Food Killer, he was eventually arrested, convicted, and sentenced to death.

As much as I don't want to, I still think about that evening. Too often, if I'm being honest. But how could I ever forget? If I hadn't left the restaurant when I did, I would have been another one of Paul's victims. It haunts me to this day, and I'm sure it will until I take my last breath.

* * *

Editor's note: Originally from Texas, Paul Dennis Reid, aka The Fast Food Killer, moved to Nashville, Tennessee to pursue a career as a country music star. In 1999, he was convicted of killing seven people at various fast food outlets over several months in 1997, and received seven death penalties. He died in 2013 of heart failure, while still on death row.

J.D. From Down the Hall
by Jane Nightshade

I moved into my first solo apartment in the early months of 1991. It was in a mid-century complex on North 25th Street in Milwaukee. Yeah, it looked dated and cheesy from the outside, totally Seventies and not good Seventies, but it was super cheap. I was on the second floor in a one-bedroom, one-bath with kitchenette. Apartment number 203, standard layout, Navajo White walls. You know the drill.

My older brother Robert laughed at the orange Formica countertops in my kitchenette and the tan shag carpeting everywhere else. "Who picked out your decor again, Meg?" he cracked. "Peg Bundy from *Married With Children*?"

"Hey, it's home," I protested. "On my own at last!" I loved Robert, but his stereotypically gay, bitchy comments sometimes got on my nerves. At least there would be no more iffy roommates with drug habits, boyfriend troubles, or other irritating characteristics in my modest new digs.

I fixed the apartment up as best as I could afford. I got a faux Persian rug that covered up most of the ugly shag in the living room. I also put up my framed posters of REM, Green Day, and Smashing Pumpkins in the bedroom. It was quite cozy, if I do say so myself, and close to both the Marquette university campus where I was pre-law, and my part-time job at a coffee shop.

The neighbors were a mixed bag of lower-middle-class and indigent people, from all different ethnic groups. Single moms struggling with deadbeat dads, elderly retirees, and newly arrived immigrants predominated. I lived among them *but not with them*; I thought of myself as a short-timer, on my way up, and different for that reason. Maybe it was a little snobbish of me, that attitude, but I was young and cocky and didn't realize it.

Most everyone in the building was struggling, but the Oxford Apartment Complex was safe, or so I thought. That was, however, before I discovered the guy in 213.

I was putting my wash into a dryer in the laundry room when I first heard about him. A couple of older women—a pink-faced white woman with a salmon pantsuit to match, and a black woman with graying hair—were gossiping about "J.D. from down the hall."

"His place smells so awful," said one. "I hold my nose when I go past it to the elevator."

"Me too. We've all complained to the management and nothin' happened," said the other. "Weird drilling or grinding sounds sometimes—what on earth is he doing in there? And you know he is one of those homos. He brings young guys home at all hours. And dumps a huge ol' pile of empty beer cans in the Dumpster later on."

"Disgusting."

"He's such a slob. He must leave food around to rot and that's where the smell comes from. He throws empty barbecue sauce bottles into the Dumpster all the time too."

"That must be it, leaving rotten meat around. Gonna bring in cockroaches to the whole buildin' and then everybody suffers."

I was intrigued by the guy in 213. Could he really be as weird as those women claimed? My apartment was close to the elevator, so I didn't have to walk by his place to use it. In fact, I'd never had any reason to go down the hall to his part of our floor. But that afternoon, when I got back to my apartment with my clean, folded laundry, I decided on a whim to check out "JD's" apartment.

That was a mistake. There was indeed a memorable stench emanating from 213. Rotten and foul as described, but also a kind of medicinal odor, as if something had been used to try to camouflage the other smell.

There was another thing emitting from 213, which was much harder to quantify. A powerful sense of evil, such as I had never felt before. Invisible and yet so, so palpable. I felt cold suddenly and shivered. *Too many old horror movies on late night cable*, I thought. *Surely evil is not something you just feel...*

I turned to go when the door flew open and I came within a few feet of Mr. 213 himself. "Oh!" I cried, startled. A tall, blond man of about thirty, wearing thick, aviator-style glasses. He had a bland look, like someone you wouldn't pick out in a crowd, even if it were a very small crowd.

"Who are you?" he said with a scowl, but his voice was expressionless, almost a perfect monotone. He was carrying a small kitchen trash can, like he was just about to go down to the Dumpster and toss its contents in it. Not even bothering to put it in a trash bag first. What a slob, I thought.

I noticed a large, empty bottle on top of his trash. I peered at the label and saw that it was a brand of barbecue sauce called Hot Stuff Extreme. I laughed nervously.

"What's so funny?" His flat, toneless voice gave me a distinct chill.

"Oh, I'm sorry! I just, uh, heard someone talking about barbecue sauce an hour or so ago. It's a funny coincidence that I see you have an empty bottle of barbecue sauce in your trash."

He stood there staring at me, unamused, while an uncomfortable silence enveloped both of us.

"I'm Meg from 203," I offered finally, in an awkward pitch. "I just moved in."

"Okay. Meg." There was another long, strange pause. And then, "Now I have to throw this trash away." He shouldered past me, gripping his plastic trash can, as if he thought I was a wooden fence post.

I went back to 203, feeling stung by his rudeness. *It's probably best to keep my distance from him anyway*, I thought. *The weird vibes are off the charts.*

He apparently worked nights during the week, and slept in the daytime, so it was relatively easy to avoid him. That was all I knew about "JD," except for the fact that he drank lots of cheap beer and he really liked Hot Stuff Extreme barbecue sauce and Clorox bleach. I would see the empty beer cans, sauce, and bleach bottles in the Dumpster when I tossed away my own garbage. Those empty bottles bothered me for some reason. *Who the heck uses that much bleach or eats that much sauce?*

I overheard more gossip in the laundry room as well. "Someone came home with him last night," confided the same gray-haired black woman I'd seen before, this time to a balding man who was probably her husband. "A really young-looking guy. I wondered if he was even old enough to go out on his own, if you know what I mean."

The man made a clicking noise with his tongue. "Ah, Bunny, that's a red flag. Maybe you should talk to the police?"

"Yeah, maybe."

A few days later, I overheard the same woman and man in the elevator. "I called the police. They listened politely and did nothing. Same as last time," she said, exasperated.

I felt an uncomfortable chill again. I tried to imagine "Mr. 213" entertaining a young lover and found it distasteful. You wouldn't call him a sparkling raconteur with that toneless, monosyllabic speaking style, and he had an apparently well-deserved reputation as a slob. I pictured him opening numerous cans of cheap beer and plying his companions with moldy pork ribs slathered in rancid barbecue sauce. Ewwww.

I'd been living at 203 for about five months, dividing my time between working at the coffee shop and going to class. Summer was coming and I was planning to work full-time at the shop over the break from school. I was looking forward to a long respite from my courses, which were pretty hard that year.

I hadn't been thinking a lot about Mr. 213 until I heard a knock on the door one warm spring afternoon. I opened it to a young, skinny Asian kid of about seventeen, dressed in a green-and-white striped rugby shirt, jeans, and Reebok tennis shoes. Actually, he was only a few years younger than I was, but he seemed so much more vulnerable, almost childlike.

"Delivery from Northside Liquor Store, ma'am," said the young man, smiling broadly, no doubt hoping for a big tip. He was holding a cardboard twin-pack containing two chunky bottles.

"There must be some mis–" I began. I would never have paid a delivery fee in those days. My finances wouldn't allow it, and the Northside store was only a few minutes' walk from the apartment complex.

I never finished my sentence. The young man began to change before my eyes. His clothes, skin and flesh seemed to melt off of his body. Strips of fabric, of bloody flesh, muscle, pink organs and white, stringy tendons fell in a pile around his feet, until I was looking at a fresh skeleton of pale, bleached bones. A skeleton with its teeth and eyeballs still intact, still smiling in a big way, still angling for a tip.

I jumped back, startled, and opened my mouth to make a huge scream, and then abruptly closed my mouth. The bleached skeleton was gone and the ordinary smiling young man was standing before me, puzzled.

"You did order this Hot Stuff Extreme barbecue sauce from Northside, didn't you, ma'am?" he asked, perplexed.

I understood then. He'd mixed up 213 with 203. The delivery order was for *Mr. 213. JD from down the hall, the man who really, really likes Hot Stuff Extreme barbecue sauce.*

"Of course. Thank you," I said. Words were spilling out of my mouth that were seemingly unconnected to my brain. As I heard myself vocalize in an odd tone, I realized suddenly that I didn't want this young kid to get anywhere near Apartment 213. Not now, not ever. For reasons I didn't even understand, I knew I had to stop him.

I held out my hands and took ahold of the twin-pack.

"That'll be $7.72, ma'am. Including delivery fee."

"What? Oh, of course. I'll get my purse." I left the door open and retrieved my purse from the Formica counter in the kitchenette. "Here you go," I said, pulling out a ten. "Keep the change."

His smile got even broader as he grasped the bill. "Thank you, ma'am. I hope you have a great afternoon."

"You, too. What's your name?"

"Tran."

"Tran. Well, Tran, be sure to go to the elevators quickly and leave as soon as you can," I said. He looked at me strangely. I nodded in a friendly way, clutching the twin-pack, overwhelmed with a peculiar, nagging sense of relief.

I stuck my head out into the hall and watched Tran walk to the elevator bank. He turned around at one point and looked at me uncertainly. I waved gaily and he waved back and then boarded the "down" elevator.

I closed my door and leaned against the inside surface of it, feeling panicky and disoriented. I was so glad to see Tran go, although I didn't know why exactly. I did know I was spooked by the strange vision of him as a bleached skeleton. I'd never, ever in my whole life, experienced a hallucination. *Maybe something's wrong with me,* I thought. *I could have neurological problems. Or maybe it's just the late-night horror movies.*

I looked down at the cardboard twin-pack with the barbecue sauce bottles in it. HOTTER THAN HOT, screamed the advertising copy on the packaging. I realized with a thud in my stomach that I had to deliver the sauce to Mr. 213, and I had to do it soon. If I didn't, he'd call the store and ask where it was and poor Tran would get in trouble. Worse, Tran might have to come back and make another delivery to the real address. I steeled myself for the task, grabbed the twin-pack, and trod down the hall, dread-laden but resolute. Tran mustn't be sent back.

I rapped on the door of 213. The stench coming from the apartment was less than it was the day I first met Mr. 213, but it was still noticeable. There was also a strong bleachy smell that almost overcame the other odor. Almost.

I felt the presence of the dark, brooding evil that had troubled me so before.

I heard a dull, whirring sound. Drilling or perhaps sawing? I wondered if Mr. 213 was some kind of artist in his spare time, who made installations out of wood or metal. I knocked again.

Eventually, the door opened and he was standing there, still pale and blank-looking, peering at me through his thick aviators.

"Yes?" he said.

"Uh," I took a deep breath and struggled to talk. "Uh, I think I got a delivery you ordered from Northside Liquor Store. Some barbecue sauce." I held up the twin-pack. "So, I'm just bringing it by."

He said nothing and just stared at me, as if he couldn't comprehend what I was saying. I was unnerved. Maybe he didn't order it after all.

I tried again. "I'm Meg from 203. We met before. The delivery guy thought 203 was 213. An easy mistake to make."

A small light appeared in his otherwise expressionless eyes. "Oh. Yes. I did order the sauce." He reached for the twin-pack and I handed it over.

I waited for him to offer to pay me for it, but he said nothing. Just stood and stared again.

"I… I paid for it, plus a tip. Ten dollars. I thought my roommate ordered it," I lied shamelessly.

"Oh… oh, that's right. I guess I need to pay you back. Hold on." He closed the door, but before he did, I caught sight of some framed pictures on his back wall. They depicted semi-nude men in various poses. I also glimpsed a fish tank and a wall plaque that looked like some kind of occult or Satanic symbol.

He was gone for a few minutes, but then opened the door again, and reached out to hand me a five and five ones. As I grasped the bills, I saw something dark hovering over and behind him. I opened my eyes wider.

The thing behind him had pointy dark wings like a huge bat, which spread out far beyond the blond man's shoulders. It also had barely visible facial features that looked demonic–I couldn't be sure. Then I heard a nasty, metallic-like voice sounding in my head.

In your heart, you know what he does with the barbecue sauce, don't you, you horrible little bitch?

I jumped back, terrified. *What on earth did I just hear?* The blond man didn't say it–no words came out of his mouth. And he sure didn't act like he'd heard anything either.

"I have to go!" I cried, and I ran back to 203, the sound of that hateful voice ringing in my mind. On the way, I dumped the money the blond man had given me into an ashtray in the hall.

* * *

I'm losing it, I thought, as I closed and locked the door of 203 behind me. *This is the second hallucination I've had in a single day. What's going on?*

I decided to call Robert that evening. He was my usual sounding board. I didn't have many close friends at college, but Robert could almost always be depended upon to offer a sympathetic ear and some good advice. It was just the two of us growing up with our widowed mother when we were young, and we were unusually close.

"I think I'm going nuts," I began, twirling the cord on my portable touchtone. "I'm having visual and aural hallucinations. They seem so real." I quickly outlined the situation with Mr. 213 and all that I'd heard from the other tenants in our building, ending with my terrifying encounter where he appeared to be haunted by a demon.

" 'You know what he does with the barbecue sauce'—what could that be referring to? I mean, what else do you do with barbecue sauce but eat it with meat?"

Robert chuckled. "You said he had a lot of barely legal-age men coming in and out. Maybe he uses it for lube?"

"*Ewwwwww…* Robert tell me that's not common in gay circles."

"I've heard worse, but no, it's not common. I'm joking. Mostly. But you said this guy was a real weirdo."

"I think he's possessed by a demon. Do you think I'm nuts?"

"I think you've had a rough semester at Marquette and are really stressed out. And you're not getting enough sleep and compounding the problem by watching horror movies on late night TV. Maybe you should talk to a professional?"

"I can't afford therapy!" I protested.

"Try the university. They probably have a student therapy service that's affordable."

I hadn't thought of that option. I made an appointment at the University's mental health service.

The therapist diagnosed "anxiety" and gave me some breathing exercises to do for relief. She told me to come back if I felt I needed medicine for the anxiety.

I did the breathing exercises every day. I didn't have any more hallucinations, but I kept away from Mr. 213 as best I could. I would peer down the hall to make sure he wasn't around when going for the elevator. I would get up very early in the morning to dump my garbage or visit the laundry room. June came and school ended, and I was working long hours at the coffee shop, glad to get out of the apartment. Robert came over more often; he was worried about me, and tried to entertain me with quirky and ribald tales of his adventures as a single man prowling the gay nightclubs in and around Milwaukee.

He never failed to make me laugh, but I was worried about him, too. One night in late July, we rented a video copy of *Goodfellas* and watched it while eating spaghetti Bolognese on TV trays and drinking lots of cheap Chianti wine. Robert drank far more than he should have, and I could see a russet flush spreading on his nose and cheeks. He was a handsome man, the one who got most of the looks in our Italian-American family. Shiny black hair, Roman statue features, and light olive skin, which he accessorized with a gold stud earring in one lobe and a ponytail. He did a lot of clubbing in those days.

After the film, I broached the subject that had long occupied my mind, a little nervously. "Oh, Robert, I hope you are being... *careful*. I don't want to see you end up as a square on the AIDS memorial quilt."

Robert looked serious, for once. "I never go out in the rain without my raincoat, Margaret June. Scout's Honor."

I was relieved. But there was another delicate issue I wanted to know about. "It's not just about the AIDS plague. I was wondering if you ever encountered any... what do they call it... rough trade? Someone who might get violent during or after... *you know*?"

My brother burst out laughing. "*Rough trade*! That's so Seventies of you, Margaret June! But I always go home with good boys, I swear. At least, if I'm not too drunk to notice."

My heart thumped. "Don't scare me like that. I worry about you too, you know. Please be more careful."

He smiled and drank some more wine. He kept drinking until he conked out on the couch and started snoring.

Great way to end a nice evening, I thought ruefully. *I guess I'm having a sleepover tonight.*

I started clearing away the dirty dishes when I heard sounds of a commotion coming from the hall. I rushed to the door to see several of my neighbors gathered there, talking loudly and gesturing. I knew at that moment that whatever had happened, it involved Mr. 213. I stood out of my door and gawked down the hall where some of my neighbors were pointing.

Standing next to me was a younger man with a mustache, who kept shaking his head in disgust. "What's happening?" I asked him. "Do you know?"

"That creepy guy in 213 had something going on with one of his boyfriends, and the boyfriend ran away and brought the cops. Now they are all coming out of 213."

Sure enough, a Milwaukee uniformed policeman soon passed by us, perp-walking a handcuffed Mr. 213 away from his apartment, toward the elevators. "J.D." stared straight ahead, not speaking or moving anything besides his feet and legs.

Behind them, another uniformed cop was walking with a very distressed and disheveled-looking black man of about thirty, well-built and handsome. He wasn't wearing a shirt.

"He said he wanted to cut out my heart and eat it!" I overheard the shirtless man say to the cop as he passed. "I got away from him!" He kept repeating "My heart! My heart!" as the group of men approached the elevators.

"What did you find in his apartment?" the neighbor standing next to me shouted at the policemen. "We told you that it smelled bad, time after time!"

"Move aside, move aside," one of the cops responded. "There will be a press conference by a Milwaukee Police Department spokesman tomorrow."

A woman yelled: "We heard a rumor that he killed his boyfriends!" The policeman shook his head and stared straight ahead. The two cops, Mr. 213, and the disheveled shirtless man entered the elevator and disappeared, apparently on their way to the nearest police station.

"My god," I said to the man standing next to me. "I don't even know his name, to be honest. I always thought of him as 'J.D. from down the hall' or 'Mr. 213.' "

"Jeff," said the neighbor. "Jeff Dahmer."

***

Multiple police and other officials traipsed back and forth in the hall all night, taking things out of Jeff Dahmer's—I now knew his name—apartment, including a large barrel full of something bystanders said was hazardous materials. For safety, some of the people who lived immediately close to 213 were sent away to stay at a motel.

All the while this was going on, Robert drunk-snoozed on my couch. I didn't sleep at all, and in the morning, I tuned into the early news on my little portable TV in the kitchen. The local stations were all over it, of course. Photos of our building flashed on the screen repeatedly, and reporters were waylaying wide-eyed residents as they tried to leave for work or school. I still didn't know exactly what happened, and I hoped a police official would provide some clarification to the media soon.

Robert stumbled into the kitchenette, bleary-eyed and rumpled after sleeping in his clothes all night.

"I swear I heard a buncha noise last night while I was out cold, but I thought it was just a dream," he muttered, sticking his head into my refrigerator door. "Got any OJ? It helps with hangovers."

"It was real, alright," I said grimly. I filled him in on the details.

"Whoa," he said. "Meg, looks like you're not nuts after all! You're some kind of psychic! You knew he was a wrong'un."

"Shh!" I said, turning up the sound on the TV. "Someone from the police is on."

The police official was a stocky black man with incongruous Jheri curls. He was giving an off-the-cuff sidewalk interview to a mob of broadcast and print reporters.

"There is strong evidence of multiple homicides found in the suspect's apartments," he began. "Human body parts in the refrigerator. Human body parts on a grill on the stove…" here the police officer stumbled… "Body parts that looked gnawed on, as if they were half-eaten. A large barrel of hydrochloric acid full of more body parts."

A ripple of shock sounded from the reporters. Then a woman reporter asked, "How did you find him?"

"A male individual was in the apartment with the suspect last night, and this individual said he got into a violent dispute with the suspect and escaped. He found two police officers cruising their beat and brought them back to the apartment. They immediately saw suspicious items and searched the premises with the cooperation of the suspect."

A mugshot of Jeff Dahmer, looking even more bland and blank than I encountered, filled the screen.

Robert made an anguished, strangling yelp. His face was a mask of shock and horror.

"What's wrong, Rob? What is it?" I cried.

Robert shook visibly, and continued making the strangling noise. Finally, he gasped out:

"I know him! I met him at one of the clubs. I had no idea he lived in your building, on your floor yet!"

"What?" I shrieked. "Are you sure?'

Robert looked around the kitchenette as if he was trying to find something to hold onto. "Yes, I'm sure. I–I–we were both drunk. He drank a lot…"

"You… you had a… date with him?"

Robert nodded, his face drained and pale. "Not the night we first met. I gave him my number. He called the next day and came over for dinner. I wasn't really feeling it when I saw him again, but he'd gone to the trouble of bringing dinner, so I let him stay. We drank a lot more and then… I asked him to leave. Because he started talking about dissecting animals and I was getting weird vibes. He was very angry, but he left eventually, and I avoided his calls after that. He stopped bugging me after a few days."

I felt the room spin and heave around me. "He could have hurt you. You could have been a body part in his refrigerator. *Damn you*, you told me you were being *careful*…" I had a sudden horrible thought. "And… and… what did he bring for *di- din- dinner*?"

"Oh god," Robert groaned, looking green around his mouth. "It was… *grilled ribs*… covered in *barbecue sauce*! I'm gonna be sick!"

He made a loud retching sound and ran for the bathroom. I stood there, staring at a wall, while I heard Robert vomiting violently in the bathroom. I wanted to puke myself all of a sudden, and I leaned over the kitchen sink. Something brushed against my neck as I did; it felt feathery, like a wing. I sensed that a dark, malignant creature of shadows was just behind me, and I froze in terror.

Now you finally know what he did with all that barbecue sauce, a metallic, nasty voice hissed into my head. *Wouldn't you like a taste, you stupid little shit?*

* * *

Editor's note: Jeffrey Dahmer was convicted of fifteen homicides in Wisconsin and was sentenced to fifteen life terms on February 17, 1992. He was later also sentenced for a homicide committed in Ohio. In 1994, Dahmer was beaten to death by a fellow inmate at the Columbia Correctional Institute in Portage, Wisconsin.

Other HellBound Books:

The Gentleman's Choice

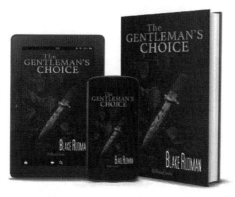

"Caught in a whirlwind of adverse publicity following a viewer's death, the streaming show, The Gentleman's Choice becomes the target for a sadistic killer – and it's up to PI Vanessa Young to put a stop to it before more young women are murdered."

A sleazy internet dating show blamed for a viewer's death, a host with a dark, secret past, and a killer with a sadistic grudge...

Someone is kidnapping and murdering previous contestants from the popular streaming show *The Gentleman's Choice* – a strictly-for-adults hybrid of *The Bachelor* and *Love Island.* Private Investigator, Vanessa Young, is hired by a victim's family to infiltrate the show as a contestant to expose and capture the killer.

Vanessa and the show's charismatic star, Cole Gianni, begin to fall romantically for each other, until Vanessa's plan goes terribly awry when they're drugged and taken to a remote location to take part in their captor's own brutal, ultimately fatal, version of *The Gentleman's Choice.*

With the clock ticking toward their fateful final night, Vanessa and Cole are forced into a battle of wills to survive their tormentor and escape with their lives before it's too late...

Goodbye Stranger

"As with *American Psycho*, Blake Rudman's *Goodbye Stranger* has a wealthy, successful man whose wonderful family life masks a much darker side. Throw in a once-trusting, increasingly suspicious wife, and the stage is set for twists and turns you'll never see coming!"

Danielle Harrington has the life many women envy: She's beautiful, rich, has two wonderful children, and is married to *the* Preston Harrington - the handsome, charismatic, retired quarterback who won two Super Bowls.

Unfortunately, something is very wrong with Preston. Having suffered more than his fair share of injuries and concussions, he becomes quiet, withdrawn, and distant. As Preston spends more time away from his family, Danielle begins suspect an affair without realizing her husband is involved in something much, much worse…

Following a series of tragic incidents and the return of an old nemesis from the past, things begin to spiral out of control for Danielle as Preston's dark side puts her and their children in terrible danger.

To Hell and Back

tep into the abyss of horror and dark fiction with To Hell and Back…where each story is a gateway to the unimaginable.

To Hell and Back serves as a mosaic of contemporary fears and timeless terrors, curated and edited by the Bram Stoker Award-winning Joe Mynhardt. This collection of horror stories brings together a diverse array of tales from both beloved and emerging voices in the horror genre, each story a unique exploration of the dark corners of the human psyche.

Published in collaboration with Crystal Lake Entertainment, with an introduction by Lee Murray, this horror anthology includes disturbing tales by Jeff Strand, Gage Greenwood, Gregg Stewart, Jasper Bark, Kenneth W. Cain, James Aquilone, Taylor Grant, Colin J. Northwood, Chad Lutzke, Felix Blackwell, J.P. Behrens, Bridget Nelson, Jay Bechtol, Nick Roberts, Kyle Toucher, Diana Olney, Devin Cabrera, Naching T. Kassa, John Durgin, Francesca Maria, James H. Longmore, and Rowan Hill.

To Hell and Back invites readers on a journey through cityscapes and small towns, into office blocks and family homes, along lonely roads, and wooded trails. It confronts external threats like predators and cults as well as internal battles with ambition, mental illness, and moral weakness. Themes of road rage, childhood trauma, the horrors of war, and the supernatural intertwine, offering a chilling snapshot of contemporary societal fears. With stories that range from political and cultural tensions to tales of creeping unease, this anthology not only aims to terrify but also to offer a means of confronting and reflecting on our fears from a safe distance.

Uncover the shadows lurking within and beyond with To Hell and Back—dare to turn the page and confront your darkest fears.

**A HellBound Books LLC
Publication**

www.hellboundbooks.com

Made in the USA
Middletown, DE
07 May 2024

54028286R00154